THE ICE

POINT OF SAFE RETURN

THE ICE

POINT OF SAFE RETURN

BILL CRAVER

Saxony Press

THE ICE: POINT OF SAFE RETURN

Cover design by Brandi Doane McCann, ebook-coverdesigns.com

ISBN: 978-1-7349713-0-9
eBook ISBN: 978-1-7349713-2-3

For Antoinette

PREFACE

The 1990s were a time of change. The decade began with the fall of the Soviet Union. Perestroika, the reformation of communism in the 1980s, and the roiling turmoil of anti-communist revolutions, along with many other things, not the least of which was the vast buildup of the US military, eventually led to the dissolution of the Soviet system, and the decline in their projection of military power around the world. By this time, I had been an officer in the United States Navy for ten years.

These were interesting times. As a Navy Officer, I followed these types of geopolitical events closely. I well remember President Reagan's historic meeting with Gorbachev, General Secretary of the Communist Party of the Soviet Union, in 1986 in Reykjavik, Iceland. I had been stationed in Iceland just one year prior. I was an experienced Naval Flight Officer and had exhaustively studied the Soviet military, their ships, and submarines, for years. I had successfully hunted many Soviet submarines in this last decade of the Cold War. It was my specialty. I was a P-3C aircraft Tactical Coordinator, with three overseas deployments under my belt.

World events like the Reykjavik Summit were soon followed by revolutions that spread across the communist nations of Central and Eastern Europe. The tearing down of the Berlin Wall and the reunification of East and West Germany were epic moments that forever changed the world in the grandest ways. They significantly impacted the US military and would ultimately shape my personal career path within the Navy.

The demise of Soviet Sea Power set in motion events that resulted in the slow and inextricable reduction (some would say decline) of the US military. In my case, that led to the draw-down of the Navy's Anti-Submarine Warfare (ASW) P-3C Orion aircraft squadrons, my warfare community, in which I was expertly trained, experienced, and deeply entrenched. By 1993 I was in the twelfth year of my career and had reached the rank of Lieutenant Commander. I was ready for my Department Head tour which would normally have been within my warfare specialty, a P-3C squadron. However, at that point, half of the US Navy's P-3C squadrons had been decommissioned. That meant half of these Naval Flight Officers, in the prime of their careers, never flew again.

I was in VXE-6 for three years, deploying to Antarctica three times for about six months each year, from 1993-1996. I became the Operations Officer in my third year. My time in VXE-6 was a challenging and rewarding experience that will remain with me forever. Unfortunately, VXE-6 was also earmarked for closure during this decade of dramatic military downsizing, and the squadron was decommissioned in 1999.

I witnessed the beauty and brutality of Antarctica. The science of many things intrigued me, like how the sun's arc moved and set so differently at the earth's poles than at the middle latitudes most of us humans experience. Or the odd juxtaposition of how a continent, so cold and covered in ice, was as dry as a desert. Antarctica's remoteness was both magnificent and treacherous. Minor accidents, a slip, a fall, a broken leg, could become life-threatening. A short walk, snow collapsing beneath your feet, a sudden drop plunging a person deep into a crevasse. There they lay—still, unconscious, unheard. Entombed for a thousand years until a glacier spits them out into the Southern Ocean. Wonder surrounding us. Peril everywhere.

This is a story that could have happened.

Bill Craver

CHAPTER ONE

ВОЭЛЕ ВОСТОК РФ
Near Vostok Station, East Antarctic Plateau
82° 40' 12" South, 106°46'04" East
February 2, 1984

Vladimir Zverev leaned forward against the strain of rope looped around his waist as he trekked across the barren ice. He wore polar goggles with glass as dark as a welder's to protect his eyes from the sun's blaze. And still, he placed makeshift pieces of cardboard with thin slit cutouts that looked like starbursts over each lens to reduce the blinding sun to a tolerable level. It was a brilliantly clear day high on the ice plateau in eastern Antarctica.

Behind him, he dragged a Nansen sled, laden with the heavy rocks he had come so far to collect. He pushed himself, conscious of his progress, keeping his pace. He hoped for another good travel day, perhaps 15 kilometers before he would camp.

He alone pulled the sled. Made of hand-oiled ash wood, it was strong, nimble, and perfect for the task. The Nansen sled was the traditional style sled used for well over fifty years on the continent. It was ten feet long and two feet wide, a design honed to perfection over decades of both Arctic and Antarctic exploration. It was low to the

ground, stable, and slipped along the ice with little resistance but was rugged enough to carry ten-times its
weight.

At the start of each day, Vladimir waxed his sled's run-
ners until they were as smooth as glass. The Nansen sled
was not too distant in concept from long-narrow cross-
country skis. It may have been no coincidence the sled's
iconic design was introduced by the Norwegian explorer,
Fridtjof Nansen, who first successfully crossed Greenland
on cross-country skis.

Vladimir's sled slid nicely on the snow and trailed
twenty feet behind him. Rather than one long tow rope
tied between the sled and himself, Vladimir preferred the
method of tying each end of the rope to the sled, which
made a giant loop. He stood in the front of the loop he
created, held it tight across his waist, and pulled. This allowed for his immediate release should he have to escape
the sled quickly.

The bright horizon split the sky from the frozen ocean
in every direction he looked. The ice beneath him was two
miles thick on this part of the East Antarctic Plateau. Vladimir walked in a straight line over the featureless ice
keeping the South Pole behind him. How curious, he
thought, no matter where you were in Antarctica, as long
as you kept the South Pole at your back, you were heading
north.

Vladimir was well south of the Antarctic Circle where
the sun stayed above the horizon 24-hours a day for
months this time of year. He was 70 miles from Vostok
Station and returned along the same route he had previously marked on his outbound journey with strips of red
cloth tied to aluminum stakes driven into the ice.

Whenever he stopped during his trek, he would look at the sky. He reached his arm up and pointed to the sun. Then, pirouetting to his left, he traced the path the sun would take above him in its 24-hour circle of time. He was so close to the South Pole now that the sun never even got low to the horizon. It looked like noon all day.

He would arrive at Vostok in a week if he didn't make any more stops, but Vladimir was a scientist. He stopped often and would stop again if he found another rock in this strewn field. His Nansen sled was now carrying more rocks than supplies by this time, twenty days into his trip.

He had been given three weeks to explore and collect samples. His comrades at Vostok thought he was a fool. They thought it was just as foolish, if not unbelievable, that the USSR had authorized his expedition. First traveling the great distance from the Port of Leningrad, USSR, by ship to Mirny Station on the Antarctic coast, followed by a two-week overland sledge from the coast to Vostok Station.

He had arrived on the first supply ship with the incoming Vostok relief crew. The USSR sent only two ships per year to resupply Vostok during the brief Antarctic summer when ships could approach the coastline without an icebreaker escort. With just six weeks between supply ships, this gave Vladimir only a few weeks to explore.

***

Two years prior, a Soviet expedition had made the overland trek from Vostok all the way to the South Pole. The 900-mile journey was conducted for no other purpose than propaganda. The team was tasked to document their journey and photograph the Soviet expedition at the South Pole. It didn't matter to the USSR that Antarctica had been a relative beehive of scientific activity for decades with at least six other nations in near-permanent residence at the South Pole. No one in the USSR was aware of this. The photos, as designed, only showed the Soviet expedition. It was national headlines for Pravda and the TASS news agency for weeks in the USSR. Mission accomplished.

On their return trip from the South Pole, that expedition reported seeing a few scattered rocks in an area on the ice about 100 miles from Vostok. This was strange. They had not seen anything but snow and ice for hundreds of miles as they traversed the flat East Antarctic Plateau. The team's photographer took a few pictures of the rocks and made one small journal entry noting the coordinates.

It was that one journal entry that led Vladimir Zverev, a geology professor at Leningrad State University, to search for the original photographs. Vladimir needed to see those images himself. He needed to know. His career needed to know.

Vladimir taught planetary science at Leningrad State University, where funding had evaporated in the final decade of the Cold War. Careers across academia were stunted in the Soviet Union during this time. Those photographs could make all the difference to his career and family.

Vladimir found those photographs, and they looked promising. This led Vladimir to seek out and interview the expedition's photographer. What did they look like in person? How did they feel? How heavy were they? And why had they not taken a sample rock home with them? These questions haunted Vladimir. The photographer had few answers. But no matter, the images, and Vladimir's interview provided all the evidence he needed, and he would bank his professional career on it.

In the waning years of the USSR, there was little money to support large University programs, much less another extravagant research expedition. Professors and researchers were scrambling to justify their jobs and preserve their government paychecks. Faculty positions were in jeopardy in this austere climate. Any good deed was scarfed up by that person's superior, and in turn, that credit was taken by their superior. It was impossible to get ahead. People were just trying to preserve their job. If Vladimir were to discover if these rocks were what he suspected, others would just selfishly steal his discovery in the every-man-for-himself environment. No, Vladimir would not share his idea with anyone. But how to justify an expedition to Antarctica?

His efforts had come at a high personal cost even before he departed. For two years he petitioned the Politburo to fund a second expedition. Even after multiple rejections, and at great risk to his professional status in academia, he persisted. He had made a pest of himself. He was one man trying to convince the USSR what a big propaganda event it would be. Vladimir insisted on having another expedition, even bigger than the earlier South Pole expedition. And this time, he would bring back more than just photos.

Finally, someone listened. He was able to contact a senior military officer with connections to the Soviet Arctic and Antarctic Research Institute program. The AARI logistics fell under the auspices of the Soviet Navy.

Everyone knew that the higher in rank the officers climbed, the more closely intertwined their military and political careers became. Soviet Navy Captain Boris Drugov was no exception. He controlled a contingent of ships from the prestigious Baltic Fleet. And specifically, the ship that transported the supplies to the small Soviet Base on the coast of Antarctica called Mirny Station.

Vladimir convinced Drugov that this discovery would be another great propaganda coup. Vladimir exploited Drugov's self-interests to authorize his expedition by promising him greatness.

The images were of meteorites. There was no doubt in Vladimir's mind. He told that to Captain Boris Drugov. They were meteorites from Mars, he strongly suspected, but he kept that thought to himself. He needed to collect those rocks. He needed to prove they were from Mars.

There were less than twenty known meteorites from Mars in the whole world. Each new find always made headlines. The value of a single Mars rock was nearly incalculable. If a staged photo at the South Pole could dominate Soviet headlines, then his retrieval of meteorites would certainly be newsworthy and help his career. If he could prove they were from Mars, he would be famous and gain international acclaim. Although a handful of his colleagues thought the rocks in the photos could indeed be meteorites, he was the only one who seemed to care, or at least care enough, to risk his career and make the sacrifice to go collect them himself.

Captain Drugov was eager to help, but not without conditions. There would be no official expedition or funding. But Drugov authorized him to go on his own— quietly.

Vladimir departed Leningrad leaving behind his wife and only child. His daughter adored him, and he promised to return home in six months, in time to see her graduate from secondary school. As the Soviet winter approached, and darkness dropped its chill on the Northern hemisphere, the summer light at the bottom of our globe was just beginning to warm Antarctica. As Vladimir departed, he shared his most sacred secret with his daughter, no one else, and began his journey to collect Martian Meteorites.

The USSR was starving. In the years following the original propaganda expedition to the South Pole, it had become clear the end of the Soviet Union was near. Now was not the time to waste money on what could be a wild goose chase. Five years hence there would be no Soviet Union. Just as some propaganda can help, bad news can become propaganda that could hurt. "Better to wait and see," his comrade in the Navy said. Then an announcement can be made.

Vladimir knew the risks. He took a leave of absence from Leningrad State University and traveled quietly, alone, practically in secret, like a stowaway. Failure would be easy to erase—as if his quest had never happened.

***

The ice was hard underfoot and there was a new strength in every one of Vladimir's steps. He was full of energy as he made his way back to Vostok. He had more than proved himself right. It was a bonanza find. He collected a treasure trove of meteorites and mapped the strewn field. He picked no less than two dozen meteorites from the ice surface. The final verdict would have to wait for a complete analysis, but he knew intuitively that these were meteorites from Mars. He would be famous and his family would be secure.

Over and over, he rehearsed to himself the speech he would deliver upon his return. He pulled his Nansen sled with youthful vigor, unencumbered by its weight, lost in a glorious trance. He imagined himself standing at the podium addressing all the political members of the Politburo in Moscow, the senior military, all the scientists in attendance, all the academic leaders, the General Secretary himself. This would catapult his standing not only in the USSR but internationally as well. While he hiked, he daydreamed.

The ice made a strange shift underfoot. Did he feel something, or was he lost in thought? His left foot slipped out to the side. There was a low groan behind him. Another shift, this one to the right. A deeper groan, again from behind.

He turned, and froze, not moving a muscle. His senses were at full alert. The heavy sled at first looked fine. But then he saw it, a very slight tremor. The sled twitched an inch.

In uncontrollable fear, he pushed the rope down and away as he saw the back of the sled drop two feet. The air crackled with a loud boom. The sled fell.

Scrambling, panicking, the rope was fighting him. A fierce pull slammed his body backward ten feet in a split second. A violent twist wrapped the rope in a tangle around his foot. He was caught. He was flat on his back, being dragged on the ice toward a hole where the now-vanished sled had been just a moment ago.

The rope was hung-up on his foot, cinched tight around his ankle like a noose. He reached desperately for his release but could do nothing. The pull was too violent, his thick gloves too cumbersome. *Just get the rope off of me!*

The crevasse was hidden by a snow bridge, and the weight of the Nansen sled had revealed it. Vladimir was yanked below the surface with a force that snapped his femur like a frozen twig.

He fell thirty feet and landed on the rocks he loved so much. His head hit so hard he saw stars. A concussion, yes, he knew, but not unconscious. Had he been knocked out? Perhaps, but not for too long, he assessed.

Stunned, laid out on a bed of rocks, his mind drifted. Hurting, he did not move. On his back, at the bottom of the crevasse, his limbs splayed limply like a rag doll. Mars rocks, he knew. The greater pain came when he thought about the promise to return that he had made his daughter, a promise he now knew he could not keep.

He looked skyward through the gapping slash of his crevasse. The bright white ice walls framed the blue sky. It was a brilliantly clear day. His heart ached. It beat in slow acquiescence. He would not see his daughter again. He slipped off his glove. There would be no point anymore. Feeling around beneath him, he closed his fingers around a fist-sized rock. He pulled it to his lips and kissed it. It had to be. Then he held it close to his chest and slowly fell into a slumber.

No one came looking for him. Drugov was right after all. "Better to wait and see." Now, it was as if the journey had never happened.

CHAPTER TWO

NINE YEARS LATER
The Dry Valleys, Antarctica
January 02, 1993

"I bet you can see a hundred miles. What a gorgeous day. Not a cloud in the sky. Zero haze." Ty, the copilot, said. He was paying more attention to the scenery than flying the helicopter.

"Another day in the twenties. *Plus twenty*," Jake emphasized.

"Hot and dusty," Ty joked.

Helo 12 zipped along at a rapid clip a few hundred feet above the Ross Ice Shelf. The steady WHAP, WHAP beat of the helicopter's rotor blades above their heads sent a pleasing guttural pulse deep into their chests. It was a good feeling, the correct feeling. It was the reassuring heartbeat of machinery that comforted the pilots and said the engines were operating in sync. Jake didn't need to look at the gauges to know—the beat said all was well.

So accustomed were the pilots to the below zero degrees Celsius normal daily temperatures in Antarctica, that saying the temperature was negative or below zero was not necessary. Every seasoned Antarctic aviator simply dropped the modifier. They only stated the temperature as a number. It was understood to be negative or below zero.

For no more than a couple of weeks of the year, during the peak warmth of the Austral Summer, around the calendar-New Year, would temperatures near McMurdo climb above zero degrees Celsius. And that's when the pilots said *plus*, or *above zero*. The summer heatwave. It was one of those quirky things they enjoyed. It's one of the things that made Antarctica so different.

Jake, the senior pilot of the pair, currently wasn't much help assisting his copilot in flying Helo 12. The helicopter, a Navy HH-1N, affectionately called a Huey by everyone, was unchanged in design for decades. It looked as if it could have come out of a Vietnam jungle, except for its bright red-orange paint job.

The two pilots sat side-by-side in the tight cockpit. The Huey allocated as much space as possible to the cabin in back, which for the purposes of this squadron, was a big open cargo bay. The six Huey's of Antarctic Development Squadron Six (VXE-6) were used to transfer people and gear between science camps like rotary-wing pickup trucks.

Instead of monitoring the instruments, Jake gazed out his side window and marveled at the pristine beauty as the red-orange Huey skimmed above the edge where the ice meets the ocean. The warming temperatures caused the sea ice in McMurdo Sound to slowly melt and recede a little closer to McMurdo each day. "There are a lot more penguins out on the ice edge today than we usually see," Jake said.

Each time Helo 12 made a loud pass close by a group of penguins, appropriately called a waddle, standing along the ice edge, most of them dove to safety into the ice-blue water. It was a response likely triggered perhaps by a primal twitch genetically hidden in their psyche.

The crew of Helo 12 was early into their morning flight itinerary. They were forty miles from McMurdo Station, flying west toward an area known as the Dry Valleys. They had twenty more miles to go before their first stop.

They were scheduled to visit three different field camps before heading back to McMurdo. The first was a science camp in Taylor Valley, the second another science camp in Wright Valley, and the third stop was the field camp at Marble Point. Marble Point served as a kind of base camp, a forward staging point for science gear and supplies used in this area.

The Dry Valleys were located less than one hundred miles from McMurdo. It was the farthest practical reach of the helicopters for routine operations. Out-and-Back in a day, usually without refueling, was good duty. Most importantly, even if they were detained by the scientists, the aircrews would be back in McMurdo for a hot dinner and able to sleep in their warm beds during the "sunlit night."

The helicopters could operate farther than the Dry Valleys, of course, but that's how the Ice Pirates, which is what the helicopter pilots of VXE-6 liked to be called, defined their "farthest practical reach." Camps farther from McMurdo were supported by the much larger fixed-wing aircraft in the squadron, the LC-130 Hercules.

The Dry Valleys are a unique environment for Antarctica. They are so named because they do not accumulate any snow or ice. As such, its uniqueness received a lot of scientific attention.

Several factors contribute to the Dry Valleys remaining snow-free. The one with the greatest impact on human survival, besides the cold, was the torrential winds that channel through these barren canyons. These powerful winds, known as katabatic winds, are the result of a unique geographical feature that juxtaposes two distinct regions of the continent next to each other; the two-mile-high East Antarctic Plateau to one side of the Dry Valleys and the much lower Ross Ice Shelf at sea level on the other.

Separating these two regions are the Transantarctic Mountains, a massive continent-wide mountain range. The mountains act like a giant dam holding back a continent covered in ice two-miles thick. The ice on the East Antarctic Plateau side of the mountains has piled up over eons nearly to the level of the mountaintops themselves. This side of the continent, although two-miles-high, is as flat as a pancake.

When cold, dense air on top of the East Antarctic Plateau wants to move, it looks for a way to flow downhill. Like water seeking its level, the freezing air spills over like liquid off the edge of a tabletop.

These katabatic winds are almost constantly in motion and pour over the edge of the East Antarctic Plateau like a two-mile high waterfall. But bottled up behind the mountain range, the frigid air always wants relief. The Dry Valleys provide that relief, the path of least resistance, like giant channels carved into the earth, it funnels the rushing winds down from the high East Antarctic Plateau to sea level below. These katabatic winds race through the Dry Valleys like rivers out of control.

Other than the few penguin rookeries that were closer to Mount Erebus and McMurdo, the Dry Valleys were one of the most studied areas around McMurdo.

If all went as planned, Jake and Ty would be back to McMurdo in less than six hours and still make lunch before the chow hall closed.

Soon Jake could see the four colorful tents that comprised the Taylor Valley Science Camp. Each tent a different color: red, green, blue, and orange.

"Approaching the Taylor Camp," Jake spoke into his mouthpiece. He turned around as best he could against the tug of his shoulder belts to see if his two passengers heard him. Helicopter Crew Chief Martin nodded and science passenger Felix Quigley, a good friend of Jake's, smiled. They looked fine. They too had been taking in the scenery. Enjoying the ride.

The traditional heavy canvas tents used by earlier Antarctic explorers were white and pyramid-shaped. Known as the Scott tent, they could be kept warm inside and proved to be a great defense against the cold winds that swept endlessly across the continent. A Scott tent had helped Jake survive for three days in his first season, so he and others preferred them. But they were not used by this Taylor science team because they were heavy and bulky. A tradition was being replaced by the multicolored lightweight fabrics.

Helo 12 hovered over their landing site. The colorful grouping of modern tents staged next to a monstrous glacier looked choreographed. Jake thought it could have been an advertisement for Patagonia or L.L. Bean. The clear blue sky and jagged mountains in the background made the setting perfect. "Should have had my camera today," he thought.

***

Upon landing, three scientists scurried over to Felix and surrounded him in a scrum. Each was vying for Felix's attention and trying to outdo the others with the great progress they were making in their latest real-world science findings. Success would mean more grant money for their research next year, maybe even the grand prize—a return to Antarctica.

Felix engaged in their passionate conversations and handed out fresh apples and oranges he had stuffed into his pockets for the team while promising to relay their good news back to McMurdo.

An unexpected person exited the fourth tent and approached Jake and Ty. A giant smile shone through his full beard, and bunches of tousled hair flowed from underneath his woolen hat.

"What are you doing here, Tim?" Jake asked, surprised. "I thought we left you in Wright Valley yesterday?"

"Yeah, you did," Tim Rogers said. He was the senior mountaineer in McMurdo. "I got a radio call from this group yesterday saying they were having problems getting their camp stove and heaters working, so I came over to straighten things out for them."

"How'd you get here?"

"I walked."

"Ten miles? Over the mountain!"

"Easy-peasy. You should try the Himalayas some time."

Ty shook his head, grinning in disbelief. The mountain range that separated Wright Valley from Taylor Valley was modest by Himalayan standards, but far from a casual stroll. There was likely no other human being in Antarctica that could make that trek and still be alive today.

"I'm done here now," Tim said, dismissing his good deed like a walk in the park. "Can I catch a ride with you back to Marble Point?"

Ty saw what he immediately surmised was the owner of the fourth tent exit and welcome the world with a full arched-back body stretch. She straightened her parka, and with a shake of her body, put everything into place. She ignored the gaggle around Felix and walked straight toward Tim, her face beaming.

Tim glanced over his shoulder as she approached. "This is a quick stop here for you, right?"

"Could be. We can move along as soon as Felix is ready."

"I think we should get going as soon as we can," Tim added while she was still out of earshot.

"Sure, Tim. Anything for you."

The woman joined the men and wrapped both arms around Tim. She nestled her head into his chest. "You're not leaving, are you Tim?" she said in a romantic tone.

"They need me at Marble Point. I have to get going…"

As wonderful and useful as Tim was, he wasn't the stick-around kind of guy. Someday, he thought. Just not yet.

The Mountaineers of McMurdo were much more than search and rescue experts that sometimes helped set up science camps. They provided world-class training and expertise in cold-weather survival to everyone who visited McMurdo, and they were always ready to help. Some referred to them as the polar handymen, but they were more like supermen, and when you were hurt, they really came in handy.

There were no more than three or four mountaineers in McMurdo, even in peak season, and as few as one at the beginning and end of the summer research season. But with the frequency that people got into trouble and hurt around McMurdo, they needed ten-times as many.

In the hierarchy of favorite people in McMurdo, the mountaineers were right up there.

***

Visiting the other camps went smoothly. Helo 12 lifted off from Marble Point after leaving Tim Rogers at that camp and turned east toward McMurdo. Felix spoke on the intercom. "Can we do a quick fly-by of Cape Royds on the way home? I want to see how that camp is doing."

"Sure, as long as we make lunch," Ty said.

"Just aim directly toward Mount Erebus," Jake said.

"Directly toward Erebus?" Ty questioned.

Jake turned his face away from his copilot. "Straight to Erebus. That'll take us to Cape Royds. Then we'll turn right and head to McMurdo."

This flight path would take them over open ocean water below. A straight shot. A short cut. Not a good idea for a helicopter in Antarctica. The Squadron Flight Operations Manual clearly stated to remain over the sea ice, and not fly above open water. Only a week ago, the sea ice of McMurdo Sound was still frozen beneath this route. But today, it had all melted away.

The WHAP, WHAP heartbeat felt strong. So, today they would shoot the gap. They wanted to make it back for lunch.

Ty stayed dutifully silent.

Jake continued to look out his side window. He seemed locked in thought far away. His eyes stayed focused on the melting ice edge, a distant shoreline that moved farther away each day, always just out of reach.

Ty kept the distinct shape of Mount Erebus directly ahead of Helo 12 to guide them on their flight. The open ocean below and the few scattered ice chunks that remained zipped beneath their helicopter, while Mount Erebus, so huge on the horizon, but only a few miles inland, never looked like it got any closer.

After a long five minutes of quiet, Ty spoke up. "I can see smoke coming out of the volcano today," he said, trying to ease the tension in the cockpit that their over-water flight path had created.

"What a sight," Jake said. "Where else can you go from sea level to 12,000 feet in less than ten miles?"

Most who visit McMurdo don't realize that Mount Erebus and McMurdo Station are on an island called Ross Island, about thirty miles off the coast of Antarctica. Millions of years ago, when Antarctica was suffocated under miles of ice, and the continent surrounded by a massive ring of permanent sea ice, Ross Island was also locked in its frozen grip. The Ross Ice Shelf, as large as a country, froze on the surface of the ocean and created a giant wedge of permanent sea ice that captured Ross Island, and it has never let go.

Seaward, north of Ross Island, away from the continent, and everywhere else surrounding Antarctica, a band of seasonal sea ice temporarily forms each winter. In places, it can extend out from the coastline hundreds of miles. And briefly, each summer, with the moderate warming that accompanies twenty-four-hour-a-day sunlight south of 66.5 degrees latitude, the latitude that defines the Antarctic Circle, the seasonal sea ice melts and recedes back to the coastline, but it never quite reaches it.

And that's one of the reasons McMurdo Station is located where it is—it's thirty miles off the coastline—the extent of the seasonal ice melt. It's the closest to Antarctica's coastline that the early explorers could approach the continent in their wooden sailing ships.

As the seasonal sea ice melts, it cracks. The thinning ice breaks and splits under the constant wind and wave action. It looks like a thousand-piece jigsaw puzzle from above. Never static, the waves endlessly jostle the floating ice pieces, their edges bumping up against one another, like a puzzle trying to fit itself back together again.

The northernmost chunks, the pieces on the perimeter, are the first to drift away. Pushed by the breezes and currents, they float north, to their fate. Eventually, like today's flight, all the seasonal ice in McMurdo Sound was gone.

After twenty minutes with no more conversation, Helo 12 went "feet-dry" near Shackleton's Hut and the Adélie penguin rookery at Cape Royds, and all tension passed. A short radio call and a visual wave to the science team confirmed all was well at Cape Royds, and Ty turned right. They passed by Cape Evans in five minutes more and gave a similar radio call to that team. Ty gently rolled Helo 12 left and right, a helicopter wave, and headed home.

To the uninitiated, this area seemed barren and completely devoid of any human presence. But if one knew where to look, and looked more closely, the remnants of early explorers were scattered everywhere throughout this stretch of coastline between Cape Royds and McMurdo Station.

Many relics of the past were virtual landmarks by this time in history. Shackleton's Hut at Cape Royds and

Scott's Hut at Cape Evans were certainly the most prominent and worthy of the legend and lore they provoked, and that still endures today. However, once the trail had been blazed, countless others followed the first explorers to this area, and many who came after Shackleton and Scott followed the same paths to launch their own treks across the continent. So many had followed these tried and proven routes that one would half expect to see a signpost that reads "Trailhead to the South Pole."

Jake looked over his shoulder, smiling again at his friend Felix. Felix smiled back.

This was the best time of the season.

CHAPTER THREE

Kronstadt Naval Base
Saint Petersburg, Russia

Oksana Zverev had waited a long time to meet with Admiral Boris Drugov, now Commandant of the Kronstadt Naval Forces, Baltic Fleet. She stood just outside of his office. An enormous uniformed person filled the doorway in front of her. Ivan was large and muscular, and he stood firm as he silently looked Oksana over from head to toe. When he was satisfied that she did not represent a threat, he stepped aside.

She paused at the ornate threshold to collect her thoughts one last time. Oksana was prepared with a speech she had ready for months. She knew exactly what she wanted to say. Like her father, she needed the Admiral's influence to get to Antarctica. She wasn't going to leave his office without it.

Admiral Drugov's reputation was that of a cunning senior military officer. Someone who, through a series of suspect maneuvers, was successfully navigating the convoluted stew of military protocols, politics, and power that swirled around the fledgling Russian Federation in the aftermath of the Soviet Union. It was a murky cesspool of money and crime. Some found fortune, but most found failure. It would be the former if Drugov had any say in the matter.

Oksana looked through the opening that separated her from the dark room inside. The massive doorway was framed in gold, its decoration so excessive it gave her the feeling she would walk through the gilded picture frame that surrounded a large Renaissance painting. Like Alice through the looking glass, no turning back. A final short breath and she stepped into the Admiral's lair.

Drugov sat with confidence behind an oversized wooden desk on the far side of the large room. Oksana saw a thick man, obviously heavy from a robust diet, but still solid from an active life. Not someone to tussle with. He wore the black winter uniform appropriate for his rank. It was covered with more gold thread embellishments than seemed necessary to Oksana, and row upon row of ribbons that meant nothing to her.

Oksana walked a full thirty feet across an open floor to approach him. The Admiral looked up as she approached. She had never felt so scrutinized before. Lonely, vulnerable, she could feel Ivan's eyes licking her back.

The dark wood of the desk looked very old to her. Historic, perhaps, also covered in ornate gold trim. It was similar to the gold braids that adorned the Admiral's ego.

Drugov customarily remained firmly planted in his seat while he received visitors, and would wait for his guests to be seated before himself standing to tower over their presence. But upon seeing Oksana's graceful approach, he rose.

Ivan raised an eyebrow at the inconsistency.

"Thank you for seeing me," Oksana said.

"The pleasure is all mine, my dear. Please sit down." Drugov held his advantaged position long enough for

Oksana to be seated and look up at him. Satisfied, he resumed his place behind his desk.

"This is about your father, isn't it? We were so upset when he died in Antarctica. What was it, nine years ago? Yes, very sad."

Oksana's body reacted imperceptibly. She knew no one had acknowledged his death. The crew at Vostok eventually found the overdue scientist by following the same aluminum stakes tied with strips of red cloth, like a trail of bread crumbs that Vladimir had planted along his route. But his recovery was too late for him to be sent home on the last ship from Mirny Station that year.

Not until his body had been returned to the Soviet Union more than a year after his death was any mention of him made at Leningrad University, where he taught, and there was never a word of any connection with the Soviet government. A rumor had even circulated that he had recklessly gone to Vostok on his own in a wholly unprepared manner.

"I am here to continue my father's research. There is a discovery for which he deserves to be recognized. It is my purpose to fulfill his dream."

"I recall he made a solo journey to work near Vostok in his field of study—geology was it? Yes. Vladimir was to retrace the footsteps of our brave Soviet expedition to the South Pole a couple of years earlier. He said he thought he could find some rocks. Important rocks, yes, possibly meteorites, I believe. He needed my authorization to get to Vostok Station."

"You were very generous to him then. Your reputation as a great naval commander and leader of sailors is well known. I need your generosity again."

"I reluctantly approved his travel on the Mirny Station supply ship. From there, he continued to Vostok. I tried to tell him it was too risky. I tried to talk some sense into him. I tried to save his life."

Oksana clenched her teeth. She knew that the Captain Drugov of nine years ago had done nothing of the kind. He only wanted to bask in the glory of her father's discovery. "I want to return to Vostok. I will bring home to Russia my father's meteorites and share them with the world. I want my father to receive the recognition he deserves—the recognition he died for."

"I can't authorize you to go, Oksana. It's too dangerous. Why should we do this again? Let your father's legacy be that he was a devoted scientist who would go to any extreme in the name of science. Let your father rest in peace."

Oksana expected she would be denied. She scanned the ostentatious trappings in the room. She knew about the power he wielded, the vast fleet of ships he commanded. She took another breath. All his gold braids, his accouterments, his ego—it made him vulnerable. She spoke his language. "Do you know how valuable the meteorites are?"

"A significant contribution to science. I think that's how your father phrased it. The first major meteorite find in Antarctica. It would have boosted his career."

And you would have taken all the credit, Oksana thought, but instead, she said, "There's more to it than that."

Drugov leaned forward. The word "Yes" crawled out of his mouth.

"The meteorites are of extraordinary value," she said.

"Go on." Drugov's interest was aroused.

"I know what to look for. I know where to find them and how to bring them back to Russia."

Oksana turned her head toward Ivan, who had been standing inside the door like a guard, listening to every word.

"Ivan is my most trusted assistant. Continue." Drugov was eager to hear more.

Oksana had no choice. It was now or never. "The meteorites are from Mars. There are so few known Martian meteorites in our world that these would be the discovery of the century."

Drugov could care less about the meteorites' origin. "Surely, they have some monetary value?"

"They are priceless. They need to be in museums and Universities all across Russia."

"But what are they worth?"

"If they were sold, they would be worth tens of millions."

Drugov tried to hide his greed, but a long inhale filled his barrel chest like he was vacuuming in a million dollars a second. Thoughts of adding to his purloined fortunes swelled his head.

Drugov stood. "We shall bring the glory of our great Soviet past into our new Russian Federation—thanks to your father, of course."

"I need you to send me to Vostok."

"There have been no supply ships to Mirny Station for several years."

"I can go with the Americans."

A momentary puzzled look crossed Drugov's face while he recalled that Vostok Station had been able to remain open. They were relying on American aircraft for resupply. It was a distasteful arrangement that the Admiral refused to acknowledge publicly.

"Tell AARI, the Arctic and Antarctic Research Institute, to send me. You have influence over them. I know you do. My father told me. Get me to Vostok and I will return the Martian meteorites to you. Recognize my father's discovery and you will receive the credit for their recovery."

"Yes, it is true that the Americans fly food and supplies from McMurdo Station to our brave men at Vostok Station. In exchange, we share some of our scientific research. Not all of it, of course, do not worry. The science we reveal is of no military value."

"We have also exchanged science personnel," Oksana added. "Both our AARI and the American's National Science Foundation have liaison programs." Oksana leaned forward in an assertive manner to submit her demand. "I want you to tell AARI that I will be the Russian liaison scientist to McMurdo Station this year."

"And I should do this for a few meteorites?"

Oksana slowed her speech for emphasis. "It would be wise not to let the Americans know *exactly* why I am going. It's best to let them believe that I am merely a scientist at McMurdo to study rocks."

Emboldened by her performance, she knew she would get what she came for, and relaxed in her seat to savor her victory. She took a moment to regard Drugov's uniform again with all the gold buttons running up and down his double-breasted jacket. Too many buttons, she smiled. Maybe there was going to be a parade later.

Something about her manner piqued his interest. There was more to her than he first thought. Her voice displayed a guarded tone. It was confident, yet elusive. She had the ambition he liked in his subordinates. It was a characteristic he looked for and fostered in his up and coming junior officers. That kind of ambition deserved praise. That kind of ambition earned respect. In Admiral Drugov's mind, she was someone to be both admired and carefully watched.

"I have to get to McMurdo before the last flight of the season to Vostok. I will collect the meteorites and hide them. No one will consider them anything other than ordinary rocks. Upon my return to Russia, you will be acknowledged as the great leader who recovered the meteorites, Martian meteorites, from Antarctica."

"You will not disappoint me, Oksana? Like your father." His last remark was unnecessary.

"Get me to McMurdo before the summer research season is over."

Drugov leaned back in a relaxed posture. "You demand a lot, Oksana." He seemed to weigh the reward against very little risk. After a dramatic pause, he spoke. "I will make the connections."

Oksana stood, "There is one more thing. Her name is Ksenia."

***

Ivan ushered Oksana Zverev out of the room after her meeting with Admiral Drugov. His stare continued to follow her a good distance down the hallway. When she was safely out of range, he stepped back from the door and turned to Admiral Drugov to listen to his assessment of the meeting.

Drugov said. "I knew her father was desperate nine years ago when he asked to be placed on the supply ship to Mirny Station. I thought he might even be a little crazy. Why else would he risk his life to collect a few meteorites? Well, thanks to his daughter, now we know."

"A worthwhile treasure, sir," Ivan said. "Millions, I heard her say."

"Tens of millions. Yes, and she will collect them for me."

"Can you trust her? Comrade Zverev wasn't fully honest with you."

"A little insurance will watch over our idealistic young scientist. Wake up, Nastasia Kidrova. This is perfect for her."

CHAPTER FOUR

Moscow, Russia

She was from everywhere and nowhere. She honed her roles like a method actor, immersing herself in character for months at a time. Most of Nastasia Kidrova's assignments were in Washington, DC, but she liked to spend her "time off" between marks getting lost among the small Southern towns in the United States.

She frequently moved, before becoming too familiar a face, or acquiring much of a distinct flavor from any one place. It was good for her mannerisms and language skills. With time, practice, and imitation, she had completely removed any accent she brought with her from the Soviet Union. But not before picking up a hint of a Southern drawl, along with a little charm, which she could turn on and off like a switch.

The Senior Senator from Mississippi, who sat on a powerful committee, was an easy mark for Nastasia. He first saw her sitting alone at the far end of the bar in his favorite speakeasy in Georgetown. These establishments were made obsolete long ago at the repeal of Prohibition, but a few remained discreetly tucked away in the hearts of older cities like Washington, DC. They kept the fun alive with the scent of misbehavior in the air.

The lights were so dim in the speakeasy lounge that Lonnie, the bartender, needed to point her out to Senator Barnes. It helped that Nastasia had dropped five one-hundred-dollar bills behind the bar earlier to facilitate the introduction.

She wore a dark evening dress, her makeup was heavy, and her naturally straight hair was styled with a loose wave rolling through it. The reflection in the mirror behind Lonnie's bar showed an older version of herself. Something she was looking for. She was glad she had decided to leave her black hair color alone. Little touches were the best.

Nastasia had been fiddling with the same martini parked in front of her for more than an hour while she waited, occasionally restocking it with an ice cube.

Barnes looked her over like a trophy waiting on the shelf. She looked classy.

"Too nice for a call girl," Barnes said to Lonnie. "Then again, maybe not."

"Looks like she's been stood up, Senator."

"Maybe I should give it a shot."

"I don't think she wants to go home alone tonight. Hard enough drinking alone," Lonnie said. He was really earning his five big ones.

"What's she drinking?" Barnes asked.

"Martini, but with vodka."

"Two more, Lonnie. Set 'em down next to the lady."

***

A savage instinct ran wild through the Soviet Union in its final year. Overwhelming odds threatened their existence, and an urgency kicked the Russian fight to survive into high gear. They were playing from behind in a last-gasp struggle for their life. Everything intensified. Cornered like an animal, they became more aggressive, desperate, took chances.

Nastasia was told to act quickly—and she responded.

Senator Barnes turned out to be a pathetically needy man that Nastasia would meet in what he thought was the secret apartment he maintained in Foggy Bottom, just blocks from the White House.

He was as careless with his information as he was clueless to her motivations.

Nastasia extracted the initial data Admiral Drugov needed in record time, and the implacable Drugov was impressed by her efficiency. She became Drugov's most effective asset in the last year of the Soviet Union.

Barnes continued to compromise the integrity of his office, and after she had sucked dry every last morsel of information from the Senator, she delivered him the ultimatum.

Predictably, the Senior Senator from Mississippi chose to live as a puppet in the shadow of his misdeeds and continued to leak useful information, like the sieve he was, to Drugov.

"He did it to himself," Nastasia said. No remorse. He forgot the first rule; don't shit where you eat.

As the final chaotic throes of revolution broke the Eastern Bloc countries away from Russia, the Soviet Union collapsed, and Nastasia's functionality in America ended, and she was recalled. Nastasia Kidrova was back in the Soviet Union for The Fall.

Today, Nastasia sat without purpose at the window of her stark Moscow apartment. Her stare took her out onto the dreary landscape of dozens of other aging apartment buildings just like hers. Each one was filled with the life of a newly democratic hopeful, each with eyes looking out, longing to live beyond the boundaries of their existence. Could they see each other, and if they did, what did they think? What was this bounty of democracy that none had ever experienced?

Her apartment was one of the thousands swallowed by these ubiquitous postwar concrete structures that housed everyone. All the buildings were covered with the dirt and grime of fifty years of communist neglect, and the arrival of democracy had not yet been able to wash them clean.

These monstrous apartment buildings, constructed to glorify the communist state, dwarfed their occupant's lives while towering over them, and blocked the sun like dark clouds.

Nastasia hated this last year spent piddling away in Russia. Once a top-level clandestine human intelligence operative, now she sat, waiting, an unused asset of a decaying superpower living on a subsistence payroll. Formerly an agent who could strike fiercely without compunction, she now wallowed in depression and regret. When she felt that way, her mind always returned to Ned Fischmann, her last assignment in America before being recalled to the Soviet Union.

Her "introduction" to Ned Fischmann had begun innocently enough, as it always did. His apartment was on the ninth floor of a newly constructed building one block off Fairfax Drive in Arlington, Virginia. Ned thought the big windows that faced east were its only redeeming value when he chose the apartment. The early morning bedroom sun worked well for Ned, who woke early, walked to work before anyone else, and until very recently, always worked late.

His building sat among many others in the center of military research labs and offices that had sprouted up in a tight grouping in this part of Arlington. The government's emphasis on research and development had doubled, and doubled again, over the last decade as the United States stayed intensely focused on defeating the USSR and bringing the Cold War to an end.

It was this small enclave of engineers and technicians that dreamed, developed, and designed the newest and most sinister military systems their bright minds could conjure up for the United States. Within these few blocks of Arlington lived a modern-day Los Alamos.

Ned met Nastasia while walking through the doors into the downstairs lobby of his apartment building after a long day thinking engineering thoughts in the nouveau Los Alamos cluster.

She was walking out when they bumped. A cleaning pail dropped from her hand, and a sponge tumbled out onto the marble floor.

"I'm sorry," he said.

"Oh, mercy, it's my fault. I'm so clumsy." She leaned over to pick up the sponge and her loose blouse dipped open. "I've been cleaning all day and I'm tired."

He picked up the pail and pushed his eyeglasses back into the bridge of his nose, trying to calculate how he would speak to a girl.

"Say, do you need your apartment cleaned, mister?" There was a bit of a Southern twang in her voice.

The accent was nondescript. He couldn't place it.

"Mister?" he said. "I'm no older than you are."

"I could really use the work."

"I don't need a cleaning lady." He felt bad calling her "lady." She was too sweet for that. Flustered, he tried to apologize. "I... I didn't mean it that way, I... uh, or in a bad way," he stammered.

"Please," she flashed.

He couldn't refuse, and as quickly as throwing a switch, she was hired on the spot to clean his apartment three days a week.

She always made sure his apartment was her last of the day—at least that's what she told Ned Fischmann.

Even when he came home late from work she would still be cleaning, and it wasn't long before she would cook dinner and wait for him. "I thought you'd be working late again," she'd say. "So, I walked to the grocery and made you *a liddle sump'n.*"

The chicken simmering on the stove filled his head with a hearty aroma the moment he opened the door. Immediately he thought of his mother's cooking, of course, because lately, he had been wondering if it was too soon to tell his mother that he may have met someone that she would approve of—someone who cooked just like her.

Nastasia had stuffed the pot with onions, celery, and carrots, as much as she could fit, and seasoned it with fresh thyme and rosemary, and sprinkled paprika all over it. It was full of all the things that were abundant to her here.

"You don't need to do that," he'd say.

"I hate to see you come home to an empty refrigerator after working so hard."

"I don't mind the work. I find it fascinating."

"But I know how much effort you've been putting into that new system you said you're working on."

"I really can't talk about it."

"I know, but it must be impressive."

He began to think that three days a week was not enough. And so the affair started.

Information flowed like wine in the evenings. Then as quickly and antiseptically as it had started, she knew she would be done with him.

And when this affair ended, he would know nothing of what she had gathered and the damage his information would cause. She would release him. She could not leave him chained in an unequal relationship.

She sipped a late afternoon tea while looking out the big window to the east on her last day with Ned Fischmann. Her gaze swept beyond the Potomac River to the Washington Monument in the distance. It was as if she had a view across all of America. This was as close to a normal life she had ever known. It was like a dream—her American Dream. She wished it would last forever.

The bed was made, the floors swept, the bath and kitchen cleaned. There was really very little to do. Ned Fischmann was a fastidious a home dweller as he was a brilliant engineer.

She heard Ned's key turn in the door.

She was Michelle now, and she knew she would never be Mrs. Ned Fischmann.

"You're still here?" Ned said, hoping she would be.

She turned from the window and discreetly wiped the driest of tears from the corner of one eye. Perhaps it had only been a feeling and he wouldn't notice. But he did.

"What's wrong?" he said.

"Nothing. I'm just happy."

"I hope so. Come on, Michelle. Let's celebrate."

"Celebrate, what?" A smile hiding a cry.

"Today is exactly one month since we started going out together."

"Really? One month? I mean, we're *going out?*" The tear reformed with a gush as she spoke. "Tell me about your workday first."

The next morning was cold and damp. A heavy mist lingered over the Potomac and didn't want to clear, so the early crab boats were almost upon him when they saw the body. Ned Fischmann was floating face down in the still of the Potomac dawn. When the authorities discovered his belly full of sleeping pills, they closed his case that day, and Michelle, who would never be a Fischmann, was nowhere to be found.

His promising life was swept away unnoticed as if it had been moved along in the unending current of the Potomac. Once here, and then gone. Like a lost day.

That memory surrounded her like a prison wall. Nastasia gathered a few pieces of chicken to cook in a pot on the stove in her one-room Moscow apartment. She added a little onion and salt, all that she could afford. The amount and quality of the chicken, nor the variety of flavors, was nothing like her culinary creations in Arlington. But the small ritual helped fight her depression and regret while it filled her meager existence with the aroma she could not forget. She remembered it smelled like freedom.

She wondered if she would ever return to America? Would she ever escape?

A knock came at her door. It was Ivan. "Come with me," he said. "Admiral Drugov wants to see you."

CHAPTER FIVE

Jake and Ty walked from the helicopter flight line to the Building 155 chow hall looking for lunch. Everyone had big appetites in Antarctica. Working in the cold required the extra calories.

Jackson Covey, better known as Jake, was a senior lieutenant with eight years of service in the US Navy. Jake is the name his little sister, Kate, had called him when they were kids. Kate couldn't pronounce Jackson correctly when she was first learning to speak, so they shortened it to Jack for her, but it always came out Jake. And from the beginning, her nickname for her brother only made them closer. The name not only stuck, but Jake preferred it.

A fit young man from the Midwest, Jake was six feet tall with light brown hair, and not quite 30 years old. He had flown the LAMPS MK III, an SH-60B helicopter, off the flight deck on the stern of Navy destroyers for three and a half years in his first tour. He enjoyed that squadron and learned he had a good aptitude as a pilot. Landing on the moving helicopter landing pad the size of a postage stamp was not easy. He had seen a couple of helicopters go into the drink. But not him. He lived. The proof of the pudding was in the eating, he figured.

The Navy alternates personnel between their sea duty and shore duty assignments every two to three years. A mediocre shore duty as a junior officer flying a desk in Washington, DC, followed for Jake. That tour sucked. He learned he did not have an aptitude for administrative work. You don't want to be a junior anything in DC where senior ranking Navy Captains and Admirals were everywhere. It's where they go to retire, which means junior officers do all the grunt work. Jake couldn't wait to leave.

At this point in his career, Jake had been in the Navy long enough to satisfy his five-year obligation after earning his wings. He could leave the Navy if he wanted, but despite his miserable Washington experience, he wasn't ready to decide if he was going to make a 20-year career of it, or not. In his own way, the decision to go to VXE-6 had made the choice for him. He was in this squadron to build flight hours, and within a year he figured, he would drop his letter and get out. He was unsure about what he might do after he left the Navy, so he just avoided thinking about it.

For now, Jake and Ty were just hungry. They had put in a good day's work by lunchtime and they both felt good about that.

Lieutenant Ty Larkin had been in the Navy for three years. VXE-6 was his first tour. His appearance was as nondescript as Jake's, and people that didn't know them well often confused one with the other. The wardroom called him Ty. Apparently, neither Jake or Ty had done anything dumb enough in their past to earn them a special nickname, or call sign, as the Navy would say. So neither had a creative call sign.

The two pilots, wearing their green flight suits and winter-weight flight jackets as they did every day in McMurdo, grabbed food trays, and entered the cafeteria line. Ty scanned the room without removing his Ray-Ban aviator sunglasses. Though not a bright day outside, he wore them anyway. The gold-toned, wire-rimmed, and classic teardrop shape were synonymous with military aviation.

"You can take your shades off now," Jake joked.

"I like the way they look. I want the new girls to see me wearing them."

"I think they know you're a pilot."

Ty continued wearing the dark glasses well into the chow hall. He thought they made him look more like a pilot. As if wearing a green flight suit wasn't enough.

The chow hall was a busy and friendly place. Because it was the only place to eat in McMurdo Station, Antarctica, it was always packed during mealtime. If you missed a meal, you were SOL, shit-outta-luck, an official Navy term.

This created an interesting chow hall group dynamic at every meal. Socialization, specifically the ability to get along well with others, was very important in such a tight community like McMurdo. It was not unlike a Navy ship. The Navy squadron personnel were accustomed to it. Everyone else was stressed, and it resulted in a natural segregation of the different workgroups. Three main groups tended to sit together, not unlike cliques in a high school cafeteria.

One group was comprised of the scientists and their assistants. They were here for research funded by the National Science Foundation (NSF). They conducted a vast array of never-ending scientific projects. Navy personnel affectionately called them "Beakers," but usually not to their faces. Beakers were mostly University faculty and graduate-level students.

Within this group, there existed a chow hall hierarchy. Faculty tended to sit apart from students unless there was an "Ice affair" going on, which were never difficult to figure out. The quarters were so close on The Ice that it was hard to hide anything. Hunger made sure everyone saw everyone else at least three times a day.

Another group in McMurdo consisted of the various United States Antarctic Program (USAP) support staff. These were the people who did everything that the Beakers and Navy did not do: Equipment maintenance, mountaineering, cooking, and cleaning. Conveniently, many of them worked in the kitchen during mealtimes, which freed up the limited chow hall seating.

And there was the Navy group, the largest segment of McMurdo's population during the summer research season, and was comprised mostly of the VXE-6 aviation squadron. VXE-6 was a large squadron in its own right. It was one of the few squadrons in the Navy that flew two different "airframes," whereas most other squadrons flew one type.

VXE-6 flew and maintained six rotary-wing Huey helicopters and six fixed-wing LC-130 Hercules aircraft. With over 500 personnel, it was more than twice as large as any other operational Navy squadron.

VXE-6 had double the mechanics, double the aircrews, and double the maintenance. "Double the trouble," their Commanding Officer would say. That added to the difficulty of deploying to Antarctica for six months every year because evidently flying in Antarctica wasn't already hazardous enough.

Their Operating Tempo (OPTEMPO), six months on—six months off—more than any other Navy squadron, required a special waiver from the Chief of Naval Operations to be renewed annually. The normal OPTEMPO for a typical Navy squadron is six months deployed, followed by twelve months at home.

VXE-6 kept about 100 of its squadron personnel stationed in Christchurch, New Zealand. This "Cheech" Maintenance Detachment, mostly LC-130 mechanics, were located 2,000 miles due north of McMurdo because the temperatures were more favorable for aircraft maintenance. LC-130 Hercs were flown between Cheech and McMurdo each week as they cycled through their routine, or "phase" maintenance schedules. There were always a couple of Hercs getting worked on in Cheech, and four good birds on The Ice. Planes and crews shuttled back and forth like clockwork.

The LC-130 Hercules was designed to land on snow and ice. It's a special variant of the otherwise ubiquitous C-130 cargo plane known throughout the world. When the engineers at Lockheed hatched some kind of crossbreed between a plane and a snow machine, the LC-130 was born, the largest plane in the world equipped with skis. No one knows where the "L" came from. Pilots said the LC designation stood for "Love Child."

The Navy had its own military rank structure, which obviously translated into their own hierarchy of seating. Officer and enlisted do not normally sit together under any circumstance in the Navy. The exception to this was for members of the same aircrew. Guys and gals that flew together could get away with loosening the rules a little down on The Ice. It was axiomatic; "Risk your life together and you can sit together."

If you asked any group which one was the most important, each would say they were the reason why McMurdo existed. There was always a little friendly tension between groups. Nothing too serious. It was a healthy symbiotic coexistence.

***

Kronstadt Naval Base
Saint Petersburg, Russia

Ivan knocked on the gold-framed door of Admiral Drugov's office in Kronstadt Naval Base, Russia. Ivan stood at attention with a piece of paper in his hand, waiting to be acknowledged.

"Enter," Drugov's hard voice bellowed from deep inside the cavernous room.

Ivan began walking toward the oversized desk to hand the oversized admiral the message. "A coded message from agent Kidrova, sir." A curt flourish from Drugov's hand cut short Ivan's approach.

"Go ahead, read it to me." Drugov had been anxiously awaiting the prearranged transmission for weeks. It would say one of two things—one good, one bad. In either case, he knew it would be brief, and he didn't want to wait any longer.

Ivan read the message. "Objective One." He looked up at Drugov, puzzled. "It doesn't say anything more."

"Excellent," Drugov said. "We fly out this week."

Apparently, that was good, Ivan thought.

Within an hour of that message, Yury Lukyanov, captain of the Russian supply ship, КЙ–222 ЕУРЕКА *(Eureka)*, received his own message. It was from the Commandant of Kronstadt Naval Forces, Baltic Fleet.

Captain Lukyanov was elated to read that Admiral Drugov directed him to reposition his ship from Buenos Aires, Argentina to the Port of Ushuaia at the southern tip of South America, and outfit *Eureka* for a long-overdue resupply of the Russian base at Mirny Station, Antarctica.

Captain Lukyanov told his XO to meet him on the bridge. "We're finally getting out of here." He handed the message to his XO with a smile. *Eureka* had been sitting at anchor in Buenos Aires, seemingly without purpose, for almost a month.

"Antarctica?" the XO said. His head snapped up in informal attention. "We are fortunate to be selected by the Admiral for this mission. Congratulations, Captain, Admiral Drugov recognizes your great seamanship."

"How long to Ushuaia?" Lukyanov asked in a concerned tone, knowing the answer.

"About five to six days, sir."

"Make it four. I've been to Mirny. March is as late in the year supply ships ever approach Antarctica. It will be April by the time we reach Mirny. It's getting too late in the season. We're a cargo ship, not an icebreaker."

"Underway in less than four hours, sir." The XO promised.

"Make it so."

CHAPTER SIX

McMurdo Station, Antarctica

In the chow line, Jake took a moment to see who was working behind the food tables. He saw the newcomer. Darn, he thought, she's standing at the vegetable section again.

Jake worked his way down the line until he got to the vegetables.

"Hi, what's good today?" he said, hoping for some conversation.

"These are good," the girl said in her soft Russian accent and picked up a heaping spoonful of Brussel sprouts.

"Uh, just one or two, please."

She dumped a half dozen on his plate and smiled. His feigned grin was evidence that he was interested in more than vegetables.

Jake liked the sound of her voice, and lingered a few more moments, struggling for small talk. "So, you came here a couple of weeks ago. Are you going to winter-over?"

"Yes," she said with an economy of words that frustrated Jake even more as he tried to keep the conversation going.

"They always bring in the winter-over staff a couple of weeks early," Jake said. "That way, if they freak out about the cold down here, they can still fly home before the last plane leaves."

"It's cold where I come from. I'm staying," she said.

"Well, I'll be on the last flight north in a few days."

"Are you the pilot?"

"No, well, yes, I mean I'm a Helo pilot. I don't fly the Hercs."

Ty pushed Jake out of the food line and into the dining area. "C'mon Romeo."

"See you later," Jake said, looking back at the girl.

"I was just about to ask her name," Jake exclaimed.

"Yeah, right."

Jake and Ty walked into the dining room and approached one of the large round dining tables. Half of the eight seats were occupied by squadron officers caught up in a light discussion. "Good morning, Commander," Jake said to Lieutenant Commander Michael Weaver, as he stood behind an open seat. "May we join you?"

"Make yourself at home. We're just talking about the last few flights as we wrap up the season," he added.

Weaver was designated to be the Officer in Charge (OIC), the top squadron officer at McMurdo, during the upcoming winter-over. In contrast to the trim Jake and Ty, Weaver's well-rounded girth stretched his flight suit out at least three sizes more. His belly was fighting a losing battle with beer. Thank goodness for Velcro.

His call sign was Weaze, not so much for the similarity to his last name, but for the sound he made when he was passed out drunk, which was a little too often. And the junior officers had pictures to prove it.

"There isn't much cargo left, we're ahead of schedule, right?" Jake asked.

"Just a couple extra flights to The Pole, and I fly one last flight to Vostok. NSF tasked us with that flight at the last minute." Weaze paused while he inhaled another mouthful of powdered eggs and washed it down with a swig of bottomless black Navy coffee. No one interrupted him. Military etiquette the OIC thought. Astonishment at his table manners is what the other officers thought.

Weaze continued. "It seems like the Russians aren't supporting Vostok Station anymore. They just canceled everything. Ran out of money, I think."

"That's messed up," Ty said to no one in particular.

The OIC continued. "The Russians were going to pull everyone out and permanently close Vostok, but the US State Department begged 'em to keep the place open. Said we would fly in more supplies and swap out their personnel if they shared their research with us."

"What's so special about Vostok?" asked Ty.

"Vostok sits on the highest part of the East Antarctic Plateau where the ice is two miles thick. By virtue of their location, they have been drilling the deepest ice cores on the continent. And the deeper you go, the older you get. I've heard they reached deep enough to get ice cores 270,000 years old. I guess we want to get access to their ice core research."

Weaze looked over to another table with several Beakers in conversation. He took particular notice of an attractive female scientist. "That's the one I'm going to fly to Vostok. The redhead. Or is it auburn? I don't know."

"So that's the trade," Ty said. "Share your ice core data and we'll shuttle in some people and supplies to keep Vostok open."

"I'll bet a few million dollars changed hands too." Weaze said, adding, "Must be nice to have a budget like NSF."

"What's left to do at the South Pole?" Jake asked the OIC.

"All the cargo has been moved for the season," Weaze said, "so the Hercs are empty inside. We're just topping off The Pole with extra fuel. The Parachute Riggers got X-ray Delta Zero Three rigged for passengers, so we can shuttle about twenty folks each to the South Pole on a couple of geedunk flights before the end of the season. We owe it to the USAP support staff. They came all the way to Antarctica and all they get to do is work in a kitchen and take a day hike to Castle Rock."

Weaze tried to disguise a little belch between gulps of his food. He was unsuccessful. Ty's nose crinkled at the sound and made no attempt to hide his disparaging look. "It sure would be a bummer to come down to The Ice and not make a trip to the South Pole and check that box before going back to the real world. Especially since they dangle that carrot in front of all these poor saps who do the work cooking and cleaning." Weaze continued his eating and talking seemingly without taking a breath. "What do you Helo guys have going on for the next couple of days?" He asked, looking at Jake.

"We're still pretty busy," Jake said. "We finished pulling out the last two camps in the Dry Valleys today. Neither group wanted to leave. I think they're all in a competition to see who can stay out the longest. They push it much longer and the weather will make them stay there. I'm not flying my Helo in bad weather or in the dark to pull them out. That's crazy."

"And we have the last flight to close the camps at Cape Evans and Cape Ròyds," Ty added. "A few Beakers are checking on the rookeries until the bitter end. I think the Adélie penguins at Evans and Royds start their migration soon. They'll travel north with the winter sun and will feed along the growing ice edge for the next six months. Not much to see once they leave."

"I've heard that Cape Evans wanted to stay past when the last Helo is put away for the winter," Jake said. "Scott's Hut and Cape Evans are close enough for the snow track vehicles to make it there in a couple of hours. But it's not going to stay open. The Beakers need to get back so they can make the last Herc flight home."

"Hey, roomie!" Lieutenant Junior Grade Jimmy Cruz energetically plopped his tray down and jumped in the seat next to Ty, his roommate. He ignored the standard protocols and avoided eye contact with the OIC. This would be a big *faux pas* in normal military settings, but McMurdo Station is far from normal. It was more like an Old West mining town than a Navy ship—and the OIC was used to it—standard behavior from this 2P and half of the other wardroom officers.

2P was the designation for Second Pilot in the LC-130 Hercules aircraft. It was Cruz's second year in the squadron, and he was well on his way to making Pilot in Command (PIC). He had an affable personality and was a naturally talented pilot. Everyone liked Jimmy. He was a bit of a jokester and always played it loose with military etiquette. He didn't care. He wasn't going anywhere after this squadron tour, except maybe Delta or United Airlines. His last name was cool enough as it was, so everyone called him Cruz, and that suited him just fine.

Just as VXE-6 was not the place for Cruz to enhance his Navy career, the same applied to the OIC. Weaze's reputation wasn't the best. He often drank right up to the last minute of the Navy's twelve-hour "bottle-to-brief" alcohol rule. The fact is, VXE-6 wasn't on any career path for anyone. It was just a place to go.

Cruz looked at Jake's plate and made a funny face. "I thought you hated Brussel sprouts."

Jake smirked, "I just like stopping at that one girl and trying to talk with her. She doesn't say much. But I love her accent when she does."

"Where's she from?"

"She said she's from Saint Petersburg. I got that much out of her the other day. Not sure how she got to work at USAP."

"What's her name?"

"I don't know," Jake lamented.

Lieutenant "Chip" Connell approached the table. "I just got the weather brief," he announced to Weaver. Wearing his perpetual smile, he took the last remaining seat. Instantly all conversation stopped to hear the latest weather update. "We'll have a clear flight to Vostok, Commander," Chip said, looking directly at Weaze, "and it'll be okay for another day or so. But then we gotta get outta here and fly North to Cheech before the next storm."

Chip's smile said it all, and he had learned to lead with that smile. Get the broken tooth thing over with right away. He chipped his tooth long ago when he and his best friend were playing catch with a rock. Not very smart, but it's the kind of thing twelve-year-old boys do. The rock knocked a little equilateral triangle out of one of his front teeth. It looked like the perfect chip to him—even on all sides. If you had to have a chip in your front tooth it was the kind you'd want, he thought. The dentist said it needed to be fixed, but it didn't hurt, so Chip was happy to let it be. Not bad for a twelve-year-old kid.

Besides, Chip thought the timing couldn't have been better. He and his best friend were teaching each other how to whistle, the really good way, without using your fingers. When he broke his tooth, or more accurately, when his best friend broke his tooth, he quickly surpassed everyone in the art of whistling. Now he could whistle better than his best friend, better than anyone else, at least better than anyone who didn't have a chip in his front tooth. He whistled for his dog. He and his friend whistled to neighbors' dogs who knew them. They whistled at dogs that didn't know them. They practiced and practiced and got very good. But Chip's whistle was the best. His whistle always got attention. He had the kind of whistle that would make a pitcher on the mound look up to single out a fan in the bleachers. You can pack a lot of meaning into a whistle, he learned. He was never going to fix his tooth.

Chip was completing this third deployment in Antarctica and was the Naval Flight Officer for the upcoming flight to Vostok. His primary duties as NFO flying the LC-130 Hercules aircraft were polar navigation and long-range communications. Weaze regarded Chip as the best navigator in the squadron and was happy to be paired with him on his last flight on the continent.

Chip was twenty-eight years old now, a Lieutenant in the Navy, and he had not seen his best friend in a very long time.

"After we get back from this flight to Vostok," Chip continued, "we get packed up, have the big party, and head home." Chip was speaking to everyone at the table. All of the officers, other than the OIC, would be on the last remaining flights north to Christchurch, New Zealand, and Chip wanted to assure them that the weather would allow them to get off The Ice.

Chip stared at Weaze. "And then the sun sets for the last time right after we leave. Say hello to three months of darkness, Commander. Then you can hunker down and deal with it."

"Have fun spending the night in Antarctica," Cruz interjected with a smile.

Weaze shrugged off the comment by turning his head and looked over again to the Beakers sitting at the other table. "Yup, I'll be stuck here—and so will she, the redhead." Weaze was obviously referring to the attractive scientist he had pointed out earlier. "We're going to winter-over together."

"You're dreaming," Cruz said under his breath.

"She arrived in McMurdo about a week ago with some of the other winter-over folks. We're flying her to Vostok," Weaze said. "That's the reason we held off the last flight to Vostok. And we're going to bring her back with their old crew. She's Russian too. Apparently, she has to go to Vostok and check out something in person. Must be important, the season's almost over."

"Lucky you," Cruz said.

"She's a Soviet scientist, or should I say, Russian, now," Weaze added.

"Where'd all these freaking Russians come from?" Cruz exclaimed.

Many eyes turned to her direction. Only Cruz spoke up. "Why don't our Beakers look like that?"

***

КЙ–222 ЕУРЕКА (Eureka)
Port of Ushuaia, Argentina

Captain Lukyanov had reported to headquarters that *Eureka* was positioned in Ushuaia, fully provisioned, and was awaiting orders to get underway.

A message arrived from Admiral Drugov in response. "Hold *Eureka* in port and await my arrival." He would presumably inspect the ship before its departure. Drugov was well known to Captain Lukyanov as a hands-on commander but thought Drugov was holding the ship too long considering the changing seasonal weather.

Two days later Drugov landed at Ushuaia airport and flew by helicopter to *Eureka*. Captain Lukyanov met the Admiral as the helicopter landed on the aft helipad of the ship.

"Welcome aboard, Admiral. The officers and crew of *Eureka* are standing by for your inspection."

"Show me to my stateroom," Drugov said.

Captain Lukyanov was stunned when Drugov told him he was embarking on *Eureka* himself for the journey to Antarctica.

Admiral Drugov had spent almost his entire career on ships. He loved the sea. He knew the better path for him to attain a higher rank in the Soviet Navy of the past would have been to build stronger political alliances and move from his ship to shore assignments earlier in his career. In that respect, the Soviet military wasn't much different than the US military. Officers built their careers in the maze of the Pentagon while only superficially "checking the boxes" in field assignments, on ships, or in squadrons. How many US Generals and Admirals had spent more than half of their careers in Washington, DC? Far too many.

The days of Admiral Drugov being recognized as a brilliant sea commander who had subsequently been promoted in rank on merit alone ended once his Navy ceased being a "blue water" Navy. After the Soviet Union, the new Russian Federation Navy was too poverty-stricken to get their ships underway. They barely left port, and when they did, it was nothing more than a coastal patrol. Certainly not blue water.

CHAPTER SEVEN

"McMurdo, this is X-ray Delta Zero Seven, position, over."

As the LC-130 reached the Vostok-Two checkpoint, Chip broadcast his position report. The Herc crew was more than halfway on its 800-mile flight from McMurdo to Vostok Station with their passenger.

"McMurdo this is X-ray Delta Zero Seven, position, over," the Naval Flight Officer repeated.

No answer.

Accustomed to the degradation in communications that plagued High-Frequency radio transmissions in the polar region, Chip persisted. He was the consummate professional, so he was never flustered. That was a very desirable trait for polar navigators. He calmly switched radios from HF1 to HF2, dialed in 8998 kHz, the primary frequency for McMurdo Center, and made the call again.

"McMurdo, this is X-ray Delta Zero Seven, position, over."

XD-07 was outfitted with two High-Frequency radios. Each radio had a slightly different configuration and antenna length to help increase the likelihood of good reception. One antenna wire was strung horizontally sixty feet, the other eighty feet, from the top of the fuselage behind the cockpit to the tip of the vertical stabilizer. Magnetic interference and atmospherics significantly affected the propagation of High-Frequency radio waves in Antarctica. Sometimes one radio would be useless while the other worked fine.

"McMurdo, this is X-ray Delta Zero Seven, position, over."

Silence.

Polar navigation was unlike anything else on planet earth. A magnetic compass was useless. The magnetic variation between the geographic South Pole and the magnetic South Pole made navigation by compass unworkable. The geographic South Pole and the magnetic South Pole were not co-located as most people thought, but almost 2,000 miles apart. The magnetic variation shifted too rapidly to be useful in navigating a fast-moving aircraft.

Chip dialed in an alternate frequency and kept trying.

"McMurdo, this is X-ray Delta Zero Seven, position, over."

Only static.

Oksana sat alone in the cargo bay of the Herc. She had been uncomfortable ever since the Loadmaster placed her in her seat before takeoff. She sat sideways with her back against the wall near the cabin door on a small mesh fabric hammock. It was more suitable for paratroopers than real passengers. She tried to imagine why they made it this way. Did it make the jumpers more likely to get out of their seats when the time came? Maybe they would be more comfortable falling into the sky.

The loud engine noise inside the Herc further isolated her on the flight and she sank deeper into her small seat as each hour passed. She wished she had earplugs.

She avoided eye contact with the salty-looking Load-master, the only other person in the cavernous cargo bay. He had never stopped staring at her. He wore a heavy intercom headset to help attenuate the noise and she occasionally saw him speak into the headset's microphone. She knew he was talking about her to the flight deck, probably making up sorted details for Weaze to enjoy.

After her first hour in the paratrooper seat, Oksana noticed a bold red stripe painted from floor-to-ceiling on the interior wall directly across from her. The word PROP was stenciled onto the red stripe, and she realized it unmistakably scribed the location where the arc of XD-07's propellers raced only two feet beyond the skin of the Herc. "Why remind us of that?"

Her academic minded brain tried to make sense of it and concluded it was used by the Loadmaster for the placement of cargo. It must have something to do with weight distribution and the center of gravity for an aircraft that often carried many tons of cargo. But still, it made her nervous.

Then, knowing the Herc had four propellers, she anxiously turned around to see the same grim red line running up the wall just behind her.

Weaze, the Pilot in Command of XD-07, interrupted Chip's position report and spoke on the intercom to the Loadmaster.

"How's our passenger doing?"

"She looks nervous," he replied.

"Always room in the flight deck for a pretty girl. Ask her if she wants to come up for a while."

It couldn't have come soon enough.

***

There was no ground-based radar support for aviation in Antarctica, no infrastructure like the FAA traffic control. You were on your own, and a good navigator was a precious commodity. In addition to the extreme shifting magnetic variation, the lines of longitude converged upon themselves until they met in a single point at the South Pole. It was completely impractical to use the Mercator projection charts to navigate in the traditional way. A whole different kind of navigation, called Grid Nav, was developed for polar operations. This necessitated that the two independent on-board aircraft gyros were kept in perfect operating condition. Chip meticulously adjusted them during each preflight, and they were closely monitored in-flight.

Also, all the NFO's in VXE-6 used a traditional sextant for double-checking their headings inflight. These gyros provided the inputs to the Bearing, Direction, and Heading Indicator (BDHI) for each pilot. Most pilots looked at the BDHI as a compass, but it was really a gyro slewed by the navigator to Grid North in preflight and updated inflight if necessary with a good old-fashioned sextant heading check.

Chip looked at his wristwatch. He trusted it more than the clock in the aircraft which tended to freeze anytime the aircraft sat for too long. Yes, he confirmed, we're late. *Aviate, navigate, communicate.* He repeated to himself again.

That's the sequence he had learned years ago, and it never failed him. Navigate came before communicate. Worry about the radio later.

By convention, the Navy designated the 180-degree line of longitude, which coincidently ran close to McMurdo Station up to the South Pole, as the sole vertical line of longitude for Grid Nav on the Antarctic continent. This line of longitude travels down to the South Pole and continues wrapping up and around the earth as the 0-degree, or Prime Meridian, and passes through Greenwich near London, England, on its way to the North Pole. All other Gridlines of longitude would lay parallel to this one for Grid Nav. No more converging lines. Furthermore, this had the effect of designating the South Pole as being Grid North of McMurdo. What? South is North? This fact alone confused more than a few navigators during their first training flights on the continent, and Chip was convinced that more than a few of the pilots never fully understood it, but Chip made it look easy.

Chip keyed the cockpit intercom. "We're past our Vostok-Two position report, but I'll keep trying. Maintain our heading." Navigate before communicate.

Chip prepped each of his position reports by writing a short code to himself in the margins of his navigation log. He penciled a vertical column of letters down the side: PTAPTP. This was the format for the position report he transmitted to McMurdo at least hourly: current Position, current Time, current Altitude, next Position, estimated Time of arrival at that position, and the next Position after that. Since there was no aviation infrastructure on the continent, no ground radar control, no transponder flight following, the position report was the only way anyone on

the ground knew where you were or where you were sup-
posed to be when you didn't show up on time. An accurate
report could save your life.

Sometimes a navigation reporting point came and went
without hearing back from McMurdo Center despite
many attempts to transmit the aircraft's position report.
Chip glanced at his watch again, always a comfort to him.
The LC-130 was already five minutes past their reporting
point and McMurdo had not responded. Unheard, Chip
sensed how alone they were on the huge and barren continent.

Five minutes past an aircraft's scheduled position report, McMurdo Center would start getting nervous. They
would call out to the South Pole and any other aircraft
airborne at the time and begin a comms search for their
plane, XD-07.

Chip had done his part by diligently broadcasting his
position throughout the full five minutes past his actual
ETA. "Balls in your court now, McMurdo," he said to
himself.

Chip knew that others would soon start to try and
reach him on their High-Frequency radios. And through
the vagaries of polar High-Frequency propagation that
bounced radio waves off the ionosphere, it would soon
likely bring in a radio signal from another location, and
Chip could give his position report and have it relayed to
McMurdo Center.

Another possibility was, of course, that XD-07 could
hear no one, and no one could hear them.

"Flight, Nav, one more time and then I'll broadcast in
the blind," Chip announced to the aircrew.

Chip decided at the five-minute mark to make what was essentially a one-way transmission. Known as broadcasting in the blind, he would transmit his position report to anyone who was listening. For Chip, this happened a little too often.

"McMurdo, this is X-ray Delta Zero Seven, position, over."

Finally, a reply.

"X-ray Delta Zero Seven, McMurdo Center, go ahead."

"X-ray Delta Zero Seven, position Vostok-Two, 15:26, Flight Level Two Four Zero, estimate Vostok-Three at 16:19, Vostok Station next, over."

"Zero Seven, good copy, out."

Technically, McMurdo should give a verbatim readback of the position report. But sometimes all you got from McMurdo was a "roger out." This always bugged Chip.

CHAPTER EIGHT

The navigator was the first to "see" Vostok as they approached the small Russian camp. "I have Vostok on radar," Chip said. "Eighty-five miles, come right to Zero Four Five."

Lieutenant Junior Grade Cruz, flying as 2P, sat in the left seat for this leg of the flight and banked the LC-130 a few degrees to the right and asked for the descent checklist, after which he gave an initial call to Vostok on his Very High Frequency (VHF) radio.

"Vostok station this is X-ray Delta Zero Seven, over."

No answer.

Lieutenant Commander Weaver, PIC for this flight, verified the VHF frequency for Vostok and repeated the initial call.

"Vostok station this is X-ray Delta Zero Seven, over."

"No joy," Weaze said.

As is typical on flights to camps of other nations, they never seemed to know when you were showing up. McMurdo had no firsthand communication with Vostok. It was too recent following the end of the Cold War to have direct contact between a United States base and an ex-Soviet station. All coordination was clumsily handled through a circuitous web of communications between the NSF, the US Department of State, the Russian Embassy, and the Russian Arctic and Antarctic Research Institute, AARI.

The arrival time always seemed to be the issue. Was it Zulu time, or McMurdo time, which used Christchurch, New Zealand time, or was it Vostok time? To complicate matters further, the International Date Line ran north-south just East of New Zealand. Aircrews couldn't be sure if they showed up a day early or a day late. No one in McMurdo ever really figured out what time zone Vostok used. It could have been Moscow time for all the Americans knew.

"Vostok station this is X-ray Delta Zero Seven, over."

"No joy," Weaze said again. "It doesn't matter. We'll ring the doorbell."

The pilots set up a gradual 1,200 feet per minute rate of descent to eventually level off at 2,000 feet Above Ground Level (AGL).

The sky was clear. The pilots looked forward out of the cockpit. "We don't want to hit a weather balloon," Weaze said. "And they have this big-ass radio tower right next to the skiway. Why'd they put it so close?"

Weaze set up XD-07 to overfly Vostok station at a low altitude while still maintaining a fair amount of airspeed. This would send unmistakably loud thunder down to everyone at the Russian camp as Weaze rudely announced his arrival. And just as the LC-130 passed directly overhead Vostok, Weeze bumped the throttles forward a bit to further enhance the calamitous roar to the people below.

"That'll wake 'em up," Weaze gleamed with undue animus.

Approaching from above, Vostok was a sight to behold. Think Armageddon meets dystopia.

"Look at this place," Cruz said, who was seeing Vostok for the first time. "Looks like a shithole."

Outbound after buzzing the station, the 2P made a gentle left hand turn to set up a second flyover of the station, lower and slower than his first pass to indicate to the inhabitants below that the LC-130 Hercules was going to land.

Cruz was too young to have any first-hand knowledge of the Cold War and he didn't know much about the USSR. This was his first up-close and personal introduction to anything Soviet. Vostok was a broken vestige of the old Soviet Union.

Inbound now at 1,000 feet AGL, the Herc's slow pass allowed Cruz to soak up all the sights. "Man, this place makes McMurdo look like the Taj Mahal."

The austere conditions of Vostok were nearly incomprehensible to Cruz. The station consisted of not much more than a scattered collection of a dozen shipping containers. And that's probably what they were. Some were connected end to end, some at right angles to each other.

"That's Vostok Station," Weaze said. "That's where they live and work."

Approaching the station more slowly from above, all eyes were out of the cockpit now as they watched the pristine white snow gradually give way to the exploded debris field of jetsam that enveloped Vostok. It appeared from above like a 360-degree junkyard at which the camp was centered in its bullseye. Like spokes of a wagon wheel, the residents had simply discarded their waste, junk, and other derelict equipment in a radial pattern surrounding the station. Their version of housekeeping was a drag-and-drop dance that had been going on for decades. You could probably date the garbage like reading the rings of an old tree.

Landing at Vostok was tricky enough, but the high altitude takeoff was going to be the real challenge for such a large and heavy aircraft as the LC-130. Weaze instructed Cruz, "Keep your speed up on approach. You don't want to get low and slow landing at this altitude."

At almost 11,500 feet above sea level, Vostok Station was the highest skiway in Antarctica. And the extremely low air pressure of the polar region easily added another 2,000 feet to the pressure altitude. This low air pressure is a result of the earth's rotation. Our globe spins around its axis much faster than many people realize. The circumference of the earth at the equator is over 24,000 miles. This means as the earth rotates each day, once every 24 hours, a person standing at the equator is actually moving at 1,000 miles per hour. The tremendous centrifugal force caused by this rotation throws our atmosphere out wide at the equator making the earth fatter in the middle and thinner at the poles.

The thin atmosphere above Antarctica placed the Vostok skiway at an elevation that seemed like 13,500 feet. VXE-6 was able to fly cargo into Vostok without much difficulty, but everything had to be offloaded before takeoff. Aircrew always flew back to McMurdo with essentially an empty aircraft and minimum fuel.

XD-07 taxied up to camp and stopped in the middle of the skiway. It seemed to Cruz to be the most likely place to park. There was no taxiway. They were next to what looked like a front door to a shipping container. It had a sign and a flag. Weaze unbuckled himself from the four-point seat harness. "Keep her warm, Cruz. Chip and I will go out."

They did not shut off their engines. The last thing the aircrew wanted was to get stuck here if an engine could not restart.

Cruz stayed in the left pilot seat, the Flight Engineer remained in his seat in the middle of the cockpit, and Weaze and Chip went outside to greet their new friends. XD-07 was tasked to bring back six Russians and their baggage. Nothing more. There was no room for any extra weight.

Oksana Zverev exited the aircraft closely following the two pilots. She walked past Weaze and firmly said to him, "Do not leave without me. I have to get something," and head down, she kept walking.

"Thirty minutes on deck is all the time we have," he yelled after her.

Fuel consumption while idling was normally not much of a problem, but XD-07 had carried only just enough fuel to get back to McMurdo. They needed to be as light as possible in order to get airborne during this extreme high altitude take off.

A half dozen Russians exited a shipping container and stood huddled around one another, shuffling their feet, waiting to get back home. "They're packed together like a waddle of penguins," Weaze muffed. When Chip did not respond to the remark, Weaze pointed to the few small duffel bags the Russians were taking home. "Not much in the way of personal belongings, either." Chip ignored him. "Man, these guys have it rough," Weaze said to no one.

Weaze looked at Chip after thirty minutes on deck. "Six bodies. Waiting on the redhead." Weaze anxiously checked his watch again for the tenth time in the last five minutes. He had exposed it to the minus forty-degree temperature one time too many. The LCD crystal on his Casio watch was blank. The battery-powered watch had frozen.

"What time do you have?" Weaze knew Chip had a nice watch. Just like sunglasses, aviators wore their watches as symbols of their profession. Chip was especially proud of his watch. Weaze knew it was from his father. He was the only officer in the squadron who wore a Rolex. It wasn't an extravagant model, but he cherished it. It was perhaps the most understated watch produced by Rolex—The Explorer. It told time, nothing more. Three hands: an hour, a minute, and a beautiful second hand that swept so smoothly that Chip often caught himself staring at it for a whole minute during its trip around the dial. Those brief respites would allow Chip the time to think of his father and to say the things he had never said before, and never would, now that his father was gone.

Just then, a small antique tractor came chugging around from behind a storage container. Belching black smoke and making a racket, the tractor carried a two by two-foot wooden crate. Oksana was walking alongside and directed the cargo to the rear of the Herc.

"What's this?" Weaze asked.

"This is my research project. It's not too heavy."

"Really, then why is a tractor carrying it?" The PIC was not happy.

"How much does it weigh?"

"Not much." Her terse comment and forced smile left no doubt in Weaze's mind that she was taking the crate back to McMurdo with her.

He read her expression correctly. Not worth it, he mused, better to be nice to her. It was going to be a long winter night. Weaze motioned to the group of Russians standing around waiting for their ride to load the crate into the aircraft. They looked back at him and continued to shuffle their feet.

Then Chip gave his short "Let's go" whistle, and they moved. It worked internationally.

The crate was quickly loaded by the Russians without further complaint, eager to speed up their departure.

CHAPTER NINE

КЙ–222 ЕУРЕКА (*Eureka*)
2,000 Miles Southwest of Ushuaia, Argentina

The seas had been very rough for *Eureka* as the Russian supply ship crossed into the Southern Ocean during its passage between Argentina and Antarctica. This 500-mile gap of angry water between the two continents is one of the most treacherous in the world. The wide band of turbulent ocean, centered at 60 degrees south latitude, wraps around the entire globe like a 500-mile wide ribbon.

Nowhere else on earth do the oceans circle the world like this, where you can trace the same line of latitude across the surface of the globe, all the way around, and never touch land. Here, ice-cold waters from the south explosively converge into warm oceans from the north, and competing currents fight each other with the forces of hemispheres behind them. Unencumbered by any landmass, hidden undercurrents forever rage beneath the surface. Anything south of 60 degrees is a gamble.

The Southern Ocean is as deadly to ships as Cape Horn and The Cape of Good Hope, at the southern reaches of South America and South Africa, the continents that dare to extend fingers of land down into the Southern Ocean. Just as the Capes are well known to be graveyards for ships, the Southern Ocean is never kind to those who cross into its path.

Most of the young sailors were seasick. None wanted to be there. They thought of themselves as one-step above a conscript. "What's the difference between a slave and a seaman?" they joked. "Slaves don't get seasick." That's how the new seamen saw it, life at the bottom rung of the ladder. Getting seasick in the Southern Ocean made it all the worse.

Eureka had made it through the most turbulent waters. A week out of the Port of Ushuaia, now at 69 degrees south latitude, about 200 miles off the coast of Antarctica, and with the roughest waters behind them, their next threat was ahead.

The ship's engine's RPM changed slightly. It was subtle. Most on *Eureka* didn't even notice, but Drugov felt it like his own pulse. He went immediately to the bridge.

"What's going on?"

"Icebergs Admiral," Lukyanov said, "hundreds of them." He offered Drugov his binoculars, but Drugov declined. It was almost an insult. You'd have to be blind not to see the acres of ice floating directly ahead, extending as far as the eye could see. Drugov turned to show he could also see the Quartermaster standing behind a huge pair of binoculars, almost two feet long, and mounted on a tripod, the "Big Eyes," helping direct the ship as it picked its way through the icebergs like a minefield.

"I've slowed to six knots, sir," Lukyanov said.

Drugov stared at the sea of icebergs in their path. He quietly breathed out a long discerning exhale. "Make it ten," he said and walked off the bridge.

Later, Ivan stood at Drugov's stateroom door. Ivan was green inside from the endless undulating motion. "A message from the radio room, sir." He only needed one step into *Eureka's* small stateroom to reach Drugov and hand him the paper.

Drugov read the brief message to himself and looked up. "Kidrova has accomplished her next objective."

Ivan leaned against the bulkhead for stability while he waited, not daring to show any sign of queasiness.

Drugov said, "Go get some rest, Ivan. We'll be there in three days."

Admiral Drugov was a sailor at heart. He was one of a very few Russian officers that had begun their careers as an enlisted man and risen to become an officer, in his case, to the unprecedented rank of Admiral. He knew how tough it was for the junior enlisted ranks. He had started his Navy career as a conscript himself.

His rapid accession in rank was attributed to both his aggressive tactics and that he was regarded as one of the strictest commanders in the Soviet Navy. But one that always saw to it that his sailors were trained, supplied, and equipped as best as the Soviet Navy could provide.

He had a genuine affection for the sailor, yet he demanded everything from them. And in return, he was supported by those under his command like no other. The devotion and sacrifice his enlisted sailors provided him had no doubt contributed to his many successes.

Privately, the Admiral's peers envied his leadership and how he was able to accomplish so much consistently. And while they worked their way through their own maze of the Politburo, they knew where best to keep the aggressive threat of Boris Drugov—they kept him at sea, away from politics, away from Moscow, and out of the Kremlin.

In this way, Drugov rose in rank, but outside the political structure. The arrangement had worked well until the end of the Soviet Union and the dissolution of the Politburo.

Drugov watched his comrades enrich themselves over the last few years while he had remained in port and oversaw ships that stayed tied up to the pier. This was not the promise of the new Russian Federation. *Keep your damn politics—I operate my way.*

Change came to Admiral Drugov's fleet. Contraband, under-counting cargo, misdirecting cargo, and bribery—all fed the lucrative Black Market in his new fleet. Not his choice. He had wanted to be a sailor all his life. But he saw it as the logical route for him. When he was forced into this new Navy, he did what he always had done, and that was adapting his tactics.

Drugov removed a large flask from his luggage and poured himself two fingers of vodka. He drank it in a gulp and welcomed the familiar warmth as he laid down on his bunk and closed his eyes. The rolling ocean comforted Drugov like the bosom of a lost lover. It was his first blue water cruise in over three years. He missed it like a sailor misses his bride.

CHAPTER TEN

McMurdo Station, Antarctica

"I'd call it Fair and Fair. There's not much contrast, but you can still see the horizon. What would you call it?"

"Fair and Fair." No argument from Ty.

Jake was half stating his own weather observations and half quizzing Ty, his copilot. The training never ended.

They were in Helo 15 flying north from McMurdo to Cape Royds, the first of two stops. It was the last helicopter flight of the season. The last flight of Jake's third and final season in McMurdo. His last flight in Antarctica. It felt bittersweet.

Jake had been an excellent instructor pilot to Ty and a good mentor, too, bringing up his student rapidly. Ty was at this time finishing his first season as a fully qualified helicopter pilot. Next season it would be Ty's turn to act as the senior pilot, the Aircraft Commander, of his crew. The year following that, in Ty's third season, he hoped to be an instructor pilot himself. Jake did not doubt that Ty would make it. The cycle continued.

Jake requested to be on this last flight of the season with his favorite crewmembers, Ty, his copilot, and Chief Martin, who was in charge of the cabin and cargo. Their only passenger on the way out from McMurdo was also a request, his best friend on the ice, Felix Quigley.

"Two Beakers at Cape Royds and two at Cape Evans," Jake said.

"The cabin will be a little crowded on the flight home. It depends on how much cargo they have," Ty said.

They were flying north from McMurdo to pick up four remaining scientists still working at the last two science camps at the close of the season.

Jake said, "Let's climb a little and see where the ceiling is. Take us to 2,000."

Ty increased power and Helo 15 slowly rose from 1,000 to 2,000 feet midway between its twenty-mile transit from McMurdo to Cape Royds.

"What would you call it now?" Jake asked.

"It's Poor, for sure," Ty said. "Getting close to Nil."

Just common words, of course: Fair, Poor, Nil, but clear and decisive terms in pilot communications. Each carried a specific multi-sentence definition in the Air Operations Manual to describe exact weather conditions for both the surface definition of the snow and the horizon definition. Critical flight information conveyed to another, distilled to a single syllable.

Jake smiled when he didn't have to remind Ty what to do next.

"McMurdo Base OPS, this his Pirate One Five, weather, over."

"Pirate One Five, go ahead."

"Weather observation, ten miles north of McMurdo. At 1,000 feet, surface and horizon are Fair and Fair. At 2,000 feet, Poor and Poor, over."

"Pirate One Five, good copy, out."

"I can't see Erebus anymore at this altitude," Jake quizzed. "Remember where it should be?"

Ty glanced down at his heading indicator. "Yeah, and pointed about 45 degrees to the right of their current heading."

Jake nodded. Ty knew right where it was. He had his shit together. "Let's go back to 1,000."

Felix keyed the intercom from the aft cabin as they started down. "Visibility is getting bad up here, huh? It's that storm brewing."

"It's a slow roller, though. Not the like that Herbie we had in our first season." Jake turned his head back and gave a quick glance into the cabin to see Felix's reaction. "The heavy stuff won't be here for a few more days."

"I'll never forget that flight," Felix said over the intercom, referring to the time the both of them were caught in a bad storm. That Herbie, a rapidly forming Antarctic blizzard, as the squadron calls it, is the storm that trapped Jake and Felix far from McMurdo during their first season together. They spent three days in a Scott tent waiting out the blizzard.

Felix sort of sounded British. That's what most people thought. You could say they were half right. His accent was difficult to nail down to any one location. Even the cleverest attempts took more than a couple of guesses. Jake asked Felix about it in their isolation together during that storm and got more than he bargained for.

Felix earned his Ph.D. from the University of Cambridge in England and had spent half of his primary school years living with his mother in London, but those early years were fragmented. He spent the other half of his youth in relative poverty living with his father in South

Africa, where school meant learning to survive in the slums of Johannesburg.

It was during that uncharacteristically long blizzard, three years ago, the first season for each of them, that Jake and Felix got to know each other well. Hearing Felix talk about his youth helped Jake more than he ever thought.

It wasn't a totally unexpected storm, it never was, but it grew rapidly, and before he knew it, they were in a Herbie. "I should have turned back," Jake said. "But if you sit around waiting for good weather, then nothing would get done." But that's not what he really meant.

Felix shared how his mother had met his father while completing her graduate research in South Africa. After Felix was born, she tried to live in South Africa, but when that didn't work, his father tried to move to England. Ultimately, neither solution worked. The undesirable arrangement that resulted saw Felix being swapped back and forth between his parents. Felix would spend a school year in England, followed by a summer in South Africa, then a year in South Africa, and another year in England. It was far from ideal.

"I kept bouncing between two worlds," Jake remembered Felix saying. "I was half black, half white. Just a little different. Just different enough, no matter where I lived, I was unsure of where I belonged." Jake was certain he had seen Felix tear up. He knew Felix had not divulged that much personal information to anyone before.

When Felix needed to continue, Jake let him. "I was neither one or the other. Not connected. Yeah, that's how I felt. Disconnected."

And when Jake needed to talk, Felix listened.

Their deep friendship began during that three-day blizzard, isolated in the cold, stuck in the most inaccessible place on the planet, waiting out the storm, and sharing their pasts, very far from the geographic centers of their pain.

Today's flight path would have first taken them directly over Cape Evans on their way to Cape Royds had Ty not flown a wide arc around the Adélie penguin rookery next to Cape Evans. Ty first saw the brown patch of the rookery ahead, and then Scott's Hut came into view.

Ty keyed the VHF radio. "See you in an hour," he told Cape Evans. "We'll pick you up on the way back from Cape Royds."

"Roger, Roger," said someone on the ground.

"That's Beaker-talk for okay," Jake joked.

Jake watched the two figures in their red USAP parkas jumping up and down hysterically. By deciding to pick up the other two scientists at Cape Royds first, they had officially made Cape Evans the last science team to remain out on the ice at the end of the season. Major bragging rights. They would have a lot to celebrate soon at the last big party. It's the simple things that can excite people in Antarctica.

The pick-up at both camps went smoothly, and Helo 15 headed home. The pilots remained quiet while the cabin celebrated in loud conversation.

Then Ty spoke on the radio. "McMurdo Base OPS, this is Pirate One Five, RTB."

Jake was saddened by that last radio transmission.

From a quarter-mile out, Jake took a final look at McMurdo as they approached from above. Strangely, it reminded him of the small town where he had grown up.

Even though smaller in size, McMurdo was similar in many ways. Mostly how everyone knew everyone.

Jake looked down at McMurdo's main street. Funny, it didn't have a name, as far as he knew. He followed along the road with his eyes and thought of the hundreds of times he must have walked on it over the last three years. It started as a wide straight road that ran gradually uphill a hundred yards from the helicopter hanger. It passed by Penguin OPS on one side, and the new NSF building on the other before the wide part ended next to Building 155, which housed the chow hall. The rest of the road was narrow and continued around town in a lazy loop as it meandered in, out, and between numerous small buildings and the only other two prominent structures in McMurdo; the Maintenance Shop and the dormitories.

The "roads" through McMurdo were not much more than winding paths. A gaggle of walkways used primarily by people, and shared with a handful of snow track vehicles and the shuttle bus, the van that drove aircrew and workers to and from the skiway and ice runway.

Helo 15 paused fifty feet above the ground to stabilize its hover before lowering itself onto the helicopter landing pad behind the hangar. Jake's last look around during their final approach found him gazing upwards to Observation Hill.

"Ob Hill," as it is known, was immediately behind the helicopter hangar and towered over them at more than 750 feet high. Jake spotted the large cross on its peak. It was silhouetted against the white sky. He vowed to make one last hike up to the summit before leaving to visit the wooden cross at the top, the private spot which had offered him comfort during his time in McMurdo.

Ty reduced power and Helo 15 settled onto the ground.

No sooner had Helo 15 offloaded its passengers and cargo than the radio burst to life. It was a crisis call.

CHAPTER ELEVEN

"Rescue, this is Base OPS, over!"

"Rescue, go ahead."

"Tim, get going, someone's been found at the base of Castle Rock! The Helo is turning."

Tim grabbed his personal rescue bag—always at his side. "Damn," he muttered. Most of his gear had been packed away for his flight home tomorrow or was already in storage for the winter season. "I'll make due," he said to himself and busted out the door and into the freezing air.

Tim Rogers was the head mountaineer in McMurdo Station, Antarctica, and looked the part. Tall, lean, and fit, with a full beard that would make any mountaineer proud. He took his job very seriously. Tim sprinted to the helicopter pad. He had made this two-minute dash many times before. He was careful. It was bitter cold out. The sub-zero air burned lungs that sucked in too quickly. Slow, deliberate breaths were required. Discipline.

The ice under his broad strides crunched like sand. Good traction. It tempted him to run faster. He knew better. Caution. Every few steps, like a trap, the ice was slippery as hell and hard as concrete. Tim Rogers had felt that pain often enough.

The essential ingredient in any rescue on The Ice was time. It was twenty-seven degrees below zero. No time to waste.

Tim reached the waiting helicopter panting hard from his run but stopped short. Thirty feet from the helicopter he bent over, trying to control his breathing and warm his lungs. They burned from their brief exposure to the frozen air. Much more of this, and he knew his lungs would suffer frostbite, on the inside.

Still bent over, heaving more slowly now, Tim looked up, facing the thumping helicopter as if in a standoff. He waited. Tim showed a healthy respect for these mechanical beasts. He paused long enough to gain eye contact with the pilot.

Looking up from the right pilot seat, Jake interrupted his pre-takeoff checklist. With an ever-so-supple nod, the pilot's head twitched back in a way that signaled to the veteran mountaineer, "Get on board."

Cautiously stooping his tall frame, Tim deliberately crouched further as he walked the last few steps, ducking under the menacing arc of spinning rotor blades, and climbed into Helo 15, through the side cargo bay door.

"What the hell happened, Jake?" Tim yelled before Chief Martin could hand him the spare headset.

The pilot knew to wait a few seconds for the mountaineer to plant his butt in the tiny bench seat and put on his headset before answering. "Some hikers at the top of Castle Rock just radioed in that they see a body at the bottom of the cliff."

"Got it. I'm ready," Tim said.

"Looks like somebody tried to climb Castle Rock again, and fell. Just like what happened a few years ago," Jake said.

"Takeoff checklist complete," Ty said.

"Ready for takeoff, Chief?" Jake asked.

Chief Martin, the helicopter crew chief, sat aft of the two pilots in the cargo bay cabin and was in charge of most everything about Helo 15 that didn't involve a stick and rudder. He was secured to the cabin bulkhead with a short lanyard, still called a gunner's belt, that allowed the crew chief some mobility around the cabin during the flight.

Martin reached across the cargo bay and gave a firm tug on Tim's seat belt. It was secure. He looked Tim in the eye and gave a thumbs up to the mountaineer. Tim knew to stare right back and return the thumbs up.

"Ready for takeoff," Chief Martin reported over the intercom.

Jake said, "Here we go again."

Jake lifted off, executing a skillful climbing turn. He twisted the throttle hard with his left hand and pulled up firmly on the collective. Airborne less than thirty feet, he pitched the cyclic stick steeply forward and to the right with his right hand while he kicked in rudder with his right foot, performing an aggressive coordinated turn. In a single motion, Helo 15 was climbing, turning, and accelerating in a beautiful synchronized dance of flight.

Helo 15 was moving fast. Jake jumped on the radio and announced his departure to Comms, the Communications Room, the radio link to the Base of Operations for all helicopter activities in the vicinity of McMurdo.

"Base OPS, this is Pirate One Five, over."

"Pirate One Five, go ahead."

"Outbound, McMurdo to Castle Rock. Four souls on board."

"Roger One Five, en route Castle Rock."

The LC-130 Hercules aircraft had their own dedicated Communications Room next door in the same building, and together they comprised the central hub for all aircraft activity and communications on the continent. This Base of Operations was simply referred to as Base OPS and served to describe both its function and location.

Castle Rock wasn't far from McMurdo and Tim knew it well. It was a 1,300-foot rock formation that sat prominently two miles from McMurdo Station. Its peak was rounded and sloped on the backside, but its front was a sheer cliff on the side that faced McMurdo.

Tim trained all his new mountaineers in the snow and ice that surrounded Castle Rock. They even did short training climbs up its steep rock face. But extensive climbing was too dangerous, even for mountaineers. It had been designated off-limits to any recreational climbing for many years. Even so, every once in a while, someone would give it a go. Tim wondered how far this one made it up before they fell. They never got very high—twenty feet, thirty? That usually resulted in a broken leg or two.

Tim remembered the last person who died. It was during his first season eight years ago. Too cute for their own good, two men had decided to take a different approach and climb *down* from the top of Castle Rock, but they fell from the top. They first made the three-mile-long trek on an established hiking trail that winds wide around behind the mountain and then gently slopes up against the backside until it finally reaches the top of Castle Rock.

This scenic route is a wonderful hike and fully encouraged on a good weather day during the relatively warm months of December and January. You can hike all the way up to the summit and stand at the edge of the 600-

foot precipice of Castle Rock. It is a beautiful and unforgettable view of McMurdo Station below and the vast Ross Ice Shelf that stretches endlessly to the horizon.

To Tim, the proximity to McMurdo Station meant that this was someone out for a final hike the day before they too were to fly home. Too bad, he thought. Antarctica, as beautiful as it is some days, can also be as hostile an environment as there is on earth. No room for mistakes.

Antarctica is almost impossible to get to, and most people that are lucky enough just to get to The Ice only come once in their lives. Their one brief visit usually only lasts from a few weeks to a few months, so sometimes they take risks to create memories, and that does not always end well.

Tim wondered who this person could be. They could be faculty or students affiliated with a university and involved in scientific research with the NSF during the summer research season. Or they could be one of the USAP support workers that do everything from the cooking, to cleaning, to maintenance. Or they could be with VXE-6, the Navy squadron that has been providing logistic support, in one form or another, since Admiral Byrd and OPERATION DEEP FREEZE following World War II.

This was the eighth season for Tim Rogers, head of the Antarctic Mountaineering Team. A real veteran. As difficult as Antarctica is to get to, for some, it can be just as hard to leave. Like a siren's song, it pulls you in. It's hard to resist. Maybe that's why Tim Rogers was still single.

Helo 15 completed its sprint from McMurdo to Castle rock in under five minutes. Tim unstrapped from his seatbelt before the first skid touched the snow. Chief Martin slid the cargo door open, and as soon as the engine's RPM's slowed they jumped out the door.

Tim reached the body first. His instinct said she would be dead. He was thankful she lay face down as he approached and called out, "Are you all right? HEY! Are you all right?" There was no answer. He dove to his knees in the snow beside the girl and placed his hand on her shoulder. Tim shook gently, as if not to startle someone who was sleeping. No response. "Hey!" he shook again more firmly. The body was frozen. Solid. Unnatural. She must have been lying here for many hours, he thought.

Jake stayed in the pilot seat and kept the helicopter idling. Ty and Chief Martin joined Tim seconds later. The three of them carefully rolled the body over. They had to look. They each recognized her as a girl who worked in the kitchen, but no one knew her other than that.

The damage was severe. It reminded Tim of the first death he had seen in this same location eight years before. Still kneeling beside the girl as if in prayer, Tim looked up to the top of Castle Rock. He spoke to no one but the rock edifice itself, "She fell from the top."

The three of them carried the girl to Helo 15. Tim picked up a glove that was lying next to the girl. Thinking it was hers, and wanting to keep it with her, he placed the glove in his pocket.

The flight back to McMurdo was silent except for the standard radio call from Jake to McMurdo.

"Base OPS, this is Pirate One Five, over."

"Base OPS, go ahead!" Quick, with anticipation.

"Inbound..." he paused, "five souls on board..., one deceased."

Anticipation drained from the radio voice. "Roger that," is all Base OPS could say.

The standard procedures followed like any routine rescue and recovery drill that had been practiced countless times. The flight surgeon and two corpsmen met the girl. They were prepared.

As the body bag was being zipped closed, Tim remembered the glove he had placed in his pocket. "Hold on," he said before the body bag was sealed. Tim went to place the glove in the bag with the girl when he noticed she was already wearing both of her gloves. "Uh, never mind," he said. A bit embarrassed and self-conscious of his interruption. He hoped the others thought he was just taking a private moment to pay his final respect.

And thinking nothing further of it, he stuffed the glove back in his pocket.

CHAPTER TWELVE

"Yes, sir. Her name is Ksenia Nikitovna." Lieutenant Commander Weaver was on the phone with the Commanding Officer of VXE-6. Jake sat quietly to the side in the OIC's office, listening to the conversation.

The OIC's office, its adjoining administrative office, the weather briefing, and scheduling rooms, and both Comm rooms, all collectively filled a two-story building that was universally known as Penguin OPS.

"Yes, sir. Yes, sir." Weaze constantly nodded his head in the affirmative as he listened to his Commanding Officer. Jake imagined the difficult time their CO must be having. His six-month deployment to Antarctica had just ended. He had returned to the squadron's home base at Point Mugu Naval Air Station in warm and sunny Southern California only the day before. It should be a time for relaxation and a reunion with his family, and now this.

"Yes, sir. She'll be on the next flight to Christchurch," Weaze said.

Jake watched as Weaze listened. Weaze's nodding grew more pronounced, and Jake sensed the conversation becoming more intense until Weaze's entire body was rocking back and forth in his OIC chair. His face grew redder and he looked like a scolded child.

Jake pictured their CO standing in his office in California and yelling into the phone. It was not one of his better traits. How could his tantrum benefit this situation?

Weaze pulled the phone away from his mouth and whispered, "As if I had anything to do with a girl falling off a cliff."

The call ended. Weaze never said goodbye. Apparently, the CO had hung-up on him. Weaze stopped rocking and sank into his chair.

Jake spoke first. "I'm glad I'm not in your shoes."

Weaze took a deep breath and looked to Jake for sympathy. "You knew her, didn't you?"

"Not really," Jake said. "I didn't know her name until you said it just now. I've only had some small talk with her in the chow line. I know she arrived a couple of weeks ago."

"Well, I gotta go talk with her roommate," Weaze said. "Maybe she knows something."

Lieutenant Commander Weaver walked the fifty yards slightly uphill along the main road that led to the dormitory used by the USAP personnel. The building was a bland brown army-style rectangular box. It looked like it was designed by the same creative mind that invented the Quonset hut. Weaze found Cynthia Brock's room and knocked on her door. "Good morning. Are you Cynthia?"

"Cinnamon," she said. "Cin for short."

"Okay, um... Hi, Cin." A somewhat casual introduction, he thought for what she knew would be a serious conversation. "I'm Lieutenant Commander Weaver. I'm going to be the winter-over OIC, the Officer in Charge. You were Ksenia Nikitovna's roommate, right?" He struggled with the pronunciation of her name.

"Yes, of course. Everybody knows. They told me what happened an hour ago."

"I'm sorry to bother you at this time. I sincerely want to offer you my condolences. This must be very difficult for you."

Not being invited in, he asked. "May I come in?"

The OIC stepped into the sparsely furnished room. It was not unlike a college dorm, but without the posters. He saw no decoration at all to personalize the room. Nothing that said anything about the occupants. Just two beds, both made, two dressers, two closets, and two chairs. Not being invited to sit, he decided he should continue to stand.

"Were you close friends with Ksenia?"

"We weren't friends. I didn't know her long. We had only been here for two weeks, but we were going to winter-over together."

"When did you see her last?"

"She and I both worked lunch yesterday, and I worked the dinner last night."

"Did you see her after dinner?"

"No, I never saw her after lunch." Cin looked over at Ksenia's bed. "She didn't sleep here last night either."

"So you weren't with her when she went out hiking to Castle Rock?"

"No."

"Do you know why she would go out alone?"

"Did she go alone?"

"Well, I don't know. We don't know anything, really. I'm just trying to figure out what happened." Now the OIC seemed to be put on the defensive, and he didn't know why.

"You're acting like a cop or something," Cin declared.

"No, I'm the OIC, like I said. Officer in Charge."

"Maybe she wanted to see Castle Rock before it got pitch black outside."

"Well, she should have known not to go alone. Is there anything that indicated to you she may have wanted to hurt herself?"

"What are you saying? No, I don't think so." Cin turned, hiding her face from the OIC for the moment, then sat on her bed. "Maybe she did. Who knows?" She let out a long sigh.

Cin became more talkative now. "This is all very stressful. I know she had kind of a bad past in the Soviet Union. She told me a little about it. And that's why she was able to come to the United States. Some kind of a refugee, or something. I don't know. Go talk with her girlfriend."

"Who's that? What's her name?"

"I don't know. She's the other Russian girl that's here— the scientist. She came down recently to winter-over too. But they don't bunk scientists and USAP together in the same dorm."

"I know who you're talking about, the redhead," Weaze said. "I flew her to Vostok."

"They knew each other from before," Cin said. "Some connection back in Russia. That was how Ksenia got USAP to send her down here. I think that scientist pulled a few strings."

"Thank you, Cin. And again, I'm sorry for your loss."

"Sure."

Weaze started to walk out but paused. "Oh, and do you mind if I had a look at your cold-weather gear?"

"My what?"

"Your parka and stuff that you wear outside. The USAP gear you were issued."

Cin opened her closet and showed the OIC her red parka. It was the standard unflattering bulky USAP issue cold weather parka.

"And your hat and gloves?"

"Here," she pushed them into his hands so he could get a good look at them. "It's all here," she said.

He gave the gloves a quick look, turning them over, but didn't notice any marking.

"Thank you," he said. "Just curious," and walked out.

An odd thing to say, he thought as he walked away. "It's all here."

CHAPTER THIRTEEN

"Nice office Felix, you're moving up." Jake got along very well with Felix Quigley and enjoyed his good-natured, if not a little eccentric, personality. Jake hardly would have guessed that Felix had his Ph.D. in Environment and Climate Research when they first met three years ago. But Felix had become one of the few true friends Jake had on The Ice outside of the squadron.

Jake had flown Felix by helicopter so many times to and from different research sites that he couldn't remember them all. But it was that one flight beyond the Dry Valleys in their first season when they were socked in for three days that he couldn't forget. No one was harder on Jake than Jake himself. He knew he should have turned back.

Felix Quigley was a sort of Jack of all trades Beaker. He liked working in Antarctica and seemed to be carving out a niche for himself as a kind of unofficial NSF liaison to all the visiting Beakers. He welcomed them to The Ice and showed the ropes to new scientists during their limited research trips. Some visits were as short as a few weeks and his assistance was invaluable. His likable personality was infectious and well suited to the role. It was good for job security.

Felix fit well into the McMurdo culture. He felt so comfortable that McMurdo became the home he looked forward to returning to—not the other way around. It was an easy decision when Felix volunteered to winter-over this year to babysit the NSF facility.

"What took you so long to ask?" and "Better you than me," were some of the comments muttered by other NSF staff. He was quickly appointed the official winter-over NSF senior representative.

"Along with the new office, I got a new title, 'NSF Resident Researcher in Chief.' How do you like the new digs?" Felix was as proud as an Emperor penguin as he showed the office to his friend.

McMurdo had been slowly built over decades from a sparse Navy base into what was now a legitimate small town whose only industry was polar science. The NSF had money to burn it seemed, and the *pièce de résistance* was their new NSF research building placed in the heart of McMurdo. It was wholly out of place in the Navy shantytown. It looked more like a futuristic space station that had landed among the otherwise unremarkable warehouse structures. Its design had most certainly been conjured up in NSF headquarters near Washington, DC by some committee of people who had never been to McMurdo. Designed perhaps, to impress on the outside as much as the inside. No expense was spared. The rumor was it cost more per square foot to build than any building in the United States. Nowhere else was the disparity between the NSF and the USAP/Navy made more apparent than after the recent construction of the new NSF building. It was officially named the Crary Science and Engineering Center, but to the USAP and Navy, it was simply called the new NSF building, probably because they were never invited to go inside.

Not only was Felix's office nice, but it was also big. About the size of a big office in DC, where it was designed. It was an absolute luxury in McMurdo. It had a large desk, several comfortable upholstered chairs and a conference table that could seat eight. The side wall was open shelving, beautifully lighted, which displayed many uniquely Antarctic items that would serve to start up small talk with visiting dignitaries, and the folks from DC, the ones who wrote the checks.

"You've got a lot of cool stuff in here," Jake said, looking around.

"I added a few things and made it my own," Felix said, picking up a couple of large eggs. "Mummified penguin eggs," he said, holding one in each hand, framing his face with a smile nearly as wide as his ears. "Found them in a pile outside of Scott's Hut."

"Hmm," Jake made a sardonic grin, but then turned his attention to a twenty-four-inch diameter classroom size world globe placed in the middle of the conference table. He gave the little world a spin as he tried to change the subject. "What's the deal with your globe? It's upside down."

In fact, Felix had unscrewed the globe from its armature, flipped the earth upside down, and replaced it with Antarctica up.

"Really, who's to say? Hey, if globes had been invented by someone from South Africa, it would be perfect. Right? Anyway, we're in Antarctica. So, the South Pole on top!"

"Okay. No argument from me, doctor."

"Honestly, we still get a few folks through here each season, usually politicians, who don't fully understand how it can be daylight down here all summer and night all winter. They may have some kind of wacky idea like the earth moves back and forth on its axis. Really, they just don't get it.

"That's when I go into my teacher role. I pick up the globe and show them it's the earth's orbit around the sun that affects the orientation of the axis, and that the earth's axis stays the same. I literally have to pick up my globe and show them before the concept sinks in."

Felix poured a few drops of water onto the soil of a potted desert cactus that was sitting on his desk. His action begged the question from Jake, but it never came. Jake wanted to say something about the odd presence of a cactus in Antarctica but thought he'd save it for another time.

"I like your stuff, Felix, but I'm really here because I needed to talk with someone about the girl that died."

Felix sat quietly. He knew to listen.

Jake spoke softly at first. "I found out her name, Ksenia. Pretty name." He spun the globe again. His head hung low. "I don't know. I kind of liked her. I thought maybe she liked me a little, too."

Then Felix watched Jake's face redden. Suppressed emotions were painful to reveal. He no longer seemed calm.

Jake's speech quickened. "What if I had been the one to take her on the hike to Castle Rock? She would have been safe with me. I should have asked her, but I didn't. I couldn't even ask her name."

Jake was torn between hopelessness and guilt. This was about more than a girl named Ksenia.

"I should have turned back on our flight. I should have known when to stop." Felix had heard him talk like this before. Something triggered Jake's remorse. No matter what happened, he always thought he could have done more, even when circumstances dictated otherwise.

"I sensed it. But you don't get to be a good pilot without a fair amount of seat of the pants insight." Jake's head was down. He was talking to the floor. "Trust your instruments. All the training. Thousands of hours of flight time. But in the end, the pilot makes the final call, right? And has to live with it, right?" He seemed to be rambling, but Felix knew. It was something deeper.

"Damn, Felix. She reminds me of Kate. Why don't I ever know what to do?"

"Maybe it was because he was too young." That's what his father told everyone. "It wasn't the boy's fault. Just a kid."

But Jake did blame himself. He was a good swimmer for his age. He and his sister were both good. Maybe that's why Jake thought his sister Kate was joking when she was splashing around so much—well past the float that they so often swam out to at the summer lake. "Don't go any farther than the float," his father would say. "Watch out for each other."

Between the shore and the float. One hundred feet, you're safe.

The splashing kept going. Kate yelled something. Jake didn't understand.

She was out pretty far. Farther than they had ever been—even that one time when they knew their father wouldn't be watching and able to catch them. *What was she doing out there so far?*

Jake decided to swim after her. From the shore to the float, Jake swam as fast as he could. As fast as he had ever swum. Like when he raced his sister in a one hundred foot dash to the float.

He climbed onto the float, a sheet of plywood and two by fours, balanced on a couple of empty fifty-five-gallon drums.

Kate wasn't making a sound any longer. Ripples surrounded an arm that reached up. Jake froze. *Don't go past the float.*

Jake dove in. He had never been alone past the float. He wasn't alone. Kate was out there.

He sprinted a few strokes and stopped to look, but the last ripples were fading away. Two more powerful strokes toward Kate. *Don't go past the float.* He had never felt so alone in his life.

I can't.

He dove down deep, but nothing.

Then he made the hardest decision of his life. He turned back. He considered it the worse decision of his life. He had waited too long. He told himself that often.

"I wish I'd never turned back, Felix."

After all those years, Felix was the only person whom Jake had ever shared his feelings.

Jake never returned to the summer lake again. And when he was older, he never returned to his small town again. Small town gossip. Too much talk. "He's the guy." Painful looks. "That's him. He let his sister drown."

He couldn't escape. Everyone knows everyone. So he left.

Jake wanted to continue but stopped when they heard a loud noise at the far end of the NSF building. With the summer research season officially over, the building was nearly deserted. They listened as the disturbance began to make its way closer to Felix's new office. Most of the building was empty with all the room lights off, yet someone was banging on every door and yelling something in each room. It sounded like a garbage truck working its way down the street. As the noise drew closer, they heard a voice. "Hello? Hello?" BANG, BANG, "Hello?"

"That's Weaze," Jake said.

"What's he doing in my building?"

"Probably lost," Jake smiled, and they waited.

Felix's office was the only room in the corridor with its lights on. "You'd think he'd check your office first," Jake said.

Weaze barged into their office without knocking the moment he saw Felix. "Hey Felix," Weaze said, ignoring Jake like he was a potted plant. "I'm looking for that red-headed Soviet... Russian scientist. We flew her to Vostok."

"Her name is Oksana Zverev. Doctor Zverev. She should be in the Geology Lab. It's in the other corridor, down the hall, and to the right."

Weaze left without a thank you, and possibly without noticing Jake.

CHAPTER FOURTEEN

Oksana sat motionless at the large rectangular soapstone table in the center of the Geology Lab. She leaned forward, looking intently through a stereoscopic microscope. Each eye glued to an ocular, one hand employed to rotate a knob, the other to move the specimen tray. She perched herself on the front edge of a tall laboratory stool, her legs and feet engaged like a runner's poised in the starting blocks seconds before a race. It was a full-body effort to examine the rock. Any closer and she would fall into the microscope. So fully engrossed, she hadn't noticed anyone enter through the open door of the lab.

Oksana was looking for clues. She examined with intense concentration a small black meteorite on the specimen tray of her microscope. Under magnification, she had already concluded the rock was a meteorite by looking at its surface. She used the stereoscopic microscope, much like a powerful magnifying glass to study the light reflecting off the rock's surface, not the light passing through it, as one might view a thin slice of material with a conventional microscope.

She saw the characteristic found only on the surface of meteorites—fusion crust—*proof*, the thin layer of material that had been superheated as the meteor passed through the earth's atmosphere. This fusion crust was very black and indicated that this was a fairly recent meteorite. But "recent" in cosmic terms, it may have fallen to earth as many as 100,000 years ago.

Oksana knew she had a meteorite, and she knew it was made of stone, not iron, it didn't weigh enough to be iron. She knew that as soon as she picked it up. That was her first test. And a magnet didn't stick to it either, her second test. That confirmed her finding.

A stone meteorite from Antarctica would itself be a great discovery. But stone meteorites are the most common type found in the world, and she did not come this far to collect a common meteorite.

It's what she didn't see that continued to encourage her. Perhaps it was the same thing her father had noticed. Other than the tell-tale fusion crust, the surface of most stone meteorites also contains small indentations, called chondrules. In fact, meteorites that have these chondrules make up the largest group of stone meteorites and are called Chondrites. The chondrules are caused by tiny grains of silicate crystals, evidence from the primordial solar nebula, the swirling dust that predated the birth of our solar system. Thus, this category of a meteorite is billions of years older than the planets themselves in our solar system, and therefore meteorites with chondrules cannot be from the planet Mars.

But some stone meteorites do not have chondrules. They are called Achondrites. No known Martian meteorite ever displayed chondrules. Her meteorites did not have chondrules.

No level of the increased power of this microscope would yield the next step in evidence for which she hoped. In order for her to *absolutely prove* that the meteorites were of planetary origin, she needed a more thorough physical examination. First, she would cut a very thin slice of the rock for visual inspection. After that, more testing by chemical analysis and gas spectrometry would still be required.

Despite the exhaustive testing that lay ahead, she was very hopeful. Her excitement at the anticipation was invigorating, and this created a dilemma for her. She knew the immediate challenge would be to contain her euphoria and not let anyone know. The Martian meteorites had to remain secret. She had to continue acting like she was only in McMurdo for a benign geology research project.

Were these Martian meteorites? That answer could take weeks to be certain, but she did have enough to tell her friend that she had found the prize they were seeking, what had taken them so long, and why so much preparation together to collect. Soon she would tell her that their lives would never be the same.

Weaze stood unnoticed in the doorway of the lab and took the opportunity to study Oksana silently. He decided her shoulder-length hair color was more red than brown. Her athletic posture seemed to accentuate her figure. He sucked in his gut and tapped on the door frame. "Hello," the OIC stepped into the lab.

Oksana looked up from her microscope, put on her eyeglasses, and smiled.

She was even more attractive wearing her eyeglasses, he thought. A tight green turtleneck underneath her open white lab coat complimented her look. The black-rimmed eyeglasses, her fair complexion, the smooth skin of her face, all framed by that beautiful reddish hair, looked perfectly coordinated. Beauty and brains, Weaze was distracted.

"Hello, Oksana," he said again and walked over to her. "You remember me from the flight to Vostok?"

"Hello, Lieutenant Commander Weaver. Yes, I do," she smiled, obviously pleased with what she had been working on.

He realized that she could not be aware of Ksenia's death. He had not thought about this. He was not prepared to be the one to tell her.

"Have you heard about Ksenia Nikitovna?" He struggled again with the pronunciation of her last name.

"What do you mean?" As innocent as a fawn, she sat upright on her lab stool, her smile fading. "Is something wrong?"

"I'm afraid I have some very bad news."

Her expression went blank while she waited.

"Ksenia was just found dead. She fell from Castle Rock."

Stunned, her rose complexion turned marble-white, eyes fixed like a Greek statue — a stare into oblivion.

Weaze had never before witnessed such a sudden and dramatic change in expression.

Not knowing how to comfort her or what else to say, he continued. "I understand that you and Ksenia knew each other."

"We were best friends." A long pause, Weaze wasn't expecting any deep connection between the two.

"Oh no," she said. "I was the one that arranged for her to come to McMurdo with me."

Both were Russian, of course, he knew that, but Oksana was a Ph.D., Ksenia was kitchen staff with USAP. Acquaintances maybe, but best friends? He never expected that. He couldn't recall seeing them with each other before or sitting together in the chow hall. He would have noticed.

Weaze found himself stuttering. "I..., I didn't know."

"No one knew. We didn't tell anyone."

Oksana became silent. Her spirit seemed to withdraw from her body, chilled by a blast from an Antarctic wind. The impact began to overwhelm her. Then a delayed reaction to hearing of the death of her life-long friend only seconds before. It became too much. She couldn't get a breath of air. Her heart and lungs were knotted in pain. Like a violent kick to her gut, she was caught between inhale, exhale and vomit.

In a moment of panic, she tried to stand. Her previously taut legs now unsteady, the room spun around, her eyes rolled up.

Weaze caught her in his arms as she collapsed.

Oksana woke in an armchair on the side of the Geology Lab with Weaze patting her face with a damp towel. She was sweating, nauseated.

"This is terrible," she tearfully choked. She could barely speak. "We were going to winter-over together."

Weaze was uncertain what to do. He wanted to go back to Felix and Jake for help, but he didn't want to leave her.

An inner strength soon supplanted Oksana's emotional display. She was stronger than he expected.

She spoke. "How did it happen? When did this happen? Who was she with?" Her staccato questions demanded answers. But Weaze sat pitifully inept. He didn't know what to say.

Oksana insisted on hearing the details of Ksenia's death.

"I don't know how it happened." Weaze realized he wasn't helping at all. He knew nothing, but he tried to match her strength and fulfill his role as OIC.

He continued to talk and informed her of the circumstances surrounding the recovery of her body at the base of Castle Rock.

"I'm very sorry," he said. "We think it was an accident." Then he began to ask questions. "Do you know why she would go out alone to Castle Rock?"

"No. She wouldn't go alone on a hike like that," she said firmly.

"Oksana, I hope you don't' mind my asking, but I am the Officer in Charge." *It sounded awkward.* She turned her bloodshot eyes toward his hoping to hear something authoritative. She was immediately disappointed.

"Do you think she wanted to hurt herself?"

"Absolutely not. Ksenia was happy. We had big plans together after this winter-over."

"What do you think happened?"

"I don't know." Oksana was clearly agitated and grew angrier with each question.

Her response was not good enough for the OIC. He should have stopped badgering her, but just like he didn't know what happened with Ksenia, he didn't know how to control his inquisition. He took her hand and could feel it shiver like she was left out in the cold. It was hard for him, but he felt now was the time to keep pressing her for more information. He stumbled forward.

"It seems a little suspicious to me that you were so close to Ksenia, but you didn't want anyone to know about your friendship."

Oksana stood up, almost defiant in her stance. Weaze was afraid she might slap him.

"Leave, please. Leave me."

Weaze stood. "I'm sorry. I didn't mean to upset you. We can talk again later."

"Leave me alone."

CHAPTER FIFTEEN

КЙ–222 ЕУРЕКА (*Eureka*)

"Attention on deck. Admiral on the bridge." A young seaman yelled out as Drugov entered the tight compartment
of Eureka's bridge. The uncomfortably low ceiling
squeezed a row of stormproof windows that wrapped the
bridge on three sides. The bridge of this Navy vessel always felt cramped, but the Admiral's presence made it
hard to breathe.

Drugov went straight to the Quartermaster, who was
standing rigidly next to his navigation station.

"Position?" Drugov said.

The Quartermaster looked down at the chart laid flat
on the table in front of him and placed his finger on their
exact position, which he had been following minute-by-
minute for six hours straight. He was too tired and frightened to speak.

Drugov looked at Lukyanov. "Make course to
McMurdo Station. Best speed."

"Sir, I understood that we are heading to Mirny Station?"

"No. McMurdo. A detour."

"That will take us south of 70 degrees," Lukyanov said. His glance double-checking the chart. "The ice will be too thick for our vessel this late in the season, sir."

Drugov stayed silent. He faced Lukyanov directly, his eyes unblinking like an alpha dog.

Lukyanov bent over the navigation chart to look more closely in a bid to break contact with the Admiral's stare. "I have maintained our track north of 70 degrees south latitude to minimize the iceberg hazard. Mirny Station is safely north of that at only 66 degrees. But McMurdo is at 78 degrees south latitude."

Lukyanov was certain that Drugov knew how far south McMurdo Station was located, but at the better part of 1,000 nautical miles farther south from their current ice infested position, he needed to emphasize the significance, and possible folly, of the Admiral's orders. Lukyanov's concern rang with a twinge of insubordination in Drugov's ear.

"McMurdo, best speed," Drugov repeated. He stood face-to-face with Lukyanov, daring him to utter any response other than "Yes, sir." He thought of relieving the Captain of his command at that very moment but knew he would be beneficial to complete the journey. He would demote him upon their return.

***

McMurdo Station, Antarctica

Weaze treaded dejectedly through the cold down the gently sloping vacant road on his way to Penguin OPS. The town's deserted state in these last days before the end of the season further numbed his thoughts. The dark sky didn't help. McMurdo seemed to be in perpetual twilight this time of year. At best, and only if it was clear, the sun peeked just above the horizon for a few hours around noon each day.

Weaze entered Penguin OPS and passed no one else in the building on his way to the Comm rooms. The radios were silent. "Pretty quiet, huh, Parks?" Weaze said to the Petty Officer on duty.

"No aircraft airborne at this time, sir. X-ray Delta Zero Three has been on deck at the South Pole for about an hour. We should be hearing from them any minute now as soon as they take off on their inbound back to McMurdo."

"That's the last flight on the continent. It's hard to believe the season is almost over. X-ray Delta Zero Seven is heading to Christchurch later today, and Zero Three will leave tomorrow."

"Yes... sir," Parks said dolefully, thinking about being stuck in McMurdo with Weaze as the OIC for months.

"How's the weather for their flights north?"

Parks pulled a clipboard off the wall. It contained weather reports from the Automated Geophysical Observatories (AGO) scattered across the continent. "It's good for now," he said without looking. "Low pressure has been building over the EAP." He had already studied the information when the reports first came in. "I'd give it a couple more days before it gets rough here in McMurdo. X-ray Delta Zero Seven and Zero Three will be in Christchurch by then." Parks extended the clipboard for Weaze to make his own assessment of the data. "You can see for yourself if you want."

Weaze shook his head. He was in no mood to interpret weather reports or listen to a Petty Officer talk back to him.

"Alright, I'll call Cheech and give them an update. Do we have a Comm Sat window?

"Soon," Parks glanced at a different clipboard. He thought twice about reaching for it and pressing his luck with the OIC. "You can make your call in another thirty minutes, sir."

Weaze sat alone and in silence at his OIC desk while he waited for the communications satellite window to make his SITREP to the Christchurch Duty Officer. He reflected on his meeting with Oksana. "I guess I pissed her off," he said to himself, brooding over his poor performance. "So much for anything between us this winter-over."

He wrote some notes in preparation for his phone call. He jotted details about the weather report he had just received, that all the helicopter flights were done for the year, and how the seasonal ice was already reforming in McMurdo Sound. What else could he say?

He opened the top right-hand drawer of his desk and took out the glove Tim, the mountaineer, had given him. Weaze had tossed it in the drawer earlier without a second look. Now, while he waited, he took the time it deserved to examine the glove more thoughtfully than he had before.

It was made of light-colored fabric, not the darker brown leather, like his, the type of working glove issued to the squadron personnel. It probably belonged to a Beaker or a USAP staff member.

Weaze tried to put it on. It was too small—probably a girl's.

It wasn't dirty or worn out. In fact, it looked fairly new—maybe a recent arrival to The Ice.

He turned the glove over and saw the numbers Tim had referred to on the back of the wrist. Handwritten—most wrote their initials. Weaze stood up purposefully.

***

A lone figure eased out the little-used side door of Building 155 in a motion so fluid as to go unnoticed. The hood of her parka was pulled out to protect the skin of her face and it slyly shielded her identity. She did not look completely anonymous, should anyone have cared. Even shrouded in a bulky USAP parka, one could see she was slight of stature.

She walked uphill in a deliberate clip toward a small group of cargo buildings that were left hibernating until next year, and away from Penguin OPS and the new NSF buildings, where human activity was still being conducted. Once behind the first structure and out of view, the figure dodged quickly to one side and slipped like a shadow between two smaller sheds before stopping. She made a determined scan of her surroundings with the stealth of a soldier clearing the streets before a conflict. The backside of McMurdo was deserted. Pleased with her safe haven, she removed a small radio transmitter from underneath her parka and waited.

After more than twenty years in service, the dated Cold War satellite from the Soviet Union continued to serve its purpose equally well for the new Russian Federation. It circled 1,500 miles above the earth in polar orbit, north-to-south, pole-to-pole, exactly once every 240 minutes. Its design was simple; receive uplink communications on a limited number of secret frequencies, record them, and then retransmit them back down to earth when the satellite was above Russia.

The timing of the satellite's revolutions was the key to its simplicity and perfection. Every 240 minutes, every four hours, six revolutions per day, the satellite orbited the earth. This meant that a spy on the ground could reliably account for the satellite returning over their position without any further information other than the time of day. Factoring in the rotation of the earth beneath the satellite's orbit once every 24 hours allowed the spy to predict the exact time to send uplink communications from their location to the satellite once per day, at the same time each day.

The time drew near. She shivered while she waited. This was the coldest mission she could ever remember. She chuckled. *I would have never complained before.* She had made many sacrifices in the past for the Soviet Union, but now she felt like a cheap mercenary.

She returned the radio to the relative warmth beneath her parka to preserve its batteries and continued to wait. Soon she checked the time again. Only minutes to go now. Good. She was freezing. The communication uplink window during the satellite's overhead pass was limited to ten minutes. Her brief message would need less than one.

CHAPTER SIXTEEN

Weaze returned to the NSF building to find Oksana weeping in the chair of the Geology Lab where he left her. He had decided he needed to be more resolute in his questioning. His superiors would be questioning him, so he needed answers.

"Tell me about Ksenia," he said. It looked like she hadn't stopped crying since he left her.

"We were going to winter-over together."

"What was she doing here in McMurdo?"

Oksana stood up, took a deep breath, poured herself a glass of water, and began to open up.

"Ksenia has been... had been... trying to leave Russia ever since her parents were killed in the revolutions that led to the end of the Soviet Union," she observed a blank expression of his, and added, "I'm sure you've heard of this?"

"Sorry to be uninformed."

"It was the two-year period we now refer to as the Autumn of Nations."

"I didn't know," he admitted.

"Revolutions were occurring all across the Eastern Bloc. It swept through many communist countries like East Germany, Hungary, and Czechoslovakia. By the end of 1991, when it was finally over, communism had been defeated throughout Eastern Europe and more than a dozen new free nations were born."

Weaze looked like he was hearing this for the first time. "I remember some of that," he lied.

"Ksenia's parents were activists in the revolution trying to help make a better Russia. But they were too public about fighting for improvement in the old Soviet Union. They were caught up in the fervor of the political movement championing for democracy. They represented a visible part of the local resistance during the chaos near the end of the Soviet Union."

"I see."

"Her parents were labeled radicals by the communist government. The closer the Soviet Union came to collapse, the more brutal it became with the dissidents. Thousands of protesters were rounded up and detained. The leaders were arrested and held as political prisoners. One day, they came for her parents, and Ksenia never saw them again."

"We both wanted to go to America. But there was no way for us to immigrate while Communism was collapsing." Tears were choking her speech. "I have also been trying to get to Vostok Station for years."

"I don't understand," Weaze said.

"I was trying to use my science background to get to Vostok before the fall of the Soviet Union, but the revolutions stopped all that."

"Vostok? For your research?"

"After the Soviet Union collapsed, the American National Science Foundation continued to help maintain the Russian Polar Science programs. I am a geologist, and I was able to be hired on with the Russian AARI, our Arctic and Antarctic Research Institute in Saint Petersburg. It's similar to your National Science Foundation. Your NSF has strict rules for whom they will sponsor to come to Antarctica. Many want to come for the summer research season, but no one wants to winter-over. So, I agreed to do my research over the winter if there was a way to bring Ksenia here with me. But it was not possible since she was not a scientist. NSF would not sponsor her. Then we found a way that Ksenia could work for the USAP support staff. USAP also has a difficult time filling the winter-over positions. A lot of senior people at NSF would not approve of this arrangement and they would cancel it if it were known that NSF was helping to arrange for friends to go to Antarctica together. So, we had to remain quiet about the arrangement."

"What were you going to do after this winter?" Weaze asked. "Go back to Russia?"

"I am never going back to Russia. You can see how much effort we put into this and how much it meant to us. I didn't want anything to get in the way of us being together in McMurdo. We kept it secret."

"You seem to like secrets," he said, looking directly at the wooden crate she had retrieved from Vostok, and which was sitting in the corner of the lab. "What's in the crate?"

"I can't tell you."

"You have to tell me. Your friend is dead. You don't think it's an accident or a suicide. I need to know more. What's in the crate?"

"Just rocks."

"You told me it was your research project. It must be something special. You flew all the way to Vostok to get it."

Realizing the inevitable, she answered with a bit more information, giving up as little as possible in the hope it would stop any further inquisition. "It's just some rocks, collected near Vostok."

"I have a feeling there is more to it than that."

Thinking of her father, her emotions started to resurface. Reluctantly she spoke. "My father, Vladimir Zverev, collected those rocks. He was a well-known Soviet scientist. The rocks are of great interest to me. They're worth examining more closely."

"Was? Where is your father now?"

"He is dead. He would want me to have these rocks."

"And is that one of them?" Weaze pointed to the small rock she was examining under her microscope.

"Yes," she nodded.

"How does it look?"

"It looks promising."

Weaze reached into the pocket of his polar jacket and pulled out the glove Tim had given him. "This was found next to Ksenia's body at Castle rock. The mountaineer gave it to me. He said there was no name on it, just some numbers—Zero Three."

He showed the glove to Oksana. "But I think there's more to it than that," he emphasized his words now as he slowly and loudly pronounced her name, "isn't there, Oksana Zverev?" Weaze was more assertive than was characteristic of him.

She was speechless. Her mouth open, her eyes still red and wet over the loss of Ksenia, she walked to her coat hanging on the wall and removed the matching glove from its pocket. There, holding her glove for Weaze to see, were the initials she had written on it, in Russian Cyrillic letters—O3. She took the glove from Weaze's hand and reunited the pair. "That's my glove," she said.

"Please, sit with me," Oksana beckoned.

"My dorm room was broken into the other night while I was at dinner," she said. "They were looking for something. Everything was turned over and gone through. I thought they didn't take anything, because I knew what they were looking for, and it wasn't in my room. That is, I didn't think they took anything, until now. I couldn't find my other glove in the morning when I came to the lab. I thought I had misplaced it."

"You said you know what they were looking for?" Weaze asked.

"I know what *she* was looking for."

"She?"

"It has to be Ksenia's roommate. Ksenia was so nice. Too innocent, too trusting. She must have told her roommate about us. Ksenia could never keep a secret."

"I met Ksenia's roommate earlier," Weaze said. "Her name is Cynthia. She goes by Cinnamon, Cin, for short. You know, the fun alter ego names people like to give themselves while they're down here on The Ice. She seemed okay to me, except for that Cin name."

"I don't care what you think."

"Let's assume she did break into your dorm room. You said you know what she was looking for. What?"

"It's something rare and valuable."

"What could be so valuable as to make someone kill for it?"

***

Jake began his final sentimental visit he had promised himself to the top of Observation Hill. He frequently made the short, steep, hike up Ob Hill next to McMurdo. He went for the exercise as much as for the peace and quiet he found there. He usually went on Sunday mornings, and always went alone. His brisk trek each Sunday was worthwhile for the view itself when the weather and visibility were good. But regardless of the weather, Jake also returned to the top of Ob Hill to stand next to the massive wooden cross that had been erected to memorialize the final expedition of Captain Scott.

Captain Robert Falcon Scott was a British Royal Navy Officer and a significant early Antarctic explorer. He had made two expeditions attempting to reach the South Pole. The first expedition from 1901-1904 fell short of the South Pole by 500 miles. He returned almost a decade later. In 1912 he did reach the South Pole but died on his return trip. The cross was an impressive structure over fifteen feet high and befitting the great explorer. Its twelve-inch crossed beams were twice the width of railroad ties. Erecting it on the summit of Ob Hill was an impressive feat in itself.

Jake seemed to be drawn to the cross just as so many other visitors to McMurdo found themselves inexplicably captivated by the solemn altar. For a reason unknown to Jake, his melancholy mood was now steering him again, as if on autopilot, to the top of Ob Hill.

Before going back down to McMurdo, Jake placed his hand on the cross as he always did. Then he turned to watch his feet very closely before carefully guiding each step upon the loose rock that covered Ob Hill. The tricky footing made the descent more challenging than the ascent. Knowing he would be looking at the ground ahead of each tenuous step throughout his downhill passage, he paused for a final gaze at McMurdo from his elevated vantage point.

The town below was peaceful and still. Then, in the distant perimeter behind McMurdo, Jake saw movement. His pilot eyesight zeroed in on a deeply hooded figure walking briskly between the buildings along the dormant backside of McMurdo. What could they possibly be doing out there?

CHAPTER SEVENTEEN

Oksana needed to talk. The burden was too much. Her life was starting to crumble and her panic was returning. But still, she resisted divulging her secrets.

"Let me think," she sobbed. Weaze leaned back and observed as Oksana seemed to fall into a trance. Her head went slack, she mumbled to herself and recounted her years of effort. She had planned long and hard to be exactly in this position.

Weaze was out of his depth and at a loss for words, so he repeated what he thought a leader would say. "It's okay. Talk to me."

Her head shook from side to side in mournful disbelief. "No, no," she quietly spoke to herself. Tears of loss trickled from her welled up eyes. Ksenia was dead and she was the prime suspect. Oksana had no choice.

She reflected on all she had done to get here. How she had been able to get NSF to sponsor her AARI research in McMurdo and fly her to Vostok. She had retrieved her father's treasure. Her plan even got NSF to arrange for USAP to have Ksenia winter-over in McMurdo as part of the support staff. Together she and Ksenia would smuggle the meteorites out of Antarctica to America.

And now her mind drifted to the future, a future that might have been, a future that would never come. She imagined the way it should have unfolded and haltingly revealed her plan to the OIC.

Once back at USAP in Denver, Ksenia was to lay low and wait. Back in Washington after the winter-over, Oksana would give a brief lecture to NSF about some made-up geology research she did in McMurdo. She would be a star at the obligatory meet-and-greet symposium. She would thank everyone profusely for the opportunity of her lifetime. She would congratulate both countries on the progress made by working together to advance science. She would emphasize that NSF had once again, as always, led the way in the improvement of international relations. She would declare that science had accomplished more in one polar season toward the advancement of world peace than the politicians could do in a decade. The hyperbole would be thick. The audience would eat it up. Later she would join fellow scientists and their spouses at an extravagant dinner party.

The following day her flight back to Russia would leave—without her. She would be on a bus halfway to Denver and disappear.

That was the plan. She was so close now, but it was all falling apart. The prize was here, literally in her hands, yet unattainable. Oksana could hear her father's voice echo in her head as it had for so many years. She was going to get retribution for her father's death. Make things right. Take what was rightfully hers. Could it still be salvaged?

She continued to talk with Weaze. "If I tell you, Commander, you will not be safe."

"I want to know."

"I will only tell you if you agree to help me."

"I'll help you."

"You don't know what you are agreeing to. If I tell you, your life will be in danger. No one who knows will be safe."

"I have to know."

After a pause, she jumped up and made a demand. "Help me hide this crate."

"So that's what this is all about?"

Oksana opened the top of the crate. "These rocks are meteorites. My father collected them near Vostok nine years ago. The Soviet Union would not support his expedition. He had to go alone and in secret. He was a brave man. But they left him to die, alone. Eventually, his body was found and returned. Some of his belonging, including these meteorites, were placed in this crate and left in a pile of worthless junk outside Vostok. They had no idea what these rocks he collected were. Everyone assumed my father was an eccentric professor, just a geologist collecting rocks and who would write another boring research paper about them."

Oksana stood proudly. "My father knew differently. He knew these were meteorites. He told me so himself. But he also told me they were meteorites from Mars. I was a child then, and I was the only person he told."

"Does that make them special?"

"All meteorites are special. But the world of geological science is just beginning to learn what my father knew. That Antarctica is a virgin landscape, perfect for the discovery of meteorites. Millions of years of space rocks have rained onto this barren continent and are waiting to be harvested."

"How did he know they were meteorites?"

"My father conducted a detailed interview with the man who originally found a few of these meteorites. That man had picked them up, handled them, and photographed them. My father knew what they were and how rare and valuable they are."

"How rare are they?"

"Until now, there have been very few meteorites found in Antarctica, only a handful, random ones found here and there. There has never been a dedicated meteorite search in Antarctica. That will all change after this."

"Is it that important? How valuable can they be?"

"Very valuable. An average meteorite, an unremarkable specimen found throughout the world, may only be worth $4-5 per gram. A rarer meteorite could be worth ten times that—maybe $50 per gram. But an Antarctic meteorite would be double that, $100 per gram."

"Wait a second. How much is a gram?"

"You see this specimen under the microscope? It's about the size of an olive, and it weighs 26.34 grams."

"That little rock, 26 grams, so at $100 per gram that's worth $2,600. Hardly worth killing someone over."

"But if it's a Martian meteorite, it would be worth ten times that, $1,000 per gram, $26,000."

"Okay, that's a lot, but still, not enough to kill someone."

"This is the smallest one of my father's meteorites. There are two dozen meteorites in that crate. A few of them weigh over a kilogram each."

"Wait. A kilogram is 1,000 grams, I know that much, so 1,000 x 1,000 is... holy shit... that's a million dollars!"

"Exactly."

"So, your father did it for the money?"

"No, of course not. He was an academic and a dedicated Communist. He wanted to bring these home to the Soviet Union. They would belong to the state."

"Then why all the secrecy of your trip?"

"I am not my father. The USSR killed my father. They killed Ksenia's parents too. I owe Russia nothing. They owe me."

"So, you're doing it for the money?"

"They are rightfully mine."

"Are they from Mars?"

"It appears so. I don't know conclusively yet. It will take a more extensive analysis."

"Wow, but they're at least meteorites, right?"

"Yes, these are Antarctic meteorites." Oksana picked up one of the larger meteorites and held it in her hand as if to emphasize that she was in sole possession of the treasure. "No one knows of these meteorites. Vostok doesn't know. NSF doesn't know. The only person besides Ksenia I told was an admiral in Russia. His name is Drugov. Telling him was the only way I was able to get to McMurdo. I told him that the meteorites should belong to Russia and be studied in our universities and displayed in our museums."

"Is he as idealistic as you?" Weaze said.

"I am under no delusions. I know he is greedy. We had an arrangement. I would return the meteorites to him in exchange for him forgetting all about Ksenia and me. I expect him to hand over a few meteorites to Russian scientists, but keep most for his own profit. I'm sure he will sell them on the Russian black market. But I have the advantage. The admiral does not know how many meteorites my father found. No one else in McMurdo knew except Ksenia. It is obvious, Lieutenant Commander Weaver,

Ksenia has told someone else, someone here in McMurdo. That someone has killed Ksenia and now they are trying to frame me with that glove. A clever plan to get rid of me. If that doesn't work, they will kill me too."

"But for now, we have to hide the meteorites. Where they can't be found."

"There is a killer in McMurdo, and they know how valuable these are. They also know Ksenia was the only other person to know besides me. If we are gone, then only the killer will know."

Oksana looked Weaze directly in his eyes. "Ksenia is dead. I know I'm in danger. And now, Commander, your life is in danger too."

***

КЙ–222 ЕУРЕКА (*Eureka*)

Icebergs rubbed and banged with disturbing noises while their edges as hard as steel scraped like sharp knives from bow to stern along the entire length of *Eureka's* hull. The queer sounds varied from deep groans to shrill peaks as the ship squeezed a path between the sea of frozen boulders on its hasty voyage south. Many of the seamen had abandoned their bunks in berthing spaces located along the outer perimeter of the hull and below the waterline. At times, the loud bangs sounded like explosions. Other times, long eerie scrapes dragged the length of the entire ship in a sound worse than a thousand fingernails running down a chalkboard.

The non-stop disorder unnerved everyone on board and had already driven a handful of seamen crazy. Any seaman showing signs of stress were quickly removed from the others. Experience had shown nervous seaman could be contagious. Sickbay, a tiny compartment with only three bunks, was already filled to twice its capacity.

Crack-Thud. A deep groan reverberated throughout *Eureka.* The bad noise was simultaneously accompanied by a jarring bump that was felt throughout the ship, and it caused the already frayed nerves of everyone on *Eureka* to jump another notch. Captain Lukyanov knew it was not a good feeling.

Each space on *Eureka* was identified by its unique sequence of alphanumerics. Compartment 3-7-5-L was located on the third deck, two decks below the main deck, just below the waterline. The number 7 indicated that space was seven frames aft of the bow. The number 5, with odd numbers counting to the right, indicated that it was the third space to the starboard side of the ship's centerline. It was next to the outer hull. The L said it was a berthing compartment.

Eight men were quartered in compartment 3-7-5-L. Four were on watch and not in the space at the time of the hull breach. Awakened to a nightmare, the other four were instantly showered in ice-cold seawater that shot into the space with the force of a fire hose. It was made worse that the berthing space was pitch black for the sleeping seamen. Before they knew what was happening, all four were up to their waists in a swirling turbulence that kept knocking them off their feet and preventing them from reaching the bulkhead door.

Half swimming, half crawling, they clawed their way to escape. With each man pulling the other, they scrambled through the bulkhead door and fell into the passageway. Untold gallons of seawater spilled over the lower lip of the oval bulkhead door opening and followed them into the passageway. The four pushed with all their might to close the watertight door behind them. They spun the watertight handle, dogging the door shut, and the water that had pooled around their feet where they stood went still. The leak was stopped. The four seamen looked in horror at each other. They had escaped their watery tomb by mere seconds.

"Flooding, flooding, flooding!" The Quartermaster's voice sang throughout the ship. Chaos ran through *Eureka* like an overturned anthill. Drugov arrived on the bridge just as Captain Lukyanov yelled, "All stop. All stop." Sirens blared and bells clanged.

Lukyanov looked to Drugov. He could not say they were too far south or that their speed was too fast. Not unless he wanted to spend the rest of this cruise in the brig. "I have ordered 'All Stop' until we receive a full damage report, Admiral."

"Very well." What else could Drugov say given the circumstances? Then he added, "How far to McMurdo?"

The Quartermaster spread the points of his metal dividers on the chart and took a measure of the span between their current position and McMurdo. Then he placed that measure along the edge of his chart. "210 nautical miles to McMurdo, Admiral."

The assessment of the damage soon confirmed that there had been a puncture to the outer hull of berthing compartment 3-7-5-L and that the small space was successfully sealed off and made watertight. Inspections of every other exterior compartment did not reveal any further damage to the integrity of *Eureka*.

Drugov knew they would have to slow down. "Resume course to McMurdo, Captain. Six knots seems appropriate for now."

"Aye, sir."

"And congratulations to your crew for their damage control performance." Then an admission by Drugov that caught Lukyanov completely by surprise. "We may not be able to approach all the way to McMurdo if the ice becomes too thick. Get us close, Captain. We have a helicopter."

CHAPTER EIGHTEEN

McMurdo Station is a research facility that is fully operational for less than half of each year. With 24 hours of sunlight each day during the summer research season, people work nearly around the clock. But it's not all work and no play. McMurdo doesn't work seven days a week, more like six and a half. Sunday mornings were reserved for a half-day off. Yes, there were a few traditional holidays, but they were always celebrated on a Sunday. It didn't matter what day of the week Thanksgiving, Christmas, or New Year actually fell because they were all moved to Sunday.

The most notable "celebrations" in McMurdo, however, were the two big parties of the season. They conveniently bookended the summer research calendar. One was early in the season, the other at the end of it. The first party was Halloween. It was the biggest and wildest party of the season. It was always celebrated on a Saturday night. So much drinking usually went on that everyone needed a full Sunday to recover. Half a day just wouldn't do.

Halloween was perfectly timed to be the summer research season-opening bash. It was not too early in the season, but early enough to act as the official kick-off party of the season. By October 31st everybody that was anybody had arrived in McMurdo, and everyone attended the Halloween party. All of the USAP and Navy personnel had been in place for weeks, and most of the science teams were there in preparation for their research during the three best weather months of the season: November through January. Most of these Beakers had not yet left the relative comfort of McMurdo before dispersing to their field camps, which would get going in earnest after November 1st. For this reason, the party was very well attended. Close to 1,000 people and a 100% participation rate. Huge by McMurdo standards.

Halloween was *the* party of the season. Costumes were optional, but everyone let their hair down. It was less about donning a costume for the evening than dressing the part to reveal your inner self. A look just for McMurdo to see. It would be our little secret. The social norms observed by the rest of the civilized world were tossed aside. As if to say to everyone in the little community, "This is how it's going to be." If there were to be a coming-out party, it would happen then.

There was a Haight-Ashbury mindset. Free to think differently. No judgment. It was uninhibited fun, full of optimism and blissful idealism. It's a party you didn't miss.

The second great party was called the End Party. It was smaller than Halloween and occurred late in the season, just before the last LC-130 departed McMurdo. Though fewer people attended, it was still a "don't miss" party with a 100% participation rate. By this date, all of the Beakers and most of the USAP and Navy were gone. This party was more intimate. It was a gathering for the upcoming winter-over caretakers of McMurdo. It was a community coming together. A ritual uniting of a select few. The chosen, who would enter into the unknown darkness with only each other. Though a somewhat somber occasion, it was still very much a party atmosphere. And as with every McMurdo party, lots of drinking.

If you thought social norms were tossed at the Halloween party in front of 1,000 people that were going to spend their summer together, then imagine the social norms being utterly abandoned when only a few dozen folks have the whole of McMurdo to themselves for the coming three months of the long Antarctic darkness.

You better have your ducks in a row going into winterover. In other words, you better know whom you're going to sleep with before, or else it's really going to be a long, cold, and celibate night.

The End party took place and included all the accepted rituals. It played out like a desperate last round in a game of musical chairs, although musical beds might be a more accurate description.

The party was over and in the early morning McMurdo was a ghost town. With nothing on the schedule this Sunday morning, most everyone slept in. No early preflight for the last LC-130 to depart McMurdo. It was still too dark to fly. Take off was not scheduled until noon.

Winter's darkness blanketed the continent more each day. There was now only a narrow two-hour sliver of daylight between sunrise and sunset centered an hour either side of local noon. It was just enough time to properly launch an aircraft northbound to Christchurch, New Zealand. The brief window of daylight provided a slim measure of safety for any Herc that should have to RTB, Return-to-Base, after takeoff. In a matter of days, there would be less than an hour of daylight, and soon there would be no sunrise at all.

McMurdo was still asleep at 05:00. The first person to find the OIC was one of the cooks. Walking outside between her dorm and Building 155 on her way to prepare the Sunday breakfast, she saw the lump in the snow that was Lieutenant Commander Weaver. Not the place to pass out, she thought, as she reached down to roust him up.

By 05:20, two more cooks, Jake, Ty, Cruz, and the Corpsman, HM2 Smith, were standing next to Weaze's dead body, wondering what the hell he was doing there. He liked to drink. It was common knowledge. This time he had obviously had too much.

He wasn't the first to wander off, get disoriented, and freeze to death. But the weather had not been too bad last night; not much wind, good visibility. The bad weather was still a day or two away. Passing out there had been a fatal mistake.

The small group of onlookers stood around Weaze's body, rudderless in their indecision. No one was sure what to do at this point. There was some small talk that speculated around what might have happened and a few words about what to do next, but no one was in charge of the situation. What to do?

Jake was getting the sense that they were looking to him for direction. He slowly came to the realization that after Weaze, he was the next senior officer in McMurdo.

With that, Jake looked at HM2 Smith and said, "Get him to medical. Ty, you and Cruz help. I'll make the call to the Skipper."

"Passed out drunk and frozen to death. Tough way to go, Weaze," Cruz said.

Within the hour, everyone in McMurdo knew about Weaze.

CHAPTER NINETEEN

"The flight is canceled. Dammit, Lieutenant! What the hell is going on down there?" Jake pulled the receiver away from his ear as his Commanding Officer ranted in an endless stream of obscenities. The CO was in transmit-only mode. All Jake could do was listen and wait.

"Just postpone the flight a day until I can figure out this mess." The CO was running out of breath.

Eventually, the obscenities calmed down enough to have a two-way conversation.

"Yes sir, we'll get everything in order and fly home tomorrow," Jake said. He was afraid of what the CO might say next.

"Listen Jake, I need an OIC down there."

Jake did not want to hear this.

"You're a Helo pilot," the CO said. "I've only got three Herc pilots left down there: Tex, Cruz, and Pyeatte. I could authorize just two pilots for the flight north to Christchurch and keep one of them in McMurdo if I had to. Chip is the only NFO remaining in McMurdo. We need him to navigate north. I think Pyeatte is too junior to winter-over. That leaves either Tex or Cruz, but one of them has to be the Pilot in Command."

The CO seemed to be thinking out loud, and all Jake could do was listen to someone who was about to decide what the next few months of his life would be like.

"I guess Tex would be a better choice than Cruz to leave in McMurdo as the OIC. He's the more senior of the two, but he's also the only one of the two designated Pilot in Command. If Tex stayed down there, I'd have to bend a few rules and authorize Cruz to fly to Cheech as PIC. Not sure I want to do that."

Jake could hear the wheels turning in the CO's head. Jake knew where this was going. He needed to stop the CO's train of thought.

Jake interjected. "I can't stay down here, sir. I'm scheduled to leave on this last Herc to Christchurch." Jake raised his voice a little. "I'm due to rotate out of VXE-6 in a few months anyway. I've already done three deployments here in three years." Jake became aware that he was starting to sound a little desperate to his own ears. It was not a sound that made him proud. He wondered how it was being perceived by the CO.

"No. I'm not going to leave either Tex or Cruz there to winter-over," the CO firmly stated. "Both have more than a year left in the squadron. Tex is married with three kids. And they'll both be right back in McMurdo for another deployment in less than six months."

Jake listened.

"You're my best option, Jake. I need you to extend in McMurdo. Let's be honest. Where are you going anyway? If you come back here to Point Mugu, you'll spend your last few months in the squadron sitting on your ass. And then what?"

The phone conversation went quite. The CO paused to let Jake talk. But Jake had nothing to add as he absorbed the inevitable news.

"Let's face it, Jake," he continued. "There's nothing for you back in Mugu. Nobody is waiting for you."

This was a truth that hurt. Jake's face went red. A tear started to grow. He turned away from the doorway. Petty Officer Parks was nearby in the Communications room. Jake was glad to be alone in the OIC's office.

Jake knew that any of his other Commanding Officers, in any of his previous commands, could have said the very same thing to him. After flying Seahawks off of Destroyers, who had he come home to? No one. And maybe the daily grind of his DC tour was a pall because he came home every day to the same empty apartment. Returning home from McMurdo after his third deployment wasn't going to be any different than coming home after his first two.

"Listen, Jake, you're my most senior Lieutenant. You're a good pilot, but dammit, that's not good enough. It's time for you to step up."

"But, Skipper..., I...," one last peep from Jake before he was cut off.

"I'm not asking you, Lieutenant, I'm telling you."

Jake listened in silent acquiescence.

"You'll be back in the states right after winter-over. Five months... six months tops. You can do that standing on your head."

"Can I think about it?"

"No, Lieutenant, you can't. But call me back in the next Comm Sat window and tell me what I want to hear."

"Yes, sir."

Click.

***

Jake made the necessary arrangements to postpone the last Herc flight by 24 hours. Then he went with Cruz to Weaze's dorm room to collect some of his personal items that would be sent home along with his body on the last Herc flight.

Because of Weaze's somewhat senior position as OIC, he had a single dorm room. A rarity in McMurdo since most everyone else had a roommate. Weaze tried to take full advantage of it. It was the perfect place to entertain his overnight guests. "My place or yours?" he was often overheard saying. It would usually be answered either "his place" or "no place." More often, the latter.

Entering Weaze's room, Jake and Cruz were immediately hit by a foul odor. "It stinks in here," Cruz said. "What is that?"

It was an unmistakable stench that Jake recognized instantly. "That's guano," Jake said.

"What?"

"Penguin poop."

Being a junior Herc pilot, Cruz had not yet enjoyed the wonderful aroma of penguin guano. The Hercs didn't fly scientists to the penguin rookeries. Helicopters did that. Jake, a seasoned helicopter pilot, knew that penguin guano and dorm rooms did not mix. Weaze, not being a helicopter guy, probably never had the pleasure of visiting any of the Penguin rookeries in the vicinity of McMurdo. If he had been a helicopter pilot, he would have known to avoid this unique experience and would have never tracked guano into his dorm room. Any person that had ever visited one of the penguin rookeries learned to clean off his or her boots meticulously before bringing them inside their dorm rooms.

Jake knew exactly where to look first. There it was. The brownish-green guano on the soles of Weaze's boots. "Not much of the stuff there, but it's potent shit. A little bit goes a long way," Jake said.

"What was he doing at a rookery?" Cruz asked.

"And how did he get there?" Jake answered with his own question. "Not by Helo," he added. "He was at the End Party last night, right?"

"Yeah, I saw him. But he arrived late."

"He must have dumped his winter-weight gear here after being at a rookery and then went straight to the party. Weaze would never miss a party."

Cruz looked around the messy dorm room. "Let's get out of here. It stinks."

"Toss his boots outside, Cruz. We'll come back later to pack up his things."

Cruz carefully picked up the boots, and holding them at arm's length walked from the dorm room and quickly out of the building into the fresh air.

"I have to call the Skipper back," Jake said. "The next Comm Sat window is coming up soon."

"What are you going to tell him—that Weaze's room smelled like shit?"

"No, I'm going to tell him that I'll be the winter-over OIC."

"What?"

"I'm not flying home with you tomorrow."

Cruz stopped and dropped the boots in the snow.

"There are no other good options. And they're not going to send another Herc down here with somebody else to be OIC, not with daylight running out. There's only enough light to get you guys out of here tomorrow, about an hour of daylight. That's just enough daylight so we're still legal per the Air Operations Manual.

***

Jake stopped by Felix's office on his way to Penguin OPS. He had a little time to kill before the next communication satellite pass would provide a good phone connection.

"Guess what, Felix? I'm going to winter-over with you."

"What?"

"I'm going to replace Lieutenant Commander Weaver as the OIC."

"Great, I... is that good news or bad?"

"I'm okay with it. How many people can say they spent the night in Antarctica?"

"I'm happy for you. And me, too."

"I just came from Lieutenant Commandeer Weaver's dorm room. Lieutenant Cruz and I were there to pack up some of his personal belonging. His cold weather boots had guano on the soles. His room stunk."

"Well, there are no penguins here in McMurdo," Felix said.

"No, it's got to be from a rookery."

"The closest rookeries are Cape Evans and Cape Royds. But both field camps are closed now for the season. The last Helo flights there were days ago."

"He could have driven," Felix said. "I've been to Cape Evans a few times driving the ice path. It's the closest rookery. We drive one of the snow track vehicles if we can't get on the Helo schedule. It takes an hour or so to get there. The path is well marked, but you have to make sure you stay on the ice path and avoid the red flag areas."

"I wonder what he was doing there?"

"By the way Felix, you're a smart-ass Beaker—"

"Is that a question?" Felix cut him off.

"I was going to say—I thought bat shit was called guano, but bats are mammals. And penguins are birds. So, why do they call it guano?" Jake queried his Beaker friend.

"And bats fly," Felix laughed. "But penguins are birds that don't fly. They swim, like fish. Who the heck knows?"

"You Beakers better figure this shit out."

"You mean guano," Felix smirked.

"Yeah, guano." Jake needed the levity. And with that, he left Felix's office, walked to Penguin OPS, and made the call.

CHAPTER TWENTY

The following day the aircrew were mulling around in Penguin OPS, preparing for their flight north to Christchurch, New Zealand. Cruz, and Pyeatte the junior 3P, were in the OIC's office saying their goodbyes to Jake, while Tex and Chip were next door in the Communications room posting their flight plan and getting their weather brief. This was the strongest LC-130 aircrew in the squadron. Every CO had their favorites, but they also knew who was their best. There was a good reason this was the last remaining LC-130 aircrew. With the CO gone, the last flight of the season to depart McMurdo needed the best.

Tex was the Pilot in Command. He grew up in Texas, not from a city like Dallas or Houston, but farther out. Someplace where everyone always woke up early, worked mostly outside, and ranches were measured in tens of thousands of acres. A place where you started to work as soon as you could ride. Work always involved horses, or cattle, sometimes both. Tex stood tall. By the time he was twelve, he could look a horse in the eye. Now he took two steps when others needed three. Tex was real Texas.

He has the record for the pilot who earned their call sign in the shortest amount of time. His given name was

Dillon, but within ten minutes of showing up in Pensacola, Florida, to start his training, the Drill Instructor pegged him as Tex, and it stuck. Anyone who met him knew right away he was from Texas. You could tell from his voice in the first few words he spoke. Sometimes you could tell in only one word, like when he said Howdy instead of Hello.

The latest weather satellite picture was two hours old, and it showed a fairly clear and cloudless flight path north toward New Zealand. The more important piece of information for this flight came from the ground-based Automated Geophysical Observatories. Half a dozen of these unmanned weather stations were strategically placed across the continent and remotely transmitted their data during every communication satellite pass. Two of the six AGO stations positioned Grid East of the Trans-Antarctic Mountain Range had been reporting a steady increase in wind speed along with a significant reduction in barometric pressures for the last twelve hours. Tex and Chip quickly absorbed this detail. The two experienced aviators knew this meant a polar blizzard was brewing and headed toward McMurdo. It was time to get going.

With no other air traffic flying anywhere above Antarctica or the Southern Ocean, and no weather balloon information, there were no reports of winds aloft or other weather information available. Without the information from the AGO stations, you may as well just wet your finger and stick it up in the air.

The limited amount of weather reporting that indicated conditions were degrading was a concern but certainly not a crisis. Tex and Chip could expect that along with this increase in surface winds and drop in barometric pressure, there would be much stronger winds aloft. Their route through the southern jet stream might get quite bumpy and require a significant crab angle to their flight path. They knew this would increase their overall flight time to Christchurch and burn more fuel.

Tex and Chip recalled flying through the southern jet stream last season and having to fight winds aloft of over 125 knots. The unrelenting jet stream hit them broadside at an angle ninety degrees to their track pushing and bucking them for hours. Chip remembered their crab angle into the wind being up to twenty-four degrees at times just to maintain their intended course. All this amounted to a flight time that lasted an hour longer than planned and burned significantly more fuel.

"Well, not too much of a problem because we're flying north to Cheech," Chip said. "I don't think I'd want to fly south to McMurdo without a better forecast."

The flight crew also had a weather report for their destination, Christchurch, on the southern island of New Zealand. It was forecast to be good weather—they just had to get there.

Their flight path would take them over the difficult 2,000 mile stretch of open Southern Ocean between Antarctica and New Zealand. It was a cold and lonely expanse of water, considered by some the most dangerous flying of their Antarctic tour. If a plane had trouble, there were no good options. If the LC-130 did have a serious enough problem that required them to look for a divert field, it would not end well. There were no divert airfields in the Southern Ocean.

Any number of things could go wrong with an aircraft in flight to reduce a plane's airworthiness. And it could happen at any time, unannounced. The loss of an engine, a fuel leak, structural damage, who knows. Endless problems for the aircrew to worry about. If the plane became unflyable, protocol in the worst-case scenario would be to conduct a controlled ditch onto the surface of the water. The NFO would use radar and steer the aircraft toward the nearest surface ship. The pilots would ditch next to it. The crew would pray for rescue. In the Southern Ocean, there was no shipping traffic. The crew knew this. There was simply no expectation of surviving a ditch. Zero.

***

"Shuttle bus is here," Cruz yelled to the aircrew. Tex, Chip, and Pyeatte gathered their gear for the van ride to the Williams Field skiway, while Tim, the mountaineer, jumped out of the van and ran up to Penguin OPS for a final word with Jake.

"Hi, Jake, I'm glad you're taking on the job as OIC," Tim said. "I wanted to tell you something but, there's been a lot going on the last couple of days, and maybe it's nothing, but I had told Lieutenant Commander Weaver that I found an extra glove next to the girl that jumped off, or fell off, Castle Rock. I thought it belonged to her, but I guess it didn't. I gave it to Lieutenant Commander Weaver, but he didn't think much about it. He said he'd look into it. I don't know... I mean... now that Lieutenant Commander Weaver is dead, I think I should mention it to you. It's probably nothing, but... I've been thinking."

"What are you thinking?"

The tempo of Tim's voice quickened. "What if she was with someone at the top of Castle Rock and began to slip and fall, and grabbed her friend's hand for help, and the glove slipped off when she fell."

"That would be awful," Jake said. "But they wouldn't have been much of a friend since no one reported her missing. The friend would have gone for help. So, we think she was alone."

"The glove had a couple of numbers written on it— Zero Three."

"All right, thanks. Lieutenant Commander Weaver probably kept it. I'll keep an eye out for it."

Tim ran back down to the waiting van. "C'mon," Cruz yelled. "I don't want to stay here any longer than I have to."

The shuttle bus made the twenty-minute drive to Williams Field, where side number XD-03, the last LC-130 in Antarctica, waited. Following preflight, the Herc would be airborne in an hour.

Jake walked out the front door of Penguin OPS to make another hike up to Observation Hill. He thought he had made his farewell to McMurdo from the top after his final Helo flight, but here he was again. The view across the Ross Ice Shelf would be clear while he watched the last Herc leave. But first, he found himself wandering through town. Perhaps, as OIC, he was surveying his domain. He passed no one on his short walk. With only the winter-over personnel in town now, McMurdo felt deserted.

He stepped both on slippery ice and bare spots that were free of ice where patches of the stony-dirt ground showed through. It looked like the ice had melted away in these spots, but that was not the case, at least not in the common sense of the word. These patches of dirt had never seen rain, never known mud. Sublimation was the scientific term, and Jake knew a little about it. So dry is

Antarctica that ice, water in its solid state, completely skips the liquid phase and disappears into the air as it evaporates straight into the gaseous phase as water vapor. He pondered this challenging factoid as he walked. Eventually, his rambling path went behind the helicopter hangar and toward Ob Hill.

He completed his vigorous trek up to the top of Ob Hill in less than twenty minutes. The air was cold, visibility good, and the wind was picking up. He had seen the same weather reports as the aircrew. They would be all right, he thought.

The sun hung low in the sky, just an inch above the horizon. It was as high as it would rise today. Jake watched the distant activity at Williams Field almost six miles away. He stood next to the massive wooden cross on the top of Ob Hill and waited. If this were one of Jake's Sunday morning pilgrimages, he would touch the cross, symbolically laying on a hand, and devote a moment of silence to the lost hero. That would qualify as a prayer for Jake. "Antarctica," he whispered, "so many had sacrificed so much in the name of exploration and science."

Today, Jake stood quietly in the cold, certain that it was his duty to wait and watch the last LC-130 take off. The only sound was the steady distant drone of the Herc's four powerful T-56 Allison turboprop engines as it prepared for flight.

Beyond the activity at Williams Field, Jake looked across the vast expanse of the Ross Ice Shelf. Endless miles of thick ice covered the Ross Sea. Were it not for the sun's extreme low angle skimming over the surface, it would look peacefully flat. But the sun rays now revealed the angry texture hidden in the hard ripples of sastrugi. In alternating patterns of shadow and light, the sun accentuated the ridges of sastrugi carved into the ice by the endlessly sweeping katabatic winds. They looked as harmless as ripples in sand dunes, but the frozen waves were as hard as concrete.

The LC-130 engine noise increased. From miles away, below his perch, Jake saw the Herc start to move. It slowly taxied to one end of the skiway before it turned around and faced into the wind. The engines roared to full throttle. The Herc accelerated for takeoff. In moments the plane was airborne. The sun, having now spent little time above the horizon, slowly slipped out of the sky.

CHAPTER TWENTY-ONE

It took little time for the winter-over routine to set in. Immediately following the last Herc's departure, the pace of life in McMurdo slowed to a crawl. It seemed like everyone in McMurdo was aware of this except Jake. They were planning for winter-over, he wasn't. This only became apparent to Jake while he and Felix sat in the chow hall talking idly after their lunch. Suddenly Jake looked up, surveying the room, his eyes swept side-to-side, nearly counting each person as they sat in the chow hall. "Well, I guess it's time to get back to work," Jake said.

"What's the rush?" Felix answered.

Though the winter-over population had dropped to three dozen, it appeared that every one of them was still comfortably seated at their tables well after lunch had ended.

Cin stepped out of the kitchen with some of the other staff during the break between serving lunch and clean-up. She selected a teabag from the side counter and poured boiling water into a cup before scanning the dining area and choosing her seat.

She waited several minutes before looking into her brewing cup of tea. It was dark, steeped longer than most, and it would be bitter, the way she liked it. She removed the teabag, pinching it between her thumb and forefinger. It was hot. It hurt. She squeezed more.

She held the pain tight in her fingertips and watched the last drops fall from the teabag. They seemed to carry the pain into her cup, and she took her first hot sip. The first sip was always the best. Her eyes peeked over her cup and across the room from her carefully selected seat with a clear view of Jake.

It wasn't long before Jake realized the chow hall was in jeopardy of quickly becoming the winter-over coffee lounge. And for the second time in two days, like the crowd that stood around OIC's body, Jake became aware of people looking at him, to him, for guidance. It's your move. If he, the OIC, was still lingering after lunch, why couldn't they? They were taking their cue from him.

Jake stood up and uncharacteristically spoke to every-one, unaware of his commanding voice. "Let's get to work people." Surprising himself, he picked up his food tray and led the way to the kitchen.

The others stood up, gathered their food trays, straightened chairs, and followed. Without complaint, and with smiles on their faces, McMurdo got to work.

"There you go, OIC," Felix said to Jake, calling him OIC for the first time. In one simple gesture, Jake went from having been appointed OIC to being the OIC. And everyone in McMurdo saw him in action. "Let's get to work people," was all it took. Like a sports team striding onto the playing field for a match, everyone filed out of the chow hall and on to their disparate chores throughout McMurdo. Teamwork, tall and proud. On to victory. They had an OIC.

Cin made sure she walked close by Jake as everyone was leaving. "Congratulations on being promoted to OIC," she said, flashing a warm smile.

"Thank you. It's not really a promotion. I'm still a Lieutenant." *I'm such a dork.* "I'm just acting as OIC for winter-over." In the small-town environment of McMurdo, Jake knew she had been Ksenia's roommate, but he was flattered that she acknowledged him as the OIC.

Cin didn't misspeak. She knew exactly what she was saying and doing. Jake was in charge, and she wanted to know him better.

***

Jake made his way over to Penguin OPS where he knew there would be an Operations Manual that offered guidance on how to conduct a winter-over. The Navy had a manual for everything. Why should winter-over be any different? He didn't have to look very hard to find it. It was laying out on top of the OIC's desk, right where Weaze had left it. The manual consisted of a three-ring binder and was a lot thicker than Jake thought it would be. It was chocked full of information, passed down year after year, from OIC to OIC. Instructions of things to do, and how best to do them, full of lessons learned, based on experience earned the hard way. It was, in essence, a survival manual—how to survive as OIC. It seemed to him like he was going to be busy.

Skimming through the contents, Jake soon realized a big function of the OIC was keeping people motivated enough to accomplish the mundane jobs required of them. The deep cleaning, repairs, maintenance, rehabbing, and upgrades would all be endless drudgery. Completing these tasks while cooped up indoors during the dark Antarctic night would just make it worse. Only near the end of winter-over, after months of boring jobs, would there be an increase in activity as the focus shifted from inside to outside, and the construction of the new ice runway began.

Reading deeper into the Operations Manual, it was obvious that the single greatest task of winter-over, beyond motivating people, was the construction of the next season's ice runway. More than anything, Jake knew his success as the winter-over OIC would be measured by how well of a new ice runway was constructed under his reign.

One of the lessons learned about building the ice runway was that it takes a long time. "Don't wait too long to start. But you can't start too soon either, before the ice is fully formed." That wouldn't be for another three months. Starting too soon, while the ice was still forming and not yet thick enough, or hard enough, would produce a poor surface for the LC-130 to land on. Prematurely grooming "soft" ice would yield ripples and bumps that could never be adequately smoothed out. It would be like landing a plane on a washboard. The lessons learned clearly indicated it was best to wait as long as possible into the winter for the ice to be as thick as possible, as much as five feet thick, before building the new ice runway. And then work like hell, 24 hours a day if needed, until the Hercs returned.

Jake could not miss seeing the interesting comment from a previous OIC many years before. To emphasize its significance, the comment had been underlined and highlighted more than once by many subsequent OIC's. It said: "Build a good ice runway and all else will be forgiven."

That sounded ominous to Jake. What would need to be forgiven during my winter-over?

McMurdo utilized two runways during the season, or more accurately, one ice runway and one skiway. This was to accommodate the incredibly versatile LC-130, which could take off or land on either its wheels, like a conventional aircraft, or its skis. It was the largest plane in the world to utilize skis. It used its wheels on the ice runway and skis on the skiway. Pilots selected their landing gear of choice depending on where their mission took them. Consider taking off on wheels from the ice runway at McMurdo, flying to a remote field camp on an Antarctic glacier, lowering the Herc's skies for landing in the snow, then returning to McMurdo and landing again on wheels. A remarkable aircraft.

To VXE-6, you could take off and land the LC-130 on the ice runway like it was pavement. All ice runway take-offs and landings were conducted on wheels. When available, the ice runway had an advantage over the skiway. That advantage is measured in weight.

The LC-130 maximum takeoff or landing weight on wheels is 155,000 pounds, but the normal landing weight for skis on an unprepared surface at a remote field camp is 118,000 pounds. This is not an insignificant difference. Let's run the numbers. The aircraft itself weighs about 85,000 pounds, and it can carry up to about 50,000 pounds of fuel. Those two weights combined put the LC-130 over the limit for operations on skis. But the whole point of the Herc is to carry cargo and lots of it. Advantage: ice runway.

Here's the kicker. You have to balance the desire to carry more cargo with the need to carry enough fuel. To operate on skis meant sacrificing fuel or cargo. NSF always wanted more cargo. Aircrews voted for fuel.

The problem with the ice runway was that it is constructed of ice, and ice melts. Therefore, the ice runway was seasonal. It could only be used in the first few months of the summer research season. By mid-December, the ice was too thin to risk landing a greater than 100,000-pound Herc on it. And by the end of the season, the ice runway and all the ice beneath it was gone. It had all melted away. All that remained was open ocean.

The skiway at McMurdo was named Williams Field and came into use when the ice runway was closed.

Jake's thoughts strayed as he sat at the OIC desk in Penguin OPS. It was his desk now. He reflected on the events of the last few days. So much had changed, and the weight of leadership sat on his shoulders.

The death of the girl falling from Castle Rock troubled him, and he couldn't explain the careless mistake of a drunken OIC. Jake knew of the dangers in Antarctica. He had seen his share of accidents that quickly escalated to be much worse, but something didn't seem right about these two deaths. Though fatal accidents can occur, they are still somewhat rare. But two deaths in McMurdo within days of each other? They were unconnected, weren't they? Both were unwitnessed, weren't they? Could they have something in common, he wondered?

Jake closed the book and stood up. He had read enough for now. It was time to get out of his office and meet some people. He promised himself he would meet the entire winter-over staff and personally speak with everyone in his first few days as OIC.

Jake decided it would be good to start his informal hello tour with the kitchen staff. He thought there were about eight to ten people working kitchen duties, but he didn't actually know how many, so it would be good to find out. He was sure it would be the biggest chunk of the winter-over personnel. Besides, he wanted to see the girl who had so nicely congratulated him after lunch on his position as OIC. Jake knew she had been Ksenia's roommate. She had apparently taken a liking to him if he wasn't mistaken. Hey, don't fight it.

The first two USAP staff that Jake met when he arrived in the kitchen were veterans of a previous winter-over. While chatting with them after introductions, he discovered they were a married couple and had completed one other winter-over together three years before.

Don and Sally were an interesting couple. White-haired, mid-sixty's and gregarious, Jake guessed they were enjoying some kind of a traveling retirement adventure. "How'd you two get down here?"

"We're enjoying our retirement—" Don started to answer.

"A working retirement," Sally interrupted. "A real retirement is at a condo on a beach." But she laughed. There wasn't a mean syllable in her. Don just rolled his eyes, something he did often. Jake smiled.

They were the perfect couple to head up the kitchen. It was like having adult parents watching over the rest of the kitchen children who were all much younger.

Jake was introduced to the others; Josh, Emily, Randy, and an extremely hairy guy named Bear, who needed to wear a hairnet on his beard and his head, although a beekeeper's veil would be more appropriate. There were two flower children who called themselves Summer and April.

They spent more time giggling than working. Jake guessed recreational drugs had something to do with that, and like Bear, he doubted the last two were their real names. Other than Don and Sally, the kitchen staff seemed to have a common thread running among them; they were all young, still searching for something in life, and they worked for peanuts; basically room and board.

After the introductions, Jake looked around the room. "Well, I think I've met just about everyone in the kitchen." Jake gave another visual sweep of the kitchen. "But where's the girl who was the roommate of the—"

"Poor thing, Cynthia," Sally interrupted, "she wanted some time off. Said she had something to do."

"It's understandable," Don said. "I figured she'd get out of Dodge after her—"

"— her roommate died." Sally was finishing every one of Don's sentences, and some of Jake's too.

"I'll let her know you wanted to see her." Sally smiled like she was facilitating a matchmaking. Something Jake felt she had a lot of experience in doing.

"No, it's okay. I'm just trying to introduce myself to everyone *(wait, I want to meet her)* and let everyone know who the OIC is, and that I'm here to help."

"I've heard that before." Sally was a pistol.

Jake said, "Goodbye," and left the kitchen.

After that, he went outside in the dark cold between Building 155 and the NSF research building to see Felix. Maybe he could introduce him to the few NSF researchers who stayed for winter-over. As he walked, he couldn't help think about the roommate he didn't get to meet yet. What was her name? Cynthia.

Maybe Don was right. Cynthia could have left McMurdo after her roommate died. It was sound thinking. No one would have blamed her if she wanted to leave, forget the whole thing, and fly back home. But she didn't. She chose to stick it out. There must be a reason. Jake saw something in her he liked. She was decisive. He admired that quality. She knew what she wanted. He wished he was more like that.

CHAPTER TWENTY-TWO

Shortly after he left Don and Sally, Jake was sitting comfortably at the conference table in Felix's office. Jake leaned forward and gave the upside-down globe on the table another spin. "I still can't get over your globe. And what's up with this?" Jake pointed to the plant that would have been more at home in Arizona than Antarctica. He had reserved comment about it previously but didn't hold back now. "You must be the only guy in Antarctica trying to grow a houseplant. And it's a cactus at that!"

"Not just trying. That cactus thrives here," Felix said. "Of course you know how low the humidity is in Antarctica. It's as low as a desert. That's why we're drinking so much extra water all the time. The air is dry as hell, so the cactus loves it."

"You should be a teacher."

"I don't know about that."

"I picture you as a high school science teacher. You'd be great."

Jake stood up from his seat and walked over to Felix's collection of interesting items that filled his shelves along the wall. He had seen them when he was first invited to Felix's office, but now he was in a more talkative mood, perhaps because of the anxiety he was feeling. "What else you got here?" He stopped in front of a section harboring a small group of rocks.

"What about these rocks?"

"Well, there's a couple of different kinds there. See those first few," Felix pointed, "... the gray ones."

Jake picked up an elongated rock that was smooth and a light gray color. It appeared to him to be shaped like a crystal.

"Those are Erebus crystals. It's a special type of volcanic rock called anorthoclase," Felix said.

"They came from Mount Erebus?"

"Yes, I gathered those myself. I picked them up around the rim of Erebus. There are thousands of them scattered around the crater."

"They do sort of look like crystals. I can see why you call them that. What makes them so special?"

"Even though there are thousands of these crystals around Erebus, they are rare in the rest of the world."

"Did they come out of the volcano?"

"Yes... well, sort of. It was molten lava when it first came out of the volcano."

"But there are volcanoes all around the world."

"But they're not as cold as Erebus. Anorthoclase crystals are formed when a volcano, like Erebus, erupts and ejects its hot lava up into the sky. Lava that is shot up very high into the sky in sub-freezing air solidifies while it's still in free fall. In other words, it's like it was weightless, and it hardens in this unique crystalline pattern before it hits the ground.

"That's fascinating."

"You can pick them up right off the ground. Erebus is one of the few places in the world this occurs. Kilimanjaro is another. So they are very rare and valuable."

"I've never flown my Helo to the crater of Erebus. Too high to reach the very top, of course."

"The researchers don't go up there very often," Felix said. "Usually they only go when Erebus starts acting up. The volcano has been quiet for a few years. No major activity lately. But I did go on an expedition to the summit last year. The Helo dropped us off at 10,000 feet. We hiked up to about 12,000 and camped a few days. We made several excursions right to the lip of the crater."

"I wish I knew about these Erebus crystals. I would have gotten on the flight schedule for one of those field camps and filled my pockets with them. If they're that rare, they must be worth a lot. Bring 'em back to the States and sell 'em."

"Can't, we're a Continent of Peace. Remember the treaty."

"C'mon, a few rocks."

"It is strictly illegal to sell anything like that from Antarctica. Absolutely forbidden. We're in it for the science."

"You don't think a Beaker doesn't help themselves to something sometimes?"

"Nope. Not only do we respect the treaty, but we also enforce it. It's up to the scientists to monitor all the activities in Antarctica. Otherwise, countries and corporations would be drilling for oil all over the place down here. Rumor had it that the old Soviet Union was trying to mine for uranium deposits, but that's all shut down now. Heck, Russia can barely keep Vostok Station open anymore."

Felix pointed to a rock on the shelf that looked completely different from the Erebus crystals. "If you really want to hold something valuable, pick up that one."

The rock was cradled in a wedge of plastic that held it for display, apparently to elevate its significance.

The rock was a dark, dull black and looked like a smooth chunk of coal. Jake took the golf ball-sized shape in his hand and tossed it up from his palm a couple of times, judging its weight. "Boy, it's heavy."

"That's a meteorite," Felix said. "It has a lot of iron in it. That's what makes it so heavy. And it's millions of years old. Those anorthoclase crystals may have only been formed the last time Mount Erebus had a big eruption. That would make them less than 100 years old. Quite the contrast in age, isn't it?"

"It's amazing. How can you tell so much about a rock?"

"Isn't geology great?"

"You really should be a teacher."

"Well, I have thought about it. Maybe someday."

"So, this is even more valuable," Jake examined the meteorite more closely.

"A lot more, but you can't sell it either."

"Did you find this meteorite?"

"No, someone else. Every once in a while, someone at a field camp stumbles across one. Remember, you can't sell them or take them home with you, so they remain here in the NSF building. Most of the research on any kind of specimen happens right here in McMurdo anyway. I mean, you can't be bringing specimens like ice core samples and penguins back to the States, can you? Everything is examined in Antarctica. It all stays here. The only thing the scientists take away with them is a bunch of data. Then they spend the next year crunching numbers and writing their dissertations.

Jake replaced the meteorite on its display stand with the care of a jewel. "You know, Felix, I'm trying to meet everyone in the winter-over group now that I'm the OIC. I've just met with most of the USAP kitchen staff. Can you introduce me to any of the Beakers?"

"There's only a few here for winter-over," Felix said. "Since we're talking about rocks, let's go down to the Geology Lab. I saw Oksana Zverev earlier. I think she's the only one in the building now."

Felix and Jake walked quietly down the featureless central corridor of the NSF building past a row of dormant laboratories and empty classrooms. All the room lights were off, making Jake feel like he was sneaking through a vacant school that was out of session.

Turning the corner at the end led to another equally sterile corridor. Light from only one room spilled onto the hallway floor. It appeared to Jake that it was the only room with activity.

"Damn, it feels like a morgue in here, Felix. Can't you turn some lights on and liven it up a little?"

"We're packed during the summer research season, but not much is going on during winter-over."

Felix stepped into the Geology Lab ahead of Jake. Wearing his customary grin, he approached Oksana. "Hello, Oksana. Are you busy?"

Jake lingered just inside the doorway, a sheepish thought holding him back.

"Hello, Felix," Oksana said. She had heard the two walking down the corridor in the dead-quite building and was expecting someone.

"This is Lieutenant Covey. He's the OIC this winter-over." Felix motioned for Jake to come much closer to Oksana. "Jake, I'd like to introduce you to Oksana Zverev."

Felix extended his arm to indicate to Jake that he should shake hands with Oksana. "Don't be shy. We're all one happy family down here." Felix was well into his role as an NSF liaison.

Jake walked over to Oksana who was standing by a piece of equipment she had obviously been working with. They shook hands. Her touch was warm and her grasp lingered longer than a brief American-styled handshake. Was she holding onto him for a reason? Was this just her customary way of meeting? Jake was unsure. Her eyes didn't leave his. He sensed despair. Something was hurting inside of her. Is it possible he could have absorbed all this in such a brief introduction? He was confused.

"Well, I can see you two are getting along just fine," Felix said, interrupting their gaze. "Oksana is a geologist," Felix continued, "She's here for winter-over as part of the new Russian exchange arrangements between NSF and Russia's AARI."

"It's very nice to meet you," Jake said. He realized he had not spoken a single word with her yet, but he knew there was some kind of connection between them. Jake glanced at the equipment next to Oksana. "It looks like you're grinding up some rocks."

"I'm trying to cut this specimen in half," she said. "I'd like to get a good slice to examine, but this saw is the wrong type, and maybe this rock is too small. I'm just ruining it. I wish I had the fine saw we have back in Saint Petersburg."

Jake barely comprehended her words. He only listened to the tone of her voice. It sounded beautiful to him. Her Russian accent was just like Ksenia's.

"We'll let you get back to work," Felix interjected.

"It was nice meeting you." Jake shook himself back to reality. "If there's anything I can do for you as the OIC here in McMurdo, just let me know."

Felix left the room first, and as Jake followed him out the doorway, Oksana stepped forward. "Lieutenant." She called softly so only Jake could hear. "May I have a word with you?"

Jake turned and paused to listen to her. "I have something very important to ask you," she said.

Felix stopped and came back to rejoin the conversation. But it was clear Oksana only wanted to speak with Jake. "I need your help," she blurted.

"What is it?" Jake was concerned.

"It's private. Can I meet you later?"

"Is something wrong?"

"Tonight. After dinner. Meet me here."

CHAPTER TWENTY-THREE

Jake sat stonelike at his OIC desk with a perplexed look on his face. He was simply unable to characterize the end of his meeting with Oksana. It baffled him so much that he dismissed the idea of introducing himself to any more of the winter-over staff for now.

He had seen Oksana enough before in the chow hall to know who she was. He was even slightly attracted to her, but he never dared to do anything about it. Could it be possible that she felt the same way about him? Then when it came time to meet her, even with a legitimate reason going to her lab with Felix, he just stood in the doorway. *I must have looked like a fool, but she wants to see me after dinner.*

Why did she want to meet with him later? Alone? What was she concerned about?

He sat at his OIC desk and planned to spend the rest of the afternoon in Penguin OPS.

Periodically Jake got up and walked from the OIC desk to the Communications room to eavesdrop on XD-03's position reports being received by Petty Officer Parks. The crackle and static of the incoming High-Frequency radio transmission blared from the loudspeaker and could be heard throughout Penguin OPS. "It seems like all is going well with X-ray Delta Zero Three?" Jake questioned Petty Officer Parks at the conclusion of the last transmission.

Parks pushed back from the Navy desk and swiveled toward Jake in his squeaky Navy chair. Every piece of furniture in OPS was painted battleship gray. Every room in the Navy looked the same. There were only three kinds of Navy furniture; desk, chair, and file cabinet. Worldwide it was all the same and always painted gray.

"They're doing good, sir." Petty Officer Parks said after recording the position report in the logbook. "They lost a little time between ELNAK and DALOS, but they shouldn't have any more problems now that they've made it through the jet stream."

"What's their latest to Cheech?"

"ETA 19:12, sir."

"Thanks, I'll call Cheech and pass along their ETA."

Parks glanced at the communications satellite schedule, which he printed out every morning and placed on a clipboard that hung next to his desk. "The next Comm Sat window is in about twenty minutes, sir."

"Right, okay, I'll wait." Jake couldn't remember ever using the telephone in McMurdo to make calls off The Ice before. In his three seasons in McMurdo, his only use of the phone was to call the helicopter hangar and check on the status of an aircraft maintenance issue. Now that he was OIC, he'd have to get used to the inconvenience of communication satellite intervals which occurred throughout the day. The phone in Penguin OPS looked like an ordinary telephone, but you couldn't just pick it up anytime and make a phone call from Antarctica to Christchurch, New Zealand, or Point Mugu, California. Just another quirk of living on The Ice that he'd have to deal with.

"Do we have a recent weather satellite picture?" Jake asked.

"The last one was..." Parks scooted his chair over to another desk, looking for yet another clipboard. The wheels groaned reluctantly as they wobbled under his seat and added another dimension to the squeak of his Navy chair. Jake smiled, thinking that all Navy rooms look alike, and they sound alike too.

"Here it is..." Parks found the clipboard that held a stack of weather facsimiles. A new weather picture was available about every ninety minutes as the weather satellite, different from the communications satellite, orbited the earth in its unique polar orbit. "The last one was thirty minutes ago, but you can't see anything, too dark." Parks flipped back that page to the one prior and handed it to Jake. "This is the last good one, more than two hours ago, at 14:17."

Jake studied the older report. "It looks a little worse than when they took off. But, they're through it now." Jake handed the clipboard back to Parks. "No worries," Jake said, adding the Kiwi flair to his voice.

No satellites were dedicated to the support of activities in Antarctica. The Navy and NSF were fortunate to be able to piggyback onto a couple of military satellites. There were certainly other satellites in polar orbits following the end of the Cold War, but the military granted only limited access to two satellites, one for the weather, one for telecommunications, as they looped around the earth, north-to-south, in their unique pole-to-pole orbits.

All Jake knew about satellites was that every time he went for a weather brief before flying his helicopter, they would say, "Here, take a look at the latest satellite picture." Now that Jake was the OIC, he was a little more interested in how it all worked.

"ET2 Parks," Jake formally addressed Petty Officer Second Class Parks by his Navy rating, ET, which indicated his expertise as an Electronics Technician in this advanced field. "Can you tell me a little about the different satellite information we get down here?" Jake was at the same time showing his respect to Petty Officer Parks and deferring to his obvious greater knowledge in this area.

Petty Officer Parks knew he could easily overwhelm the college-educated OIC with his knowledge of anything to do with radio signals, telecommunications, and satellite transmissions. Parks could probably talk circles around Marconi. Instead, he sat a little straighter in his chair, appreciating the subtle recognition.

"Well sir, we get to use two satellites down here. But they're not orbiting the earth in the traditional sense that most people think. They're not going around the earth above the equator."

Jake looked more closely at Parks' rating insignia sewn on the upper arm of Parks' uniform. It was a red and white patch on a black background. It looked to Jake like an image of satellites flying around, or was it electrons around an atom? Jake thought he should figure that out some other time.

"These two are in polar orbit," Parks continued. "They circle the earth North Pole-to-South Pole. Actually, they're offset a little from going exactly over the poles, but that doesn't matter for us." Parks scribbled a little diagram on the back of a weather fax.

Jake took a seat next to ET2 Parks, continuing to absorb his lesson at eye level.

"Anyway, see the weather Sat is in a very low orbit, only about 150 miles above the earth's surface. Its job is to take pictures. Pictures of Russian shit in the northern hemisphere, pictures of clouds in Antarctica. The closer the better for pictures. Since it's in low orbit, being so close to earth and all, it has a much tighter orbit. So it returns overhead frequently, about every ninety minutes."

"Okay," Jake nodded his understanding.

"But our Comm Sat orbits about 1,500 miles above the earth," Parks said with a flourish of his pencil. "It's also in a polar orbit, but since it's higher than the weather Sat, it takes longer to go around. The interval between its overhead is about 4 hours. It stays above the horizon longer. That's why we get a Comm Sat window of up to an hour."

Parks sat back in his chair and looked over at Jake. "We can't use any of the Comm Sats that orbit around the equator, not at our latitude. They put those satellites up at about 25,000 miles. At that altitude, they basically position them over the same spot above the equator in geosynchronous orbit. There's got to be one of those above Australia that we could be using. I guess it just costs too much money to piggyback our stuff on it."

Parks tapped his pencil on the desk. "What we need down here is a few satellites for aircraft communications. That's coming, but still a few years away."

"Thanks, Petty Officer Parks. You know your stuff. It's good to have you here. I'll stay in OPS until the next position report, and then I'll head to chow."

***

About an hour later, XD-03's position report for BOSLA could be heard throughout Penguin OPS. Jake approached the Communications room and listened to the transmission in its entirety. He took comfort in hearing the aircrew's safe passage.

VXE-6 aircraft reported their position to McMurdo about once an hour on these long transoceanic flights. Six navigation points had been established, one every five degrees of latitude, along the 2,000-mile route between New Zealand and Antarctica.

A wonderful Navy tradition recognized some of the unsung heroes who were indispensable to the early Antarctic expeditions and named each of these navigation points after one of the many courageous sled dogs that were part of Admiral Byrd's sled dog teams. The famed polar explorer and aviation pioneer, Admiral Richard Byrd, a person of many accomplishments, was often best known for his acknowledgment of the famous sled dogs that were inseparable from his many successes.

Jake could picture in his mind where the aircraft was along its route based upon the name of the sled dog. He glanced at the large air navigation chart on the wall. In its flight from McMurdo to Christchurch, XD-03 had already passed KALVA, GULAN, ELNAK, and DALOS. This report was for BOSLA. The sixth and final position to report on their route would be APORO. They're going to make it safely to Christchurch, he saw.

Jake sometimes mused that one day he would be married with a couple of children. He'd get a dog too, maybe a Labrador, with that perpetual dolphin-like smile, and name him after one of these historic canines. He liked the name BOSLA, and he liked KALVA, too.

CHAPTER TWENTY-FOUR

Jake couldn't wait for dinner. He wasn't very hungry, just eager to meet with Oksana again after the evening meal. What did she want to talk to him about?

Entering the chow hall, the first people Jake met were Don and Sally. These two seemed inseparable, and Jake watched as they were still placing hot food out in preparation for the dinner buffet.

"You're the first one—" Don began.

"Oh, go ahead," Sally blurted out, "help yourself and start eating."

"I'll wait a few minutes for some of the others to show up," Jake said.

"Then stay right here," Sally added, "I'll get Cynthia. You didn't get to meet her earlier."

The first few hungry winter-over staff began to arrive in the chow hall and gather their meals. A minute later, Sally returned from the back of the kitchen with Cynthia.

"Here you go, Cynthia, this is Lieutenant Covey. He missed you this morning."

Cin grabbed a food tray, and ignoring the kitchen staff protocol looked directly at Jake and pronounced, "Let's eat."

More of the USAP staff entered and went straight for the food. The dining room started to fill.

Jake followed Cin's lead as they each selected their choice of food from the self-serve buffet table.

"No vegetables for me," Jake remarked.

"Too bad. I can't get enough," Cin stated.

Cin selected an open table and indicated for Jake to sit with her. She waited for him to put his tray down first and then placed her tray next to his and sat in the chair beside him. This seemed a little forward to Jake. *If she's putting the moves on me, she's trying too hard.* Had Sally been putting some of her matchmaking ideas into Cin's head?

Jake felt like Cin had barely taken her eyes off him while they were seated.

"Sally told me you wanted to speak with me," Cin said.

"I've been meeting everyone who is here for winter-over." Jake noticed her attentive look that hung on every one of his words. He scanned the dining room. Other tables were filling up, but people were avoiding his. Cin and Jake were alone.

Jake refocused his attention on Cin. She was about his age, a thin girl, a little too thin for him—no, that wasn't it—just thinner than she should be, he decided. Her hair was black, short and straight, her eyes pleasantly dark.

"You're the Officer in Charge. I remember Lieutenant."

"Please, Cynthia, call me Jake. My name is Jackson, but I go by Jake."

"And you can call me Cin. It's what I prefer."

Part of a tattoo revealed itself on the inside of Cin's wrist as she reached across the table. He wasn't sure if she meant for him to see it or not. "Okay, Cin, but Cynthia is a very nice name."

"I like Cin. Rhymes with sin, S-I-N."

Jake was examining his plate and picking at his food as he spoke. "How did you come about taking a job with USAP and winter-over in Antarctica?"

Cin's eyes stayed glued on Jake. She hadn't touched her food. "I moved to Denver, that's where USAP is headquartered. Someone I knew said to just go for it. So I did. It's a cool job—Ha." She laughed at her pun.

"Ha, good one." Jake smiled comfortably with her now. She was becoming easy to talk with.

The tension he had felt when he first met Cin softened. In a matter of minutes, their strained exchange had evaporated, and a fondness inserted itself. Words drifted as they learned little bits about each other. Their conversation suddenly flowed with ease and rambled aimlessly like two young hearts flirting at the entrance to a new world. Jake was somewhat shocked at his own behavior. Initial casual conversations with women always seemed artificial to him, and he figured pheromones must be filling the air. It was odd—he had never felt so relaxed with a woman as he did with Cin. Perhaps his initial concerns about her had been misplaced. It happened quickly. Efficiently.

The last of the diners arrived, and soon the chow hall was filled as much as it ever would be during winter-over. Jake watched as Felix walked in with Oksana. They sat together at a table on the other side of the room. Jake's stare followed Oksana to her seat.

"Do you know her?" Cin asked.

"Who?"

"The one you're looking at. The Russian scientist."

"I met her today, that's all."

"My roommate was Russian, too. Did you know my roommate, Ksenia?"

"Yes, well no, I mean, I just met her in the kitchen before she—"

"Ksenia didn't like her—that Russian scientist."

Jake saw a concerned look on Cin's face. Her demeanor flipped like a switch. He was beginning to like Cin and he didn't want to see her upset. "What's it like in Denver, where you came from?" Jake tried to deflect her concern.

"Not so great. I hadn't been there very long. Why do you think I came here? Haven't you ever just wanted to go for it?"

"Sure, I went for it in the Navy. I worked hard and got to fly Helos."

"Is it everything you wanted it to be? Are you everything you ever wanted to be?"

"I guess they'll be more, later—after the Navy."

"What will it be? What do you want?"

"I don't know. What do you want?"

"I want everything. I want it all."

"You have a lot of ambition, Cin, but I don't know how you're going to find it all down here in Antarctica."

"I'm here for a piece of Antarctica—whatever that is. Who knows what I'll find."

"I suppose we're all looking for something."

"I found you, didn't I?"

Jake was shocked. He hardly knew this girl. He didn't know what was happening. But it was happening, and fast.

"The Ice has a funny effect on people. I think you're just talking." Jake redirected the conversation. "What was your roommate Ksenia like?"

"Ksenia told me her parents were dead." Cin seemed not to want to talk about it and turned to her food for the first time.

Jake looked across the room again at Oksana. "And what about her, the Russian scientist? You said your roommate didn't like her. Why do you say that?"

"Ksenia said that Oksana and her family were from the academic class and deeply connected to the old Soviet government." Cin raised her voice in an annoyed fashion.

"You know her name?"

Cin continued without skipping a beat. "Her kind hated to see the end of the Soviet Union because it brought the end of their hold on power." Cin pressed her fork down firmly onto her plate. "They resisted the change. Even today, after the new democratic Russia was formed, the old communist types still thrive throughout Russia."

"What do you mean?" Jake's furrowed eyes emphasizing his question. A moment ago, Cin didn't want to talk about Ksenia, and now she was railing against Oksana.

"How do you know all this? Did Ksenia tell you about Oksana?"

Frustration replaced annoyance as Cin continued. "Don't you know what the promise of democracy and freedom meant to the people of Russia? Communist corruption was simply replaced with a new generation of corruption. Criminal elites and the Russian Mafia now control most Russian politics. And their connections with a vast underworld run the huge Russian Black Market. They act as if they are still in power, and their network of corruption influences everything; politicians, government, and the military."

"For a girl from Denver, Colorado, you sure know a lot about Russia. Did Ksenia tell you? Did she know about this?"

"All Russians know, and you should know too. Russia is run by ruthless billionaire moguls of untold power and wealth, where trading in the unobtainable is a sport. They are brutal. They do whatever they want."

Cin was convincing. She spoke passionately. "Ksenia told me that she was afraid of that scientist. I wonder now what really happened to Ksenia?"

Jake and Cin were the last to leave the chow hall after dinner. Their conversation together made Jake lose track of time. He said goodnight and walked away. He had heard some interesting things, but his head was bouncing around with thoughts about this girl. He liked her, but she was a contradiction. She seemed nervous and uptight. Not with him necessarily, just a tense personality. She changed like a chameleon — warm-hearted one minute, intense the next.

Maybe that's why she was so thin. She was certainly direct. She was adventurous, after all, she made it to Antarctica, but he sensed she was running away from something. And then there was that tattoo. He saw that it covered a scar on her wrist. When he asked her about it, she quickly dismissed it—a childhood accident, nothing more. But by covering the scar with a tattoo, Jake couldn't help but think there was something more to it. "Who knows," he said to himself. "She's a contradiction."

The one thing he was certain of was that Cin didn't like Oksana. She had practically accused her of being responsible for Ksenia's death. "That's absurd, right?" Jake spoke out loud to himself. And now he was going to meet Oksana.

He didn't tell Cin where he was heading next, but he was going to be careful around Oksana. That struck him as odd since earlier he had felt an attraction to her. He felt he needed a different kind of weather report so he didn't get caught in zero visibility.

CHAPTER TWENTY-FIVE

Jake walked through the deserted NSF research building and found Oksana in her Geology Lab. "What did you want to see me about?"

"I saw you eating dinner with Ksenia's roommate," Oksana quizzed Jake.

"Yes, her name is Cin. She talked a little about Ksenia and said some things about Russia that Ksenia told her."

"I don't think Ksenia's death was an accident," she said abruptly.

"Neither did Cin," he said. "Why haven't you told someone about it?"

"I did. I spoke with Lieutenant Commander Weaver. And now he's dead. I don't think his death was an accident either."

"That's quite an assertion. I admit two deaths so close to each other is a rare occurrence, but they're probably two unfortunate accidents. There doesn't seem to be any connection."

"Yes, there is."

"What? Tell me."

"I explained it all to Lieutenant Commander Weaver, then he knew too much, and he was killed to silence him. Ksenia knew too. And that's why she was killed."

"Knew what? What's this all about?"

"I have to tell you the real reason I am in Antarctica. There is a discovery I came here to collect. I have it now, and it is extremely valuable. It is potentially worth tens of millions of dollars." She shook her head. "I was foolish, driven by hatred and greed. I have been wrong. That greed made me lose Ksenia. I have been blinded by my hate." She seemed to dwell on her shame, unsure of what to say.

"Why don't you start at the beginning."

Jake listened to Oksana explain in detail the history of the meteorites. She described her father's devotion to his quest and how she was continuing in her father's footsteps to introduce the meteorites to the world. She blamed the Soviet Union for making her father go alone to Antarctica and then abandoning him to die near Vostok.

"I will never forgive them for what they did to my father. But don't tell anyone about this," she begged. "I have first to verify the meteorites are from Mars. Please, if you tell NSF now, I'll be punished and unable to complete my work on the meteorites. I will be sent back to Russian, not only a failure and in shame, but I will most likely be killed if I return empty-handed."

"Why would you be killed?"

She revealed the arrangement she made with Admiral Drugov and that he was the same Navy Officer that had sent her father to Antarctica. "For him to coordinate my research in Antarctica, I had to agree to collect the meteorites, remove them from McMurdo, and sneak them back to Russia. I knew I couldn't trust the Admiral. He thinks I will return them to Russia. But why should I? He will just sell them on the Black Market. He'll leave me nothing."

She listened to herself describe her convoluted plan, and it seemed like a different person was speaking. The more she spoke, the more devious she sounded. At the core of it, she was humiliated, Jake surmised. Her regret poured out like a confession.

She admitted that she and Ksenia were going to keep the meteorites and not return to Russia. "It took the death of Ksenia to shake me to my senses." She realized all her scheming to justify stealing the meteorites and profit from them was pointless, and it was poisoning her soul and ruining her life. "I have been on the wrong path," she admitted with a heavy sigh.

Oksana's remorse was palpable. "I thought the best retribution for my father's death and revenge against the Soviet Union would be to steal the meteorites for myself. All that has resulted in is death. I know that is not what my father would have wanted. If the meteorites are kept a secret, then I am not safe. There is no reason to hide the truth anymore. There never was a good reason. I realize now that if they are kept hidden, no one who knows the secret will be safe. The only way for everyone to be safe is if everyone knows about the meteorites."

Her voice cracked and sniffles mixed with her tears. "Lieutenant Commander Weaver helped me hide the meteorites. Someone got to him in order to find the location of their hiding place. I..., we, have to retrieve them before anyone else. Then I will announce their discovery to everyone. My father's discovery. No more secrets."

There was a long silence. Jake watched Oksana straining under an emotional burden that was more than she could bear. It seemed Oksana's thick outer veneer was not so tough after all. She was not the stern, unemotional person that she portrayed herself to be."

Will you go with me to collect the meteorites from their hiding place?"

"Where are they?" Jake asked.

"They are away from McMurdo now. Lieutenant Commander Weaver and I took the meteorites to Scott's Hut to hide them."

"That would explain the guano we found on his boots."

She pleaded. "I had them, and then I let them go. You can get a snow track vehicle without any questions. Please, take me to retrieve the meteorites." She was convincing, hard to resist.

"We'll have to go in the morning."

"No! I want to go now. Right away!"

"We need to travel during twilight," Jake said. "It will be safer driving then."

"Then you must not say a word to anyone about the meteorites. Please, promise me. I want to be—*I have to be*— the one to announce their recovery.

***

КЙ–222 ЕУРЕКА (*Eureka*)

The endless thumping and scraping of ice along *Eureka's* hull became a continuous grinding chaos. Nerves were raw. Many of the crew believed they were on a doomed ship. It was more than obvious to Lukyanov that it was no longer safe to continue farther south, even at the reduced speed of six knots. Something had to be done. The captain and his XO secretly began plotting ways to reduce their speed further. The thought of taking command of his ship back from Admiral Drugov was not far from Captain Lukyanov's mind.

"The engines are operating at an increased RPM just to push us through the thick ice and maintain the ship's headway," the XO said. This RPM would normally have allowed *Eureka* to travel eight knots or more over smooth water, but the thick ice was holding them back. Captain Lukyanov and his XO had remained together continuously on the bridge for more than twenty-four hours.

"We can't keep going," the XO said under his breath to Lukyanov. It wasn't an unexpected comment. In fact, had Admiral Drugov not been embarked, the XO would have voiced his opinion long before they were put in this predicament. "Remember the fate of Shackleton and *Endurance*," the XO whispered.

He was referring, of course, to Sir Ernest Shackleton captain of the ship *Endurance*, who attempted to travel too far south into the Southern Ocean to reach Antarctica during the winter of 1914-15. As punishment for their error, *Endurance* became trapped in the encroaching winter ice. Eventually, the ice crushed their wooden sailing ship into splinters. With *Endurance* hopelessly imprisoned in ice, the crew was forced to abandon ship and set out on an incredible journey of survival. It was nothing less than a miracle that the entire crew lived through the ordeal. The story of their nearly two-year struggle to escape the clutches of unforgiving Antarctica is legend.

"Echoes of Shackleton," Drugov's voice spoke up from behind the CO and XO, startling the officers. He seemed to have appeared from nowhere. Consumed with their survival, and constantly looking outward from the ship to the ice, no one had noticed Drugov enter the bridge. Lukyanov wondered how long Drugov had been behind them. Was the mention of Shackleton by Drugov just a coincidence of their obvious similar circumstance? How much had he overheard of the discussion between him and his XO as they weighed the misfortune of their current situation against the disaster of Shackleton?

"Attention on deck," the XO belatedly called out. Exhausted seamen jerked their depleted bodies to a rigid stance.

"We should be getting close to McMurdo by now." Drugov asserted.

"Distance to McMurdo?" the XO barked to the Quartermaster.

"One hundred and twenty miles, sir," the Quartermaster's swift reply.

"And the distance to Cape Royds and Cape Evans?" Drugov asked.

The Quartermaster froze. The young seaman had never heard of Cape Royds or Cape Evans before. Lukyanov joined the Quartermaster and leaned over the chart. He was vaguely familiar with some of the early Antarctic landmarks that dotted the coastline near McMurdo.

"Ninety miles to Cape Royds, Admiral. A little farther to Cape Evans."

"Very good. Get us as close to Cape Royds as you can." Drugov placed a hand on a shoulder of each the CO and XO, and with a coy smile that emphasized he had heard everything between the officers, he said. "Maintain a position near Cape Royds, Captain. Then keep *Eureka* moving—small circles and figure eights—so we don't get locked in the ice.

CHAPTER TWENTY-SIX

Jake told Petty Officer Parks the following morning that he would be out in the field with one of the scientists for much of the day. Then Jake and Oksana went together to the Mechanics Shop where the snow track vehicles were kept during winter-over.

A dozen snow track vehicles were kept in McMurdo for use by the NSF and USAP. They were nothing more than square box enclosures large enough for two passengers that sat atop a set of conveyor belts tracks for wheels. Painted the same red-orange as the helicopters, these odd machines were constantly seen scurrying around town like bugs during the summer research season. But most of the vehicles would remain in hibernation, just like the helicopters, during winter-over when it was too dangerous to travel in the dark. No use of a vehicle would be authorized until the new ice runway was constructed months from now.

The snow track vehicles reminded many of little cube-shaped tanks. They were very basic. Windows help keep out the cold wind, but the only heat inside was what wafted up from the loud gasoline engine that sat beneath the occupant's butts. Despite their uncomfortable ride and crude makeup, they did have a certain quaint look about them. Some even thought they were cute, and in that fondness, they each acquired nicknames like "Herbie" and "Chilly Willy" that were stenciled on their sides. There was one large snow track vehicle that could carry eight people inside, and it was called "Ere-bus."

Jake and Oksana climbed into the awkward-looking snow track vehicle named "Ice Cube" and began their journey to Scott's Hut.

They drove inland toward Mount Erebus and away from the relative safety of McMurdo. First, they went by the area of Castle Rock on their left, and next, they passed the New Zealand research station on their right, but they could see none of these landmarks in the featureless terrain. Near whiteout conditions had reduced the visibility to less than one hundred feet and obscured all but the closest points of reference. They planned to stay on the ice road that would eventually lead to Scott's Hut. Although used by track vehicles and snow machines, it could hardly be referred to as a road. It was just a marked path.

The polar twilight brightened the white sky uniformly as if they were surrounded by a cloud. The ground and the sky were uniformly white. The air was white and without definition. The only variation in color was spread on the snow path ahead of them, dimly illuminated by the two pale-yellow headlamps of the track vehicle. They drove slowly and cautiously, keeping their vehicle centered on the path. One by one, they watched as bamboo poles with little green flags passed beside their vehicle, and which marked their safe passage.

Jake's eyes stayed focused ahead, always straining to find the next flag. "Help me keep the green flags in view. They mark the path."

"I'm watching!" Oksana said excitedly.

As soon as one flag passed, each of them tried to predict where the next flag would materialize out of the fog. At first, a little game played out between them to see who could spot the next flag first, but soon they settled into the seriousness of their routine.

There was no heater in the vehicle. Both were bundled up for the long drive. Jake wore his Navy winter-weight flight gear and thick black leather flight boots. Over that, he wore his military-green jacket and heavy snow pants. Oksana wore the bulky red polar parka issued to her by USAP. On her feet, she wore the bulbous white "Moon Boots," which made the wearer look like some kind of cartoon character. They were issued by USAP for protection against the freezing air, but the indignity of their ungainly appearance seemed more like some kind of cruel Antarctic joke.

Oksana saw Jake glance at her feet comically. "These boots aren't very flattering," Oksana said.

"Don't worry. You look great. They keep your feet warm, don't they?"

"I saw some red flags earlier," Oksana said to shift the topic quickly. "What about them? Danger?"

"You haven't heard about the flags?"

"No, what?"

"We have three kinds of flags down here. They're easy to remember: green, red, and yellow; good, bad, and piss."

"Oh my," Oksana laughed.

"Green flags mark the roads and paths. Stay close to them, of course. But you want to stay away from the red flags. They mark unsafe snow and ice conditions, lots of crevasses in places. Some of the crevasses are big enough for a Herc to fall in. Some are just the right size to swallow a human."

"Don't tell me someone has fallen into a crevasse?"

Jake looked straight into Oksana's eyes and took a moment to debate how much horrid detail he should express to her about these hazards. He decided not to ruin the mood.

"You don't want to know," he quipped. "Many crevasses are hidden by snow bridges because the wind covers them over with a thin layer of snow. Most of the dangerous crevasse areas around here have been marked off with red flags by the Mountaineers."

"And yellow?" she smiled, anticipating the answer.

"Yellow, well, you know. After many years of explorers and researchers, people realized it wasn't just the sled dogs turning the snow yellow all over the place. So, when you have to go, everybody goes in the same place. And we mark that spot with a yellow flag."

"Even women?"

"Yup. We all gotta pee," Jake smiled. "Everyone respects everyone's privacy. Remember, it's all in the name of science."

***

Time began to pass more easily. Their playful banter hinted at a budding friendship. They were enjoying each other's company. The sky grew whiter as noon approached, and there was no definition to the horizon. They continued to follow the green flags carefully.

As they approached the area near Scott's Hut, Jake stopped and turned off the loud motor. "Just listen," he said. Hidden in the nebulous white distance ahead, the sound of thousands of Adélie penguins roared. Jake started the motor again and crept forward. Gradually the path in front of their vehicle darkened, and the pristine fields of white snow gave way to more frequent guano stains, and eventually it became the solid brown mass of guano that blanketed the entire penguin rookery. Simultaneously, the fetid odor of the penguin rookery revealed itself.

Along with the changes in sight and smell, a chorus of thousands of penguins raged. All individually squawking their melancholy song like loons on a lake, they joined together to fill the air like the united cheers of a crowd in a stadium. It would be easy to mistake their calls for the forlorn cries of despair. But this was their home. This was their safe haven. Together their vast numbers perpetuated their existence. This is where they mated, where they warmed their eggs, where their chicks were born. This is where they fought for survival, always together. The wind, the cold, the predators all conspiring against them, but still they survive. This is where new life is created. Where they live and die. And together, they survive.

Jake stopped the vehicle once again to listen and observe the immense field of the rookery that lay before them.

"It's a beautiful sight," Oksana said. "I'm amazed that they can survive here. It's truly remarkable."

"They huddle together," Jake said. "Survival in numbers. They'll start their seasonal migration soon to the ice edge. But the odds are against them. And it's not just the weather—look." Jake pointed to the side, reaching across Oksana, he singled out a large bird that seemed to be standing guard just outside the perimeter of the huddling mass of Adélie penguins. "See that big seagull-looking bird. That's a Skua."

The large bird was light brown in color and looked similar to a seagull in shape, but nearly twice the size of any seagull that Oksana had ever seen. The Skua wasn't standing guard. It was watching, waiting patiently for an opportunity to prey upon weakness.

"Those are tough birds. They are very aggressive too. If any of the young penguins get separated from the group, the Skua will snatch them up."

"That's awful."

"Yeah, it is too bad. But they're trying to survive just like the penguins. The Skua is a very hearty bird. They can survive all the bad weather that Antarctica can throw at them. And they can fly through anything. They're the LC-130 of seagulls."

Jake continued driving the remaining few hundred feet to Scott's Hut. They were adjacent to the rookery. He parked next to the front door, turned off the snow track vehicle, and stepped out.

"Let's go into the Hut. But don't get too close to the penguins. We don't want to disturb them. And don't step in any of their guano."

***

Next to the front door sat a bright red emergency survival box that was a common sight at every location USAP conducted operations. It contained all the signaling devices one could expect in an environment like Antarctica: aircraft signaling mirrors, day smoke flares, night flares, and a flare gun. Every visitor to McMurdo was instructed by the Mountaineers on its contents and usage as part of their orientation on The Ice.

As they walked into Scott's Hut, Jake asked with a wry smile. "You gonna lick the blubber?"

"Excuse me?" Oksana quizzed Jake, giving him a cute look, but at the same time baffled by what he was referring to.

Just inside Scott's Hut, Jake pointed to a two-foot-long pile of seal blubber that was resting on a side table. "Now that you're in Scott's Hut, you have to lick the blubber if you want to be initiated."

"Initiated in what?"

"The club."

"What club?"

"The club of everyone that has ever been in Scott's Hut and licked the blubber. It's a tradition."

"Another one of the Antarctic traditions I've heard about," she said wryly.

"You don't want to go against tradition, do you? It's not like I'm asking you to take off your clothes and jump in Lake Vanda."

She looked down again at the blubber. It had been sitting in the same spot on the table for over fifty years.

"You're kidding... I'm not..." making a sour face, and then another cute look at Jake, she leaned over the blubber. "Oh God, I can't believe I'm..." She turned her head, stared Jake directly in his eyes, and smiled. Then, turning her head back down, she touched the tip of her tongue to the moldy seal blubber.

"Aargh!" Wiping her tongue on her sleeve. "I can't believe you made me do that," and spit on the wooden floor of Scott's Hut.

"Hey, you can't spit in here. It's a historic site."

"I can't believe I did that."

"You should have seen your face!" Jake gave a bellowing laugh.

"I can't believe everyone that visits here does that."

"Well, I didn't say everyone did it. Most probably don't. In fact, I don't think anyone has ever really done it. More folklore than fact."

"Jerk!" She hit him and hit him again, playfully. "*Лодбнок*," she blurted a Russian word that sounded like pa-DOR-nik to Jake.

He laughed, thinking it probably did mean something like "jerk" in Russian. Or something worse. He didn't care. He deserved it.

"You tricked me. You made me do that!" Now she was laughing too.

"All right, let's get serious. Where are the meteorites?"

"Over here." Oksana led the way across the wood floor to the far side of the shelter. The structure had been kept just as it was fifty years ago. Even the contents were left undisturbed.

Following Oksana, Jake moved through an interior full of the clutter of everyday early Antarctic life. As a helicopter pilot, Jake had visited this rookery and Scott's Hut many times before, but it never failed to fill him with a sense of wonderment. Old tins of soda biscuits, cans of pemmican meat, and wax candles stuffed the shelves everywhere you looked. The contents were legitimately considered artifacts having survived decades of pilferage, Scott's Hut had become a museum of early Antarctic Explorers. It was *the* Antarctic museum, preserved *in situ*.

Walking through the kitchen area toward a group of four bunk beds, Jake soaked up every detail. A dog leash was hanging on a peg here, a glass jar with tea in a cupboard over there, dinner plates with cups and saucers neatly stacked on shelves. Awestruck at the simplicity of daily life, frozen in time. The feeling was enchanting.

Tucked beneath a wooden bunk that looked impossibly uncomfortable for sleeping were the meteorites. "Hiding in plain sight," she said. The Vostok crate didn't look all that different from the dozens of other old wooden crates among which it was buried. Kneeling beside the bunk, Oksana pulled hard, sliding the heavy prize free from underneath it. The top lifted off easily. She paused, straightened from her low crouch, and admired her treasure.

Jake stood behind Oksana in the cramped space looking down over her shoulders. "They look like meteorites to me," he joked.

Oksana jumped up. She turned rapidly toward Jake and grabbed him in a strong bear hug. Jake was startled. What was happening? Thoughts stirred in his head about Cin's suspicions of Oksana. He had been warned to be cautious around Oksana.

He pushed back—certainly she wasn't going to confront him. She was no match for him physically. He leaned back farther, pushing free of her grasp, not knowing what to expect, or what to do. She leaned in closer to him again, hugged him effusively, and kissed him.

"Thank you." She was jubilant. She pressed her lips firmly to his again and held a long sensuous embrace.

The interior of Scott's Hut glowed with the ambient light of peak twilight. The pale light was warmed as it bounced off the raw wood interior that had been seasoned to a mellow patina from decades of exposure to the cold, dry Antarctic air.

Although cold outside, the interior of Scott's Hut was a pleasant temperature, and rapidly heating up. The anticipation of reaching the meteorites, along with the excitement and Oksana's exertion while dragging the crate, seemed to have overheated her. Perhaps there was something more. "It's warm in here." She took off her bulky jacket, hat, and gloves, and placed them carefully on another bunk.

Jake didn't share the same sense of passion over the meteorites that had overheated Oksana, but he was sharing in the warmth. He watched Oksana as she knelt down again beside the meteorites. She picked up several from the crate, one at a time, and held them up. She examined their features closely and admired their beauty.

Her shoulder-length red hair, unbridled after she had removed her hat, repeatedly fell forward as she continually looked down into the crate. She pulled her hair back several times. Jake admired a slight brownish tint he had not noticed before—an auburn hue that shimmered as it flowed.

Eventually, she flipped her head back, aware now how Jake was watching her, aware of how men often looked at her. She used both hands to collect her hair neatly behind her neck. She lifted her arms above her head, raising her breasts, and slowly pulled her hair up, exposing the bare skin on the nape of her neck. She twisted the bundle together in a loose knot. It wouldn't last long before it fell loose and she would repeat the overture.

CHAPTER TWENTY-SEVEN

The opportunity was there. She presented all the right signs. He could easily agree that it was warming up in the Hut and remove his heavy parka as well and continue this frisky interaction. Would it lead to an encounter, a passionate crescendo?

Jake stayed resolute. This cannot happen. "I am the OIC," he told himself. We are in Scott's Hut for God's sake. To go any further would be to desecrate a historic site.

"Let's get your crate and head back to McMurdo," Jake commended himself on his self-control and threw cold water on his mischievousness.

Oksana looked deflated. She had not expected the encounter to end this way. She removed one of the larger meteorites and replaced the top cover on the crate. Then she pushed hard on the crate to slide it under the bunk again and back into its hiding place.

"I thought we were going to get all of them?" Jake said.

"I just need this one."

"I don't get it. Weren't you going to bring all the meteorites back to McMurdo and tell the world about your discovery? That would guarantee their safety, you said."

"I need to examine this sample a little longer before I make an announcement. Don't tell anyone until I have finished. Promise me."

Jake grew cautious. Echoes of Cin's mistrust of Oksana entered his mind. "It seems you've misled me."

"Let's just go," she said abruptly. Oksana was eager to leave.

What was Jake to do? If she only wanted to bring back one meteorite to examine in the Geology Lab there wasn't much he could do about it.

"Here," Jake picked up her coat like a gentleman and wrapped it behind her as she put it on. Her intoxicating red hair that he had come so close to swimming in, draped temptingly over her neck and shoulders, just out of reach of his desires. Jake bent over the bunk to collect her hat and gloves.

There, delicately handwritten on her gloves, Jake read not numbers, but letters—O3—Oksana's initials. Written in Russian Cyrillic script, they looked just like the numbers 03. Exactly what Tim said was written on the glove he found next to Cin's dead roommate, Ksenia, at the base of Castle Rock.

Jake turned to look at Oksana and carefully handed her the gloves. "Here you go." He slyly examined her face to see if she had picked up on his epiphany. He was in a life and death game of poker now, and he didn't want to reveal his tell.

"Let's go," she said and put on her hat and gloves.

He was nervous. "After you." He didn't want her walking behind him. It was troubling to him that she was leaving the box of meteorites behind.

He had to play it cool. Had she killed before for these meteorites? Would she kill again? Would she kill me? When? Today? Now?

Jake decided he knew the answers. But he couldn't let on that he knew. He just had to make it back to McMurdo—alive.

Despite driving too fast for conditions, Jake somehow made it back to McMurdo without careening off the green flagged path and killing themselves. They exchanged few words on their journey. Jake hoped Oksana would think he was just staying focused on the drive. But Oksana was quiet, too. She felt hurt that Jake had rebuffed her delicate suggestions in Scott's Hut.

Once back in McMurdo, they separated. Oksana went straight to the NSF research building to start examining the new meteorite. Jake desperately wanted to see his good friend Felix and confide his suspicions to him, but he was in no way going to follow Oksana into the NSF building. He didn't want to be anywhere near her.

***

Jake picked up the phone as soon as he got to Penguin OPS. "Hey, Felix, come over to my office, I need to talk to you right away."

"Sure, it sounds urgent."

"Just get over here."

"I'll be right there." Felix dropped everything and made the brisk walk to Penguin OPS in less than two minutes. "So, where have you been all day?"

"What if I told you I know where to find a whole bunch of Antarctic meteorites? A couple of dozen of them, in fact, and larger than the puny one you have in your little collection on the shelf in your office."

"I'd say great, and I'd say we're in luck. We have a geologist staying with us right here in McMurdo for winter-over."

"Right, I know, but she's the one hiding them."

"What!" Felix jumped. "Let's go see them."

"No," Jake was firm. "She doesn't want anyone to know."

"Why not?"

"She doesn't want me to tell anyone."

"Well you blew it, you just told me."

"She says she needs time to examine them. She thinks they could be Martian meteorites."

"That would be absolutely incredible. Are you sure?"

"I'm not sure, and I don't think she's sure either. That's why she needs me to stay quiet."

"It's not like a scientist to keep secrets. I don't get it."

"She's not just any scientist. Listen, Felix, I think there may be more to it. A lot more."

Jake stepped to the door of the OIC office and looked each direction down the hallway to see if they were alone.

"I've been talking with a girl who works in the kitchen. Her name is Cin. She was Ksenia's roommate."

"The girl who died?"

"Yes. Ksenia was Russian, too, like Oksana. Cin says Ksenia and Oksana had a connection before they came to McMurdo, and she thinks Oksana may have been involved in, or at least know something, about her death."

"Does Cin know about the meteorites?"

"I don't think so. Oksana told me the only other person who knew about the meteorites was Ksenia and a Russian Admiral who arranged her research trip to McMurdo. She thinks Ksenia must have told someone else down here, and that person killed Ksenia, and then Weaze too."

"How is Lieutenant Commandeer Weaver connected to this?"

"Because he took Oksana to Scott's Hut to stash the meteorites. They hid them after Oksana's dorm room was broken into. Someone was looking for the meteorites. Oksana needed to hide them where they couldn't be found, and she knew the Geology Lab wouldn't be safe. It would be broken into next."

"But who is this other person that Ksenia told?"

"We don't know."

Jake paced back and forth and then closed the door to his office to make sure they could not be heard.

"But I think there could be another scenario. Maybe there isn't another person. Maybe Oksana got greedy and killed Ksenia herself. Then she got Weaze to help her hide the meteorites where they couldn't possibly be found, and then Oksana killed him too."

"That sounds far-fetched. And there's nothing to connect Oksana with Ksenia's death."

"There is. Listen to this. Tim, the mountaineer, told me just before he flew to Cheech that he gave Weaze a glove that he found next to Ksenia's dead body at the base of Castle Rock. He said it had a number written on it, but I just figured out that it wasn't a number at all. It was Oksana's initials. The letters OZ, written in Russian, is O3 and looks just like the number 03. And I just saw those initials on her gloves when I was in Scott's Hut with her."

"You were in Scott's Hut?"

"Yeah, I went with Oksana to where the meteorites are hidden."

"Okay, you've put together a pretty wild story. I don't know who would believe you."

"Someone has to believe me. I think I'm onto something down here."

"Jake, listen to me. If there's one thing I've learned about being in McMurdo, in fact, it's the reason I'm here in McMurdo, is that no one gives a shit about what happens down here. You could kill somebody and no one would notice."

"What did you say?"

"Nobody gives a shit."

"And no one would notice."

"Petty Officer Parks," Jake screamed loud enough to be heard everywhere in Penguin OPS. "Have we got a Comm Sat window to the States now?"

Jake called his Commanding Officer in Point Mugu and explained his theory in excruciating detail. The CO gave Jake the courtesy of listening to all of it. He didn't want his winter-over OIC thinking his CO didn't care. But that's exactly how the CO felt.

Then Jake made his pitch.

The point of the call was to keep XD-03 in Christchurch before it continued home to Point Mugu. Jake wanted to hold XD-03 long enough to get a Naval Criminal Investigative Service (NCIS) agent on board and fly back to McMurdo. Jake guessed the closest NCIS office was in Pearl Harbor, Hawaii. It would mean at least one extra day delay to get some law enforcement help down in McMurdo.

"I want you to arrest Oksana," Jake pleaded with his Commanding Officer.

"C'mon, Jake. Denied. Don't make me question my selection of keeping you as the winter-over OIC."

Jake could hear the disappointment in his Commanding Officer's voice from 8,000 miles away.

The line went dead.

CHAPTER TWENTY-EIGHT

The next day Jake was in the OIC office preparing for his daily phone call to Point Mugu. It was a routine update that took no more than ten minutes. The report consisted of boring information on the fuel oil levels for heating and power, freshwater production, progress on rehabbing the dorms, and so forth. Later in the winter-over season, after the ocean next to McMurdo had frozen over again, the report would include updates on the construction of the new ice runway.

Jake waited a few minutes past the start of the communications satellite window to begin the call to ensure a good two-way conversation over the satellite phone transmission. He was startled when his phone rang first.

"Jake, this is OPSO. Hey man, the CO's got to talk with you. Hold on—" Jake hadn't had the chance to say hello.

A minute later, the CO picked up his end of the phone in Point Mugu. "Jake, this is serious. I guess your suspicions were right."

"What's wrong?"

"As soon as Tex landed in Cheech, the local Kiwi authorities took possession of Weaze's body to prepare him for his next flight. The Kiwis are great. They were going to send him on an Air New Zealand flight direct to LAX. Then the US Navy would take him straight to San Diego Naval Hospital."

"What for?"

"Per some regulation, when any active-duty personnel dies outside of the USA, they have to be immediately received at a designated military hospital. And they always do an autopsy as part of that procedure. Well, guess what?"

"What, sir?"

"Well, the Kiwis have their own procedures when they receive a dead body from The Ice, and they did their own examination of the body, not a full autopsy, but the initial toxicology results indicate that Weaze was poisoned."

"What?"

"Not poisoned as in arsenic or something, but he had enough sleeping pills in him for it to be considered poison."

"Oh no," Jake realized he wasn't much of a comfort speaking to his Commanding Officer in only one and two-word sentences.

"This is a crisis, Jake. The Admiral is hot. I had told him that Weaze just drank too much when we first heard about it. He said that if I knew he was such a lush, I should have never designated him to be the OIC in the first place. Man, I'm screwed."

"This is incredible, sir—," Jake was cut off.

"Listen, I already told the Admiral that you're a good OIC and that you're on top of things down there. Then I said you had requested an NCIS agent down there to look into things, and you thought the death of the girl that fell was suspicious. He didn't even know about the girl that died. The Admiral is furious that I didn't get NCIS down there right away, especially if you, as OIC, requested it. My career is over."

"Sir, it's a little late to get NCIS down here. There are no more flights—"

"He told me just to make it happen. Whatever it takes. I'm turning around X-ray Delta Zero Three as soon as possible. I'm sending Tex and his crew right back down there, ASAP."

"What about the daylight? It's nighttime down here. The sun has set already. You know it won't be sunrise again for months."

The CO didn't hear a word that Jake was saying. "Two NCIS agents are flying to Cheech from Hickam right now. Tex will be waiting for them. As soon as possible, they'll board X-ray Delta Zero Three and take off for McMurdo."

"Wow, I can't believe this, sir." Jake was wondering how all this coordination was going to take place.

"Sir, the weather is still pretty bad here in McMurdo." Jake realized this wasn't helping the CO feel any better, so he added, "Hopefully it will improve in the next twenty-four hours. I'll double-check the weather forecasts and we'll make it happen, sir."

In an instant, Jake's life went from boring to blizzard. Suddenly, he had more to do than he could handle. He needed help. First, he called Maintenance and told them to drop everything. Anyone with skiway maintenance experience was to go to Williams Field and start grooming the skiway to receive a Herc.

The handful of USAP maintenance personnel who had remained for winter-over were now recalled from the mundane tasks of cleaning, painting, and rehabbing. Everyone capable of helping at the skiway reported immediately to the Maintenance Shop where they were reassigned to prepare the skiway.

Then Jake called his friend, Felix. Within minutes, Felix joined Jake and Petty Officer Parks in Penguin OPS. Together they gathered the latest weather reports, satellite pictures, and AGO meteorological data for the last 48 hours. Even though the current weather picture was bleak, they hoped it would improve. The same storm that had threatened the last aircrew's departure from McMurdo just two days ago had behaved and held off long enough for them to make it safely to Christchurch. "Now it needs to continue behaving and move the hell out of here," Jake mused.

"As I see it, if this weather pattern continues in its current state, it should be moved through McMurdo sometime after noon tomorrow," Petty Officer Parks sounded confident. But the fact that it would pass around noon was just part of the logistical puzzle. The darkness would still be a threat to be considered.

Jake wasn't as confident. The storm seemed to want to linger. To him, something was different. Was it the storm, or was it that Jake was OIC for this storm? He had seen dozens of polar storms in his three years on The Ice. He never had a problem with the Go or No-Go decision for his helicopter. Either the weather was above minimums or it wasn't. He looked out the window of Penguin OPS at the blowing snow. There was a knot in his stomach. This storm needed to be gone before the aircrew returned.

"The aircrew." It was such a sterile term. That's thinking like an OIC. The thought weighed on him. They were more than just aircrew. They were his squadron mates. His friends.

Jake started planning for the arrival of XD-03. The Herc should land shortly after local noon tomorrow. There would be no daylight technically. The sun would not be above the horizon, but local noon would be the period of brightest twilight.

Throughout the regular season, the skiway was touched up a little each day. But the skiway had now been neglected for several days, and a polar storm had just blown through. It would need extensive grooming to be smooth enough to land XD-03. It was up to Jake to make sure the workers provided a smooth surface by the time XD-03 landed the next day. He directed everyone to work around the clock. The aircrew would be all right, he thought.

Felix raised a dilemma. "All of McMurdo will know a Herc is returning, and everyone will want to know why."

Jake knew what Felix was thinking. "We can't tip off the person that must have spiked Weaze's drinks with an overdose of sleeping pills. McMurdo can't know about the toxicology report. If there's a killer among us, I want them to have their guard down."

Together, Jake, Felix and Petty Officer Parks formulated a plausible scenario for the Herc's return.

Jake called the corpsman to the OIC office in Penguin OPS. He arrived shortly eager to help and expecting a medical situation that required his skills.

"HM2 Smith, listen carefully."

Hospital Corpsman Smith was nervous.

"You have a patient with severe pain. You have diagnosed them as having acute appendicitis in need of emergency surgery. You are not capable of performing this procedure here in McMurdo. Not by yourself, not during winter-over, not without a doctor."

"Sir?" Now he was perplexed.

"We're bringing X-ray Delta Zero Three back to McMurdo, and we need to disguise its purpose."

Petty Officer Smith grew more nervous.

"We'll tell everyone that since it's only just past the end of the season, and that we still have a Herc in Cheech, we can send it right back here to pick up our patient."

A medical evacuation during the winter-over season was very rare. It is only done in an extreme emergency because of the danger. There had not been a MEDIVAC in the three years that Jake had been in the squadron.

"Petty Officer Smith, you are sworn to secrecy," Jake directed.

"And we have to make this look like a real emergency," Felix added. "We need a real patient."

"Yes sir, absolutely," Smith wasn't exactly sure what he was agreeing to. "Who is going to pose as the patient?"

"We need everyone in maintenance to work on the ski-way, so it can't be any of them," Jake said.

"Probably one of the kitchen staff is best," Felix suggested.

"I have the perfect choice," Jake said.

"Who's that, sir?" Smith was trying to fill in the blanks.

"Her name is Sally. She works in the kitchen." Jake's voice swelled with confidence. "I'll go talk to her. She'll do it." The plan was going well.

"We'll sell it real good," Jake looked directly at the corpsman. "I'll call you to the kitchen after I've explained it to her. Then you pull her out to medical."

"Put her on a stretcher for everyone to see," Felix insisted. "Make it look authentic."

"No one else can know. Understood," Jake commanded.

Soon it was no secret to anyone in McMurdo that one of the USAP staff was gravely ill. The aircrew that had just said goodbye to McMurdo was coming right back. They were to pick up their patient and bring her to a New Zealand hospital.

***

XD-03 was airborne out of Christchurch at exactly 05:00 the following day. The aircrew that had been planning to be flying back to California at this time was now returning to Antarctica. They carried just two passengers.

NCIS Special Agents Ronald Saunders and Isaac Morrow, from the Pearl Harbor, Hawaii Field Office, had caught the last commercial flight out of Honolulu to Christchurch. Undercover work was a specialty of every NCIS agent. In McMurdo, these two would assume the identity of two extra Navy personnel. They would blend in with the winter-over staff while surreptitiously conducting their investigation. Other than Sally and Don, only Jake, Felix, and Petty Officers Smith and Parks would know their true role. And Jake would make sure they knew where to look first: Oksana.

***

The parade of well-wishers to Sally's bedside in medical continued non-stop since the news broke. The visitors initially consisted of kitchen staff who worked directly with Sally, but she was so well-liked that quickly the numbers swelled to include every one of the three dozen winter-over personnel in McMurdo.

Jake congratulated himself for picking the perfect choice for his little charade, and Don agreed, at first. Sally played her part to the hilt, of course. She wailed in pain as each visitor approached her bedside. Don never left her side. Eventually, Don was shaking his head with each new visitor. Finally, he said to her, "Sally, I can't wait for your miraculous recovery at noon when the plane arrives."

"I don't know. I could get used to this."

XD-03 conducted its initial climb to 8,000 feet out of Christchurch, heading east over the South Pacific Ocean. After a short while, they chopped from Christchurch Departure and were cleared by ATC to climb to Flight Level 240 and turn south toward Antarctica. As they passed abeam of Dunedin, they took their last glimpse of land before the handoff to Auckland Oceanic for the next hour of their flight. There would be another weather satellite picture in less than two hours. McMurdo would watch it closely and keep the crew updated after that.

Tex and his copilot, LTJG Cruz, had been quiet for more than ten minutes, a very long time to go without the usual aircrew banter on a long flight. Tex's mind was focused on the weather. Silently, he reviewed the worst-case scenario: a whiteout landing. He had already convinced himself to fly all the way to McMurdo. He knew the stakes. And in committing himself to fly into marginal weather, he was fully aware that he was committing everyone on the aircraft to his decision. He had to be right. But sometimes, Go or No-Go was more than just a weather decision.

Chip, the NFO on XD-03, broke the silence in the cockpit and informed the pilots they had reached APORO.

"Auckland Oceanic, this is X-ray Delta Zero Three at APORO. Thank you for your services. Good day," Cruz announced over his radio.

CHAPTER TWENTY-NINE

XD-03 was flying from Christchurch to McMurdo into what the crew hoped was an improving weather picture. That was the most optimistic way you could phrase it. The weather en route was marginally acceptable. The recent satellite photos of Antarctica showed patchy clouds in a large swath grid east of the Transantarctic Mountain Range. The satellite picture two hours earlier had shown a mostly cloudy sky above the Ross Ice Shelf. The trend should be for a clearing sky. Again, the most optimistic way of looking at it.

At APORO, Chip switched the aircraft into grid navigation mode for the remainder of the flight to Antarctica. He disconnected the two gyros from magnetic influence, one at a time for safety, and slewed each of them to grid north. This had the indication of swinging each Bearing, Direction, and Heading Indicator (BDHI) almost completely around 180 degrees. A few moments previously, the aircraft was flying south. Now it looked like they were flying north—grid north, to Antarctica. Within the hour, while they were still close to New Zealand, Chip would conduct a sextant heading check using the sun before it went below the horizon and verify the proper functioning of the gyros.

Before reaching their first reporting point, Chip had scratched his usual pencil marks in the margin of his navigation log: PTAPTP.

"McMurdo Center, this is X-ray Delta Zero Three, position, over."

He repeated the call.

"McMurdo Center, this is X-ray Delta Zero Three, position, over."

The return signal was weak and full of static, but it did indicate that McMurdo had heard the transmission, so Chip gave his report. "McMurdo Center this is X-ray Delta Zero Three, position APORO, 06:22, Flight Level Two Four Zero, BOSLA at 07:29, DALOS next. Over."

The Herc's report heard in Penguin OPS was barely audible.

"X-ray Delta Zero Three, roger out," Parks spoke loudly and clearly into the microphone.

Jake stood in the back of the Communications room with Felix listening to the position report. Jake stepped forward, faced his audience of two, and summed up his thoughts. "The CO said go. If the weather goes to shit we can always recall the flight before PSR."

Petty Officer Parks and Felix nodded in agreement. They knew the significance of the Point of Safe Return (PSR).

"Let's keep the Herc coming," Jake said. "We need NCIS down here. I want them to grab Oksana."

Chip had completed his preliminary PSR calculation during preflight as he did on every flight over the Southern Ocean from New Zealand to McMurdo. Subsequently, he updated this PSR calculation inflight prior to reaching the first reporting point. In typical Navy fashion, PSR was another benign term for a very critical piece of information. The Point of Safe Return was the farthest point at which the LC-130 could fly toward McMurdo and still have just enough fuel to turn around and safely return all the way back to Christchurch. After PSR, you're committed. There is no turning back.

The PSR was essentially a fuel calculation problem but heavily influenced by wind and, to a lesser degree, aircraft weight.

Why would you fly two-thirds of the way to McMurdo only to turn around and fly back? Well, normally you wouldn't, of course. It would be a big waste of time, effort, and fuel. The better question might be: Why fly into McMurdo when the weather is so bad that you can't land, and there isn't an alternate airfield near McMurdo to divert too? The answer is, you don't.

A few minutes later, a new weather satellite photo came into McMurdo. It was a crude black and white facsimile. The quality was poor and made all the worse by the low illumination of the weak Antarctic twilight. Parks handed it to Jake.

Jake stared at it as if studying a puzzle, searching for a clue. But there was nothing promising in it. He tossed it aside. "No change," he said. "Get a call into Cheech while we're still in the Comm Sat window. Let 'em know Zero Three has passed APORO. No change in the weather en route. Same here in McMurdo. No change. Williams Field weather is at minimums."

In the unlikely event that an LC-130 arrived overhead McMurdo with the weather having so rapidly deteriorated that it could not land there, it would normally continue to another field camp with better weather. But all field camps were closed during winter-over. There are no divert fields.

The South Pole, though manned during winter-over, was too far away after the long flight from New Zealand. Not enough fuel. The only option would be a whiteout landing. This is a very rare occurrence. It had been more than five years since the last whiteout landing. No one in the squadron had any personal experience with that event.

It was called whiteout because it was a landing attempted during an Antarctic storm, and pilots said the view from inside the cockpit looking out was similar to the one you could imagine having from the inside of a ping-pong ball.

Aircrews did practice the whiteout landing procedure, but only just enough to be superficially familiar with it.

A whiteout landing was basically a blind controlled crash into an open field near McMurdo.

The open field space where this ostensibly harmless inconvenience was to take place was innocuously designated the whiteout area. It was an area near the Williams Field skiway, but several more miles from McMurdo—miles farther away from McMurdo—not closer. Just in case. It was a relatively flat patch of the Ross Ice Shelf that the Mountaineers had surveyed and declared to be free from sastrugi and crevasses. There were no structures, vehicles, or any man-made objects allowed in the whiteout area, not even a bamboo flagpole. Other than a practice area for newly-qualifying pilots to learn the art of the ski drag, it was kept pristine.

"McMurdo, this is X-ray Delta Zero Three, position, over."

Chip repeated his position report two more times. "Flight, Nav, I think they can hear us. I get a lot of extra static after each radio call. I'll just send it in the blind."

"McMurdo this is X-ray Delta Zero Three, position report in the blind. Position BOSLA, 07:33, Flight Level Two Six Zero, DALOS at 08:42, ELNAK next, out."

The High-Frequency radio crackled in response but was unreadable. "I think they heard me."

"Yeah," Tex said. "How much farther to PSR?"

"Just past ELNAK, 10:04."

"Okay, we'll see what they say when we hit ELNAK."

***

Jake sat alone at his OIC desk, where the minutes passed like hours.

"Weather imagery, sir." Petty Officer Parks walked briskly into the OIC office and handed another muddy black and white facsimile to Jake.

"Doesn't matter," Jake barely glanced at the paper. "I can look outside and see the visibility sucks." He was nearing a decision point.

"What are the winds?"

"Zero Seven Zero at Twenty Six, gusts to Thirty Four at Williams Field," Petty Officer Parks reported.

"Ceiling?"

"Five hundred feet."

"Damn."

Alone in his office, Jake sat and waited for the aircrew's next position report. The slow passage of time between reports was excruciating. Jake heard the static of the next report. The quality of the radio transmission for DALOS was no better than the one before.

After what seemed like another eternity, Jake returned to the Communications room to listen to the ELNAK position report he was expecting at 09:46.

As long as the aircraft arrived at an upcoming position reporting point within five minutes of their previously announced time, early or late, the aircrew was under no obligation to update their ETA. They would simply make their position report with their actual time of arrival as they passed through it. If their updated ETA had them more than five minutes ahead or behind, the aircrew should update their position report prior to arrival.

Petty Officer Parks looked up at his OIC. "Nothing yet, sir."

By 09:41, Jake knew XD-03 had not arrived early. By 09:46, he knew they were not on time. Now at 09:50, four minutes late, Jake knew they had only one minute remaining before they would be overdue.

"McM... kshh-ta... X-ra... kshh... sion... kshh... Eln... five... kshh..." came scratching over the loudspeaker.

The report was garbled and with too much static to comprehend. But there was just enough information hidden in the radio transmission for everyone in Penguin OPS to realize that XD-03 was making its position report at ELNAK, and they were still headed to McMurdo.

"These comms suck," Parks exclaimed. "They can't hear us."

"Keep trying to reach them," Jake made up his mind that very second.

"Send Zero Three the message: RTB. RETURN TO CHRISTCHURCH."

"Flight, Nav, I know they can hear me 'cause they keep coming back when I call, but I can't make them out." Chip was desperately trying to understand the garbled transmission, but it was hopeless.

"Get Cheech on the phone," Jake ordered Petty Officer Parks. "Tell them we can hear Zero Three but they can't hear us."

"Sir, the Comm Sat is dark," Parks stated. "The next window is in forty-five minutes."

"What's the latest PSR we have for them?" Jake knew what it was, but he needed to hear it again."

"PSR is soon, 10:04."

"Flight, Nav, we're approaching PSR. What do you think, Tex?" Chip wasn't saying anything that Tex didn't already know.

"I think I wish we had an updated weather report and better comms," the PIC continued his assessment out loud. "So, what's our abort criteria?" It was a silly question. Everyone was intimately familiar with the abort procedures in the Squadron Air Operations Manual.

"If negative comms with McMurdo and the last forecast were below minimums, then we would RTB at PSR." Cruz piped up like a 2P student being quizzed on his PIC exam.

Tex referenced the Air Operations Manual he had memorized in his head. "If all equipment status is good, and the last weather report was at minimums, or above, we could continue with negative comms, at PIC discretion."

"I just double-checked radar, it's good," Chip said before Tex could ask. It was an extra bit of information that the PIC could use right now. One key piece of equipment was the radar. All equipment was important, of course, but if the radar was down, it would be a no-brainer. Abort.

"The last weather report for our arrival time had forecast minimums at 1,000/3, right?" Tex asked the aircrew over the intercom just to confirm what he knew. The cockpit nodded in unison. A 1,000-foot ceiling and three miles horizontal visibility were the required weather minimums at Williams Field. It was just then that Tex realized that he might have overlooked a critical detail.

"Take the controls," Tex suddenly directed Cruz.

Tex reached down low and behind his seat into his helmet bag and pulled out his Aircrew In-flight Reference, an abbreviated copy of the Squadron Air Operations Manual. Opening to Polar Procedures, he quickly located the section about weather minimums that he knew by heart. And there it was, he found it, a small note next to the 1,000/3 minimums, one word: SEASONAL.

The next line in the procedures stated minimums of 3,000/3 were required during WINFLY. But Winter Flight OPS, WINFLY, would not occur for another five months, before the start of next season. And this current season had officially ended. Where were the procedures for flight operations during the Antarctic night—between the regular season and WINFLY? Tex flipped the pages back and forth, hunting for an answer he knew was not there. Technically, they were flying after the season ended, but before WINFLY started. No Polar Procedures in the Air Operations Manual addressed this deficiency. They were in uncharted territory.

"Keep trying McMurdo until we reach PSR." Tex shoved the In-flight Reference back into his helmet bag.

"Less than ten minutes later: "Flight, Nav, 10:04, PSR."

After a long moment of silence, Tex said, "We'll stretch it a little bit. Let's keep going another ten minutes."

"Roger that," Cruz spoke for everyone with as nonchalant an answer as there could be given their situation. No one else even blinked.

Well before the self-imposed ten-minute deadline was up, Tex had made up his mind. "I guess the season isn't really over because we're still here."

None of the aircrew expected anything less.

"Oh boy. I can't wait to get another McMurdo cheeseburger," Cruz said mischievously.

***

Oksana walked down the lonely corridor of the NSF research building. Her shoes made a hollow sound that echoed off the hard floors and bare walls. Each step seemed louder than the one before. All the rooms she passed were empty and dark. She quickened her pace, anxious to reach the familiarity of her Lab.

At the Geology Lab, she reached her arm through the doorway to the inside wall feeling for the comfort of the room's light switch. Finding it, a dozen fluorescent tubes in the ceiling popped to life and flickered for a moment in a crescendo of brightness that at the same time both comforted and spooked her. She stepped in, and to her right when from behind a cold voice spoke out and startled her.

"Hello, Oksana." Cin was standing against the wall on the far side of the Lab. Her voice was calm, but her look was fierce.

Oksana jumped back frightened and fell into the lab counter knocking over several chemistry flasks. Glass shattered on the floor. Cin took one step closer to more fully reveal herself. In Cin's hand, she held a twelve-inch kitchen knife.

CHAPTER THIRTY

The men at McMurdo Penguin OPS waited for the next report. The minutes dragged by. They never heard the position report for GULAN. If nothing was heard soon, the aircrew would be over two hours without any communication.

There was a squadron procedure for re-establishing contact with an aircraft that was overdue for more than two hours. It consisted of having everyone with a radio begin calling for the aircraft on all frequencies. During the regular summer research season, this would include at least one or two other LC-130 Hercules that were out and about flying around Antarctica. It would also bring the support of the South Pole and a half-dozen field camps. A large-scale radio search would usually yield positive results in a short time. But this was not the regular season. No other aircraft were on The Ice. No field camps were open. Only the South Pole and McMurdo were able to conduct the lost communications procedures.

Why wait any longer? "Make preparations for lost comms," Jake told Petty Officer Parks.

"All ready to go, sir. Been ready."

Both the South Pole and McMurdo tried continuously for the next hour to reestablish radio contact with XD-03. No joy.

Jake reviewed the emergency procedures section of the Squadron Air Operations Manual for the third time this day. It said if after *three hours* without communication with an aircraft, the situation would be escalated. The squadron would enact lost aircraft procedures. The transition from lost communications to lost aircraft procedures was a rapid one in VXE-6. The squadron redirected every available aircraft to fly to the lost aircraft's last known position and to search other likely positions where the lost aircraft might be.

Jake threw the Air Operations Manual against the wall in frustration. This was just a hair away from becoming a Search and Rescue. There were no LC-130 aircraft in Antarctica. "How did we let ourselves get into this position?"

KALVA was the last scheduled transoceanic reporting point for XD-03 before reaching McMurdo. The ETA for that position had come and gone. The High-Frequency radio search continued at a lesser pace as a somber mood drenched everyone in Penguin OPS.

Suddenly, the radio speaker crackled.

"McMurdo, this is X-ray Delta Zero Three, over." The signal was weak but readable.

Elated, Petty Officer Parks jumped in response and yelled down the hallway for his OIC to come.

"X-ray Delta Zero Three, this is McMurdo, good to hear from you!"

"We've had bad comms on HF. What's the weather at the field?" Chip asked.

"X-ray Delta Zero Three, the weather is below minimums. I repeat, below minimums. Currently a 500-foot ceiling and one quarter mile visibility at Williams Field. Winds Zero Five Zero at Twenty, gusts to Thirty, over."

Jake came running in while the winds were being reported. "Where is he?"

"X-ray Delta Zero Three, say your position, over."

"McMurdo, this is Zero Three, we are one hundred fifty miles from McMurdo," Chip said. "We'll contact you on Victor at one hundred miles, out."

Jake picked up the telephone and should have called Christchurch right away. Instead, he called Helo Maintenance.

"Helo Hangar, this is Chief Martin."

"Chief, Lieutenant Covey here, I need you to get a Helo ready for flight right now. Can you do it?"

"I can get Pirate One Five ready, sir. We haven't prepped it yet for hibernation."

"Good. Pull it out on the Helo Pad. We're taking off in fifteen minutes."

"But sir, no other Helo jocks here on The Ice now. Who's going to be your co-pilot?"

"You are."

"Hot damn, yessir!"

Ten minutes later, a second speaker in the Communications room sparked to life.

"McMurdo, this is X-ray Delta Zero Three, over," Lieutenant Junior Grade Cruz announced on the VHF radio.

"Got 'em on Victor!" Petty Officer Parks yelled to the world. "Go ahead, Zero Three, we got you five-by-five!" He could barely contain his excitement.

The Very High-Frequency (VHF) radio, referred to as "Victor" by the aviators, transmitted and received its signal in a direct line of sight. The atmospherics that plagued High-Frequency (HF) transmissions had little effect on

VHF. The trade-off, however, meant a shorter range. You were lucky to hear anything at distances greater than 100 miles on VHF. But, at least it was clear now.

"McMurdo, this is X-ray Delta Zero Three, we are approaching one hundred miles to McMurdo, over."

"Zero Three, McMurdo, roger that. Williams Field is ready for you."

Jake recognized Cruz's voice on VHF and picked up the microphone. "Cruz, this is Jake, is Tex in the seat? Over."

"Jake, this is Tex. I'm in the left seat for landing."

"Roger that. Everyone in McMurdo has been grooming Williams Field for you. Don't worry about that. You'll have a smooth skiway." It was good for Jake to know that the most experienced pilot was in the left seat for this landing. "You have a little weather to deal with. The field is below minimums. So, you'll have to be at your best."

"Piece of cake."

"I'm flying Pirate One Five down to the skiway in a few minutes. I'm going to get you the actual ceiling and visibility, over."

"Thanks, Jake. Out." Tex was done talking. He had to get his mind right for this landing.

***

Helo 15 hugged the snow road that led to Williams Field flying only fifty feet above the ice. Green flags zipped by beneath the helicopter at a rapid pace. The VXE-6 helicopter pilots spoke about their IFR flying on The Ice. The conventional meaning referred to Instrument Flight Rules, but the Ice Pirates often joked that it meant "I Fly Roads." Today, that term applied literally.

Jake and Chief Martin could only see one or two flags ahead as Helo 15 skimmed low over the snow road to Williams Field. As they flew past each green flag, their eyes strained to locate the next. It reminded Jake of his drive to Scott's Hut with Oksana just the other day. Why was he thinking that now? "Just wait, Oksana. NCIS is coming to get you." So much had changed in such a short time.

"Visibility is a lot worse than one-quarter mile," Jake said to Chief Martin. After flying six miles dead straight from McMurdo, the snow road to Williams Field curved sharply to the left and terminated at the small group of maintenance huts. Helo 15 pulled into a hover and then proceeded to crawl forward, searching for the skiway. Everything was white.

The skiway is marked along its side every 1,000 feet with four by five-foot red banners. The strong fabric is stretched between two poles that stand fifteen feet high. Each marker also displays a large single-digit number from one to nine, indicating 1,000-foot increments along the length of Williams Field. These markers are augmented with strips of metal woven into the material that act as radar reflectors to help the LC-130 navigators locate the skiway and guide the Hercs to a safe landing.

Jake found a skiway marker and hovered over it before turning Helo 15 to fly along the length of the skiway at one hundred feet altitude. He never saw more than one marker at a time. He estimated the visibility to be less than 1,000 feet.

"X-ray Delta Zero Three, this is Pirate One Five, over."

"Hey Jake, this is Tex, we're about 30 minutes out. What have you got for us?"

"I just flew down the skiway at one hundred feet. Visibility was less than 1,000 feet. Then I elevated to three hundred feet and I couldn't see a thing. It's not zero/zero, but it's close."

"Roger. We're going to extend the downwind and set up for a long straight-in approach. I'll come in at three hundred feet and see if we can pick up any markers."

"Roger that. I'm going to set Pirate One Five down next to the maintenance huts. You've got the sky all to yourselves. Pirate One Five, out."

Jake located the giant number five on the marker in the middle of the skiway and turned Helo 15 toward McMurdo. The few maintenance huts slowly differentiated themselves from the white fog. He set the Helo down, and he and the Chief went inside and joined four maintenance crew members who were inside monitoring comms.

Tex, PIC of XD-03, pulled his seat and shoulder straps a little tighter. He squeezed the yoke with both hands. Cruz, 2P, was comfortably planted in the right seat, his youth seemingly oblivious to the potential of death. The Flight Engineer sat nervously between the two. His seat was about one foot behind and slightly elevated from the pilots. He maintained a vigilant scan of every dial and gauge in the cockpit. Chip had his head buried in the radar scope. His eyes focused on the radar reflectors that marked the full length of Williams Field. He frequently glanced at his other navigation aids, BDHI, TACAN, Altimeter, and others. The closer XD-03 got to the skiway, the greater emphasis Chip would give to his radar.

At a distance of thirty miles, the 10,000 foot-long skiway at Williams Field resembled nothing more than an elongated blob on the radar display. The skiway was no bigger than the size of a grain of rice on Chip's radar display. But experience showed Chip what he needed to see. He was lining up nicely. Patience. The grain of rice fluoresced a bright green with each pulsing sweep of the radar. Slowly, XD-03 approached the field. Chip constantly adjusted the range of the radar display—smaller and smaller. The blob lengthened its appearance as they got closer to the field. Only when the Herc reached ten miles to the skiway would Chip be able to distinguish the individual markers.

"Ten miles. Good radar picture," Chip said to the cockpit.

"We'll bring the field down the left side on downwind," Tex said. "I want to extend this downwind a little and have a nice long straight-in approach." That made perfect sense. No one replied.

As XD-03 settled to its pattern altitude, flying the downwind leg of their approach, Cruz called out their altitude. "Level at one thousand feet."

No reply. Everyone heard it. No extraneous talk now. Only necessary announcements from here on.

XD-03 was one-quarter mile offset from the field as the skiway passed down the left side of the aircraft. They were now flying in the opposite direction from which they would land. Tex couldn't help but peek out his side window as they passed just over 1,000 feet abeam of the field. He stared longer than he should have to try and spot some indication of the field during this close pass. He knew he wouldn't be able to see anything, but he looked anyway. The skiway slipped by. Nothing but a ping-pong ball.

They continued the downwind leg heading 250 degrees until their TACAN read four miles. "That should be good," Tex said. "Turning base." The Herc banked gently to its left and completed a 90-degree turn. "Steady on One Six Zero," Cruz said as they rolled out on base heading.

The banked turn that set up XD-03 on its new heading also had the unfortunate effect of rolling the radar antenna, which was mounted low in the aircraft's nose, away from the field. This caused the radar antenna to break contact with the skiway and Chip to lose sight of the field on the radar image briefly.

XD-03 was rapidly approaching the intercept to an imaginary line that extended out from the skiway. Just seconds after the turn to base was completed and wings were level Tex initiated another 90-degree turn to the left to line up for the skiway heading. "Turning final," Tex said.

The aircraft leveled out on the skiway heading of 070 degrees. The radar needed two more sweeps before reacquiring the skiway image. "Continue left to Zero Six Zero," Chip said. The aircraft had overshot the extended skiway heading.

It could have been the result of several things. Maybe the call to final was late. Maybe the aircraft skidded a little too much while Tex was trying to roll the aircraft as gently as possible and preserve the radar picture for his Navigator. Or, maybe it was the wind. Maybe the wind was different than announced. Chip thought it was the wind. He assumed his pilots were perfect. "Call for a wind check," Chip said.

"McMurdo, say winds," Cruz chirped on the VHF tower frequency.

"Zero Four Zero at Twenty Five."

Okay, the winds shifted to the left a little. His original ten-degree correction to the heading of 060 would not be enough. "Flight, Nav, come left to Zero Five Zero."

A nearly imperceptible roll to the left indicated that Tex heard the command, and XD-03 was heading 050 degrees.

"Right of centerline, correcting." Chip was happy with this heading for now. "Three miles to threshold."

"Five hundred feet," Tex declared. The Flight Engineer reached forward and positioned his hand just behind his pilot's hand to guard against any misintended throttle movements as Tex carefully pulled back the four throttle levers simultaneously to reduce speed and sink to the new altitude.

"Two miles, approaching centerline, come right to Zero Six Zero." Chip's attention was now completely devoted to looking at the radar display. The skiway and its radar reflectors were elongated from that earlier grain of rice image to one that now more resembled a shape about the size of a matchstick on his radar scope.

At this point in the approach on normal flights, the co-pilot would be looking forward out of the aircraft and calling that he had the field in sight. The pilot would look up from his instruments, acquire the field visually, and declare "I have the field." The Nav would have done the best that his equipment would allow delivering the aircraft to the pilots on final approach. The pilots would tweak their approach, select the final flap setting, establish the rate of descent, and land.

But the call "field in sight" never came from Cruz. So, Tex never looked up. And Chip continued his calls over the cockpit intercom.

"One mile, on centerline, come right to Zero Six Five." Chip's eyes stayed glued to the radar. Cruz and the Flight Engineer both strained to see any indication of the skiway. White on white.

"Three hundred feet," Tex called out. The aircraft settled slightly.

"Over the threshold," Chip said.

"Marker!" Cruz yelled. A skiway marker passed below and to the right of XD-03.

"Marker!" another passed under and away.

"Marker! Off to my right again," Cruz said. "We're too far left."

Tex maintained their 300-foot altitude for another ten seconds. No other markers were seen.

"Going around." Tex pushed the throttles forward. XD-03 accelerated and climbed.

XD-03 extended on the skiway heading of 070 degrees for a mile before turning left to set up for another 250-degree downwind.

Safely up to 1,000 feet, Tex spoke in his best pep talk voice. "Okay, that was pretty good. Just poor vis. We'll shoot the same approach, but this time we'll get down to 200 feet before the threshold." The reassuring timber of the big voice from Texas soothed the cockpit.

A second approach followed. It was no better than the first, third, the fourth, or fifth. Try as they might, one approach after another, the field would just not present itself to the aircrew. They were becoming exhausted.

"Climbing to 3,000 feet. Set us up for a safe orbit, Chip. Let's think this over." Tex knew what was next.

CHAPTER THIRTY-ONE

Stealing a snow track vehicle from the Maintenance Shop was simple. There was no one in Maintenance to stop them. Everyone had gone to Williams Field to help with the skiway, and they had taken with them all but one of the snow track vehicles.

Cin escorted Oksana at knifepoint and forced her into the driver's seat of the snow track vehicle. Cin removed one of the remaining portable radios from the rack of VHF radios that were available for all the vehicles and tucked it in her parka. Safety procedures dictated that no vehicle leave McMurdo without a radio. Safety was the least of Cin's concerns. She was only interested in listening in on the activity surrounding McMurdo.

Oksana trembled as she held the steering wheel and began to follow the ice path out of McMurdo. "You killed Ksenia."

"Shut up and drive," Cin's words spit out like venom.

"Why did you have to kill her?"

"You were the one that brought her down here."

"You're an evil person. You can't get away with it."

"Just take me to the meteorites."

"You killed Lieutenant Commander Weaver too."

"Whose fault is that?" Cin demanded. "You told him about the meteorites. You should have never done that."

"You're blaming me? You're sick."

"I know the two of you hid them in Scott's Hut. You used him to take you there. He told me all about it at the End Party after you came back together. But you still kept it a secret. That proves you were going to steal the meteorites and keep them for yourself. You would have killed him yourself soon anyway to keep him quiet. You're no better than me."

"That's not true."

"And you would have gotten rid of Ksenia after you were done with her."

"You're mad."

"You were just using her to help remove the meteorites from Antarctica."

"No, that's a lie. I don't know why Ksenia told you about the meteorites."

"She didn't tell me."

Oksana didn't hear what Cin was saying. She was frightened for her life and focused on the knife clutched in Cin's fist. Its blade was held tight to Oksana's ribs, poised to strike her like the coil of a viper. The snow track vehicle veered off the path and hit a green flag.

"Watch where you're going."

"I had to remove the meteorites," Oksana said. "I had no choice. We needed to escape. You don't know what it's like."

"I know." But Cin's retort went unheard again.

"Ksenia and I were willing to sacrifice everything to be free."

"I just want the meteorites. It's my way out too," Cin said.

"Out of what?" Slowly, Oksana started to hear what Cin was saying.

"My prison. My life." Cin pulled back the sleeve of her parka to reveal the scar on her wrist. "I was almost free, once." She needed to talk, but there was too much buried in her past holding her back.

Oksana didn't comprehend the significance of Cin's gesture and continued to dwell on her own situation. "I wanted to get out of Russia. We all hoped things would improve after the Soviet Union. It changed, but it was no better than before the end of the USSR. The Soviet Union killed my father and killed Ksenia's family too. I needed a life away from Russia. I just wanted to do the right thing."

"I always do the right thing," Cin said. They were talking over each other like they were in two different conversations.

"Ksenia and I were going to use the meteorites to get away," Oksana said. "We were sure that would make things right. Trade them for our freedom. Buy our freedom."

"I know the Soviet Union changed," Cin said. "You'll never know how it changed me."

Oksana gave a perplexed look at Cin. The once threatening knife now sat relaxed in Cin's lap. What did she mean?

"We both want to be free," Cin said. "We both want to do what's right." A somber expression appeared on Cin's face as she looked to the path ahead, and Oksana saw a tear form in her eye.

The drive was quiet for the next minute.

"You're going to kill me too, aren't you?" Oksana said.

No answer from Cin. They continued to drive in silence, and Oksana watched the green flags on bamboo poles pass by at regular intervals like they were timing the countdown to her execution. The road to Scott's Hut looked no different now to Oksana than the other day except it no longer resembled a winter wonderland. It was bleak and barren.

The radio in Cin's parka broadcast a loud voice. She removed it to listen. Cin and Oksana recognized Jake's voice. It sounded like there was trouble at Williams Field.

CHAPTER THIRTY-TWO

"We got this, right?" No one spoke. "Then let's do it." Tex was authoritative.

The aircrew had reviewed their whiteout landing procedures three times while orbiting safely at 3,000 feet above the Ross Ice Shelf ten miles grid east of McMurdo. At the easternmost portion of their next orbit, XD-03 turned toward Williams Field heading 250 degrees. Chip used his radar to keep them safely between the mountains as they slowly descended to 1,500 feet above sea level and to their eventual whiteout landing on the Ross Ice Shelf.

The TACAN, the military Tactical Air Navigation system, became a key means of homing in on the field and would be used to locate the aircraft within the boundaries of the whiteout area. Inbound to Williams Field, but not to land the aircraft, only to Mark on Top the TACAN that was adjacent to the field. The 30-knot tailwind pushed the aircraft from behind faster than the less experienced 2P had anticipated. Cruz's job was to watch the TACAN's bearing needle swing as they flew over the TACAN and audibly call to everyone in the cockpit their exact MOT. The needle started to swing slowly back and forth, then wildly, left, right, left, uncertain which side of the TACAN the Herc would pass. Then it quickly flipped around 180 degrees—a good MOT.

"Mark on Top," Cruz sang out.

"Come right to Two Seven Zero. We're outbound now to ten DME," Chip restated what they had all just briefed. XD-03 settled to its next altitude of 1,000 feet.

There was a minute of silence while XD-03 flew assuredly away from Williams Field and over the whiteout area before Chip broke the tension and repeated the plan. "At ten DME we do the big left turn and steady up on Zero Five Zero."

DME was the acronym for Distance Measuring Equipment. It was essentially the range measurement used by the TACAN. One DME is the equivalent of one nautical mile.

Exactly as the DME counter turned to ten, Tex made his final turn to the left. It was a long sweeping arc that carried XD-03 more than just turning around 180 degrees, and they continued a full 220 degrees forming a teardrop, and rolled out on a new heading of 050 degrees.

"Flaps to fifty," Tex called. "One hundred and twenty knots, setting 200 feet-per-minute rate of descent." He announced it out loud not for everyone's instruction, but to assure his confidence.

The cockpit remained quiet.

Chip's radar picture showed the Herc equally positioned between the eight-mile gap separating McMurdo and White Island. They were pointed into the wind, heading 050 Grid. This was good, but all Chip could do at this point was observe.

Chip felt like a passenger at this point. He tried to ease his mind by doing what he often did on flights, distract himself. "Let's do some math," he thought.

Okay, we're flying at 120 knots into a 30-knot headwind. This makes our groundspeed only 90 knots. Oddly,

Chip thought about how some people often survive car crashes of 90 miles per hour. Why did he think like this now? Maybe he didn't have enough to do during this phase of the approach. He continued to distract himself. Let's see. He knew a nautical mile was longer than a statute mile. That would make the speed in miles per hour more than nautical miles per hour for the same number. He couldn't remember exactly, but he recalled that MPH was at least ten percent more than knots. So, maybe 90 knots is more like 100 MPH, hmm. Okay, so a few less survive a 100 MPH crash.

But many people do survive a car crash. He had survived a terrible one himself. The same wicked accident that took the life of this father and best friend many years ago. The three of them were broadsided while driving home from a baseball game. It always made Chip think about how the seconds in life make all the difference. A few seconds earlier or a few seconds later, and they would never have been hit, and everything would have been different.

Chip looked at his watch, trying to keep busy. He appreciated the simplicity and function of his father's Rolex Explorer. Just time. No date, no day, no stopwatch chronograph. Chip had other gear for that. He admired the smooth rhythmic sweep of the second hand but pulled himself back from the daydream.

Tex and Cruz had it covered. Chip followed their heading. It looked good. TACAN looked good. Radar looked good. They were now comfortably centered in the middle of the whiteout area. Chip knew they had about seven or eight miles remaining ahead of them before they exited the far boundary of the whiteout area.

The eight by ten-mile patch of ice that comprised the whiteout area seemed like a huge space when studied in the Squadron Air Operations Manual. But today, flying blind, tired, and stressed, it felt like threading a needle.

As was often the case, a little more math to calm the situation. "Okay," Chip said again to himself. Our ground speed is 90 knots. That's 90 miles in 60 minutes. So, 90 divided by 60, that's 1.5 nautical miles per minute. A 200 fpm rate of descent. We started at 1,000 feet. That's five minutes until touchdown. So, at 1.5 miles per minute, we will have traveled 7.5 miles in those five minutes. But we only have seven or eight miles to the boundary of the whiteout area. "This will be tight." Chip kept that thought to himself. Tex and Cruz had enough to do.

Below 1,000 feet, Cruz had called out the altitude of the radar altimeter in 100-foot increments. Below 200 feet, Cruz began calling out the altitude every 50 feet.

There had been no other words spoken during this final phase of the approach.

"Two hundred feet... One hundred fifty feet... One hundred feet..."

"Maintaining Angle of Attack." Tex's voice was elevated. There would be no flair today.

Chip watched the TACAN bearing needle as it crept past the 330 degrees grid mark—the edge of the whiteout area. They were going to touch down just outside the boundary of the whiteout area.

"Fifty feet."

Tex would maintain their AOA and fly it all the way to the ground. At their 200 fpm rate of descent, the remaining fifty feet of altitude took only fifteen seconds.

Chip sat strapped in tight, a passive observer in the final minute before XD-03's whiteout landing—a controlled crash. He wasn't afraid. He just looked at his watch and counted the seconds.

***

The whiteout landing, the controlled crash, did not go well.

XD-03 first hit "ground" one-half mile beyond the whiteout area. The left main gear ski hit first. *The plane is level,* was Tex's first thought. *Maybe the ground isn't.* An instant after that thought, the right main gear ski hit. It hit harder than the left—much harder than any other landing that any of the aircrew had ever experienced.

Sastrugi. That was the first thought Chip had immediately followed by the realization they had overshot the whiteout landing area. XD-03 bounced and briefly went airborne again. It rolled right wing down. Tex corrected. They hit again, the force so strong it jarred their spines. The left wing was too low now. "Wings level!" yelled Cruz.

Tex heaved the yoke with all his might to correct their roll, but the Herc was being beaten up by the uneven terrain of the hard ice sastrugi.

The left wingtip touched the ice at the same time the left main gear ski hit. The wingtip dug into the snow. The number one propeller, the left-most propeller, bore into the ice. Instantly, hydraulic control of the ailerons was lost. Fluids, still pumping through vital hydraulic lines, gushed from the severed arteries that fed the ailerons. XD-03 pirouetted ungainly to its left in a violent twisting whirl. Finally, the plane stopped. "Fire," the Flight Engineer yelled. No one heard him. He was the only member of the aircrew that was conscious.

The Flight Engineer pulled all four E-handles to secure the engines and was just able to push the fire bottles for number one and two engines before he too passed out.

"X-ray Delta Zero Three, this is Jake over."

"X-ray Delta Zero Three."

"Come in, Tex, over."

"X-ray Delta Zero Three?"

"X-ray Del—," Jake stopped. He set the microphone down on the counter in the maintenance hut. He looked at the other people stuffed into the small room listening to his desperate calls. "Let's get the Helo out there."

Jake and Chief Martin jumped into Helo 15 and flew in the direction of the whiteout area.

The poor visibility and lack of any landmarks in the whiteout area made the going excruciatingly slow.

"X-ray Delta Zero Three," Jake continued calling as he flew. "Tex, Cruz...?"

"I see it!" Chief Martin pointed to his left. They approached XD-03 from a distance of fewer than 1,000 feet and an altitude of only fifty feet. Slowly the outline of the smothering aircraft revealed itself. XD-03 was awkwardly settled onto the snow. Its left wing was flat on the ice and shrouded in smoke. It looked to Jake like the Herc was pointed in the opposite direction it should be to have just landed facing into the wind. Its left wingtip was buried into the snow. The right wing pointed wrongfully skyward.

"They must have had a fire," Martin said.

Helo 15 set down next to XD-03. They ran to the aircraft, a twisted hulk laid out on its side. "Tex, Chip!" Jake called and ran. He couldn't imagine how anyone could have survived in the wreckage. The Herc looked more beast than machine. Rolled up in a fetal curl, it writhed in agony, holding in its pain after receiving its mortal blow.

"Cruz!" They ran and stumbled as best they could over the uneven terrain and yelled for their friends. They trudged in an ungainly panic to reach XD-03. Deep soft snow valleys interrupted by the hard ice peaks of the sastrugi ridges slowed their progress. Nearly to the fuselage, Jake tripped and fell. He got up, covered in red fluid. Only now did he see the snow all around was splattered and stained in bright red like blood pooled around a dying beast.

Chief Martin said, "It's hydraulic fluid. The number one prop is missing. The propeller must have cut the hydraulic lines."

Jake wiped away the caustic fluid that stung his eyes. The gruesome scene made him pause and gaze at the once-powerful Herc. Purple-blue and black smoke rose from the carcass. Life's fluids oozed from mortal wounds, and steam hissed from its pores.

Jake saw that the propeller for the number one engine was missing. "It must have slammed into number two and started the fire." Martin's assessment was correct. "They must have shot the fire bottles to put out the fire. That means they're still alive." Mercifully the fire was out, but the cloying smell of oily kerosene from the sickening mix of burned and unburned JP-5 jet fuel filled the air. The fire could flare up again at any moment.

The main cabin door to the Herc was located a few feet in front of the number two engine, the second engine from the left. Jake struggled to open the cabin door, which was half-buried in the snow. Folding it down part-way, he climbed up the few steps to the flight deck where he found the aircrew.

"I think we're all right," Chip moaned. "Dazed, but alive."

"Check the Pax," Tex cried. "We hit hard."

Chief Martin went back down a couple of steps and turned aft into the cargo area closely followed by Jake.

When the propeller hit the hard sastrugi, it broke free and cartwheeled at 4,500 RPM slamming into the port side of XD-03. It first ripped through the number two engine fuel lines and then tore open the hydraulic lines in the tender underbelly of the left wing. Then it slammed into the fuselage underneath the leading edge of the left wing.

The detached fifteen-foot spinning metal propeller had sliced into the soft aluminum skin of the aircraft. Four deadly propeller tips reached into the fuselage like blunt daggers, one after the other in a rapid blur as it tried to enter the cargo bay. Each bite of a propeller tip stabbed and ripped another hole as it raced from front-to-back along the side of the aircraft and split it open like a crude can opener. Blow-after-blow, the propeller ruthlessly hacked away through metal, cable, wires—flesh.

Unfortunately, the propeller found the two passengers. The NCIS agents never had a chance.

Jake leaned over one of the agents and pressed his fingers on the carotid artery in the man's neck. Nothing. Jake pulled open the agent's jacket and placed his hand over his heart, trying to feel life. Nothing.

What Jake did feel next to his hand was the cold steel of the agent's 9mm Beretta. Unthinking, Jake snatched the handgun from its holster and stuffed it in his jacket.

Chief Martin examined the other man. He looked up at Jake and shook his head.

Jake was furious. "I'm going to get Oksana myself."
"Chief, you stay with the aircrew. I'm taking the Helo back
to base—solo."

"McMurdo, this is Pirate One Five, over."

"One Five, go ahead."

"X-ray Delta Zero Three had a hard landing. Send
medical. The aircrew is shaken up, but they'll be okay. The
two Pax are dead. I'm RTB McMurdo. Tell Felix to meet
me."

Felix was waiting for Jake when he landed at the helicopter pad. "I have to warn Cin. Oksana may be out to get
her."

They ran to the chow hall. "Cin... Cin!" Jake yelled. The
dining room was empty.

They ran to the kitchen. "Where's Cin?" Jake demanded.

"Not here." The startled kitchen staff claimed as if
apologizing.

"Come with me," Jake told Felix. "We're going to the
Geology Lab, I want to get Oksana."

There was no sign of Oksana in the lab.

Jake looked at Felix. "I know where she went. Let's
go."

"Where?"

"Scott's Hut."

They ran to the Mechanics Shop. It was empty.

"Come on—we're taking Pirate One Five."

CHAPTER THIRTY-THREE

Once again, Jake found himself in Helo 15 flying low over an ice road shrouded in white cloud. Green flags passed beneath. Jake and Felix were searching for a snow track vehicle—hunting for Oksana.

"I see something," Felix said as his vision began to separate out a shape from the white fog. "It's Scott's Hut. We're here." He peered into the fog, looking for movement. "There's the snow track vehicle. She's almost to Scott's Hut."

"And what's that?" Jake pointed to an unexpected shape. A strange dark form lay just beyond the recognizable ones. He continued his cautious approach, trying to decipher its meaning and purpose as it was slowly unveiled from the white.

Helo 15 wasn't the only helicopter at Scott's Hut. Expecting to see Oksana in a snow track vehicle, Jake now looked at another helicopter and two men looming beside it on the ice. The black helicopter had landed on the far side of Scott's Hut. "It doesn't look like an American Helo to me. Not from New Zealand, either." Jake said. "Does it look Soviet?"

The snow track vehicle pulled up to the front of Scott's Hut and stopped.

Jake eased in closer, wary in his approach. He began to circle around the unexpected grouping in a slow hover much as a predator might surround its prey. Observing every detail below, Jake kept a measured distance as he maneuvered Helo 15 in front of the snow track vehicle to get a better look at the occupants. "I see two people in the vehicle," Felix said. "Oksana is driving. Not sure who the other one is."

Both occupants exited the vehicle in unison and walked uncomfortably close to one another to the front of Scott's Hut. Jake squinted as he tried to identify the second figure.

The two large men walked over and met the occupants of the snow track vehicle in front of Scott's Hut. Who are they?

"Wave at them," Drugov said looking skyward. "Smiles everyone. We want them to think we're here doing research." Drugov grinned from ear to ear. "Come on, wave."

Ivan cracked a frozen smile and held up a hand in an unnatural wave. Oksana stood still. She looked petrified. The other figure stayed silent and turned away.

Drugov raised both arms over his head and waved a generous welcome. He continued to pull Helo 15 toward him with big rounding swoops of his hand, signaling them to land.

"I'll set down over there," Jake said. He continued to eye the odd grouping with suspicion as he began a low hover and prepared to land.

246 · BILL CRAVER

Cin stepped to the front door of Scott's Hut and opened the red emergency survival box. Moments later, a red streak shot skyward nearly hitting Helo 15.

"That's a flare," Jake said.

"Чет, чет, Анастасия" (No, no, Nastasia), Drugov said, still grinning and waving. "You won't shoot them down with that toy. Let them land. Then Ivan can shoot them."

"Nastasia?" Oksana's voice shivered. "Who are you?"

"Oh, what shall I call you this time, Nastasia?" Drugov asked. "I'm curious as to the name you have chosen for this task. You were always so creative."

"I am Cin," she affirmed.

Jake backed off Helo 15 for a few seconds in reaction to the flare before creeping in closer again.

"Where are you going?" Felix cried.

Another flare whizzed by almost hitting the helicopter.

"Get us out of here," Felix was adamant. "They're shooting at us!"

A flare gun against my helicopter, you lose.

Jake jinked Helo 15 quickly to his right and dropped within feet of the ground in a split second. He moved in with a zig and a zag to make himself a more difficult target as he tried to get a closer look, and was dumbfounded to see Cin holding the flare gun.

Jake tried to absorb the situation. What is going on?

Another flare fired by Cin. Jake backed off. Was it Cin all along?

Drugov glared at Cin, incredulous at her actions. "You bitch. Warning shots?"

Cin pulled the radio from her pocket. "Get out of here, Jake."

Ivan snapped his gun level with Cin's head, awaiting the command.

"Have you taken a liking to these swine? Too much time undercover in America? It happens." Drugov said. "And we don't need her anymore either." Drugov swatted the back of his hand at Oksana like she was a fly. "Kill them both. Oksana first, so "CIN" can watch her friend die."

"Sorry," Ivan smirked to Cin, firmly confident he had the upper hand. "You know how it is."

Ivan panned his gun in a deliberate fashion back to Oksana. He seemed to be savoring his dramatic delay of the inevitable. Cin turned to Ivan and smiled. He returned a confused glance.

It was the moment she needed. Cin shoved her flare gun into Ivan's abdomen and punched a flare into his belly. His body quaked. His intestines boiled out before his eyes spilling in front of him like noodles onto the white snow. Expanding guts popped from the searing heat and gurgled up into his bloating thoracic cavity. His eyes bugged out, and his jaw was forced open in a painful dragon's roar. Innards spewed from his mouth in an uncontrollable puke of red chunks.

Cin pointed the flare gun at Drugov and pulled the trigger, but it was empty. She held her ground. Her stare was purposeful but woefully blank.

Drugov laughed. He removed a pistol from under his heavy coat, extended it at arm's length, and pointed it at Cin. "You bitch. I'll kill you myself. But you can watch her die first."

Drugov swung his aim toward Oksana and pulled the trigger. At the crack of Drugov's gun, Cin jumped in front of Oksana to take the bullet herself, and a round black dot seemed to magically appear in the dead center of Cin's forehead. The ink-black void was slightly larger than the caliber of Drugov's pistol. A wet crimson ring appeared along the raised edge of the bullet hole. The single bullet sprayed a lethal cone of lead and bone fragments as it ripped through Cin's head. The back of her skull, a catcher's mitt, shielded Oksana from the flak and protected her from harm.

Cin's face looked expressionless but peaceful. Her knees bent slowly, letting her down until she was kneeling on the ice. Then, as gentle as a feather, her body lowered as if cradled by invisible arms to lay her down in quiet repose on the ice. In the briefest of final moments, as her mind was wiped away, a last thought passed through Cin; "I did the right thing."

Jake and Felix were stunned at the scene playing out a few feet below them. "What the hell is happening down there?" Felix said.

Drugov calmly walked to Cin and stepped over her dead body, and picked up her radio. "Jake? Jake, is it? It's time for you to go. Fly back to McMurdo, and I will leave Oksana behind. You can return for her in one hour."

"Who the hell are you?"

"My friend, leave now, while you still can."

Jake and Felix were trying to process the unbelievable mayhem they had just witnessed playing out below their perch. Cin's body lay dead on the ground at Oksana's feet. One of the two men was dead on the ground in a bloody mess. "What's going on?" Felix cried.

"I thought Oksana was going to steal the meteorites," Jake said. "I thought she must have pushed Ksenia off the cliff at Castle Rock. But we just saw Cin kill one of the men and then sacrifice her life to save Oksana."

"This is too much, Jake. Get us out of here."

"I can't."

Jake had to save Oksana. There was no other choice to make.

He flew in very close. He brought the spinning main rotor blades to within a few feet of the shooter—within striking distance. Helo 15 was his weapon of choice.

Felix gasped, expecting a meat grinder. "What are you doing?"

Jake pulled up hard on the collective and twisted the throttle. That rocked Helo 15 back nearly vertical like a valiant stallion rearing up on its hind legs. The sudden blast of rotor wash funneled down and forward in an explosive burst. The blast of air knocked down the two surviving figures and hurled them like leaves in a tornado. Drugov tumbled over and over and slammed into the side of Scott's Hut. Oksana was blown thirty feet past Scott's Hut and got up running in a full sprint. "That's Oksana," Jake said. "Good, she's running away."

And just as Jake had anticipated, the black helicopter was also flipped over on its back like it was a dried up dragonfly.

"Now what are we going to do?" Felix blurted.

"We're going to land."

Drugov chased after Oksana and threatened to shoot her if she didn't stop. Oksana kept running. The undulating snow became steeper. Oksana passed a single red flag.

"Stop, or you're dead," Drugov yelled. But he had no intention of killing her. Not yet.

Oksana ran past a pair of red flags. A moment later, she tripped and fell into a crack in the ice. It was small and she struggled to get up, and Drugov was upon her.

"He caught her," Felix said.

"Just wait."

Drugov walked Oksana at gunpoint back to the front of Scott's Hut and picked up Cin's radio again. "That was a very foolish thing you did, Jake. Land immediately or I kill Oksana. I have some unfinished business here. I need your helicopter."

"I know."

Cautiously, Jake set Helo 15 down next to the bloody carnage.

"Both of you get out. We have a little cargo to load onto your helicopter. I'm sure you know about the meteorites."

Jake and Felix exited Helo 15 and walked cautiously toward Drugov and Oksana.

CHAPTER THIRTY-FOUR

Jake and Felix removed the heavy crate of meteorites from Oksana's hiding place inside of Scott's Hut and carried it together to Helo 15. Jake whispered to Felix, "I've got a gun." Felix's hand slipped.

"Careful you imbeciles, don't drop it," Drugov shouted.

Felix stared at Jake. "Don't get us killed."

"It might be too late for that," Jake returned.

They set the crate down on the ice next to Helo 15 and Jake slid open the cargo door. Jake and Felix huddled close, leaning over the crate while they struggled under its weight and heaved it into the cargo bay.

"Strap it down tight," Drugov said.

Jake whispered again. "I took a gun from one of the NCIS agents." Felix's eyes went wide, and he gasped a small breath.

"Shut up, you two."

Jake climbed into the cargo bay and pulled the crate while Felix pushed it from below. They began to wrap the crate with straps connected to tie-downs built into the floor. "As soon as we finish strapping in the crate, I'm going to shoot Drugov."

Jake looked out through the cargo door opening past the crate, beyond Felix, and to Drugov. He was already lining up his plan of attack. "You get ready to run to Oksana and get her away from here in case it gets ugly. Run as far and fast as you can."

"Hurry up, hurry up. You're finished," Drugov said. "You have more than enough straps to hold it down. It's not going anywhere."

Felix turned, stood erect to face Drugov, and began a brave march straight toward him. Jake slowly crawled out of the cargo bay. Felix was directly in line between Jake and Drugov. *Get out of the way.* Then Jake realized Felix was purposely giving a critical few extra seconds of cover to Jake by blocking Drugov's view—time enough for Jake to quickly prepare the gun.

The Berretta felt awkward in Jake's hand. He had fired a gun a few times before, but he knew he was no expert. He tried to recall his Navy small arms training as he glanced down to locate the safety. His pistol coach had drummed home the important connection between a calm mind and improved accuracy. *How can I stay calm now?*

He fumbled with the safety before he could flick it off with his thumb. *There's the red dot.* Jake looked up, grateful for Felix's cover.

Having no way of knowing if Jake was ready, only hoping he was, Felix turned toward Oksana and stepped out from the line of fire, exposing Jake.

The moment Felix was clear, Jake jerked the pistol to Drugov and fired. *Damn, that was too quick.* He should have taken more time to aim his first shot when he had Drugov unaware. Even a second more might have made all the difference.

Drugov spun around, half in pain, half from surprise. The bullet had slammed into the muscle and bone of his right shoulder—a second shot by Jake. But with Drugov's erratic spinning and falling, the bullet missed and hit the wall of Scott's Hut.

Felix grabbed Oksana and pushed her ahead of him. "Run, Oksana!"

Drugov tried to return fire. He had fallen face-down and struggled with the agony of his shredded shoulder. It was difficult to raise his right arm and shoot back at Jake. His arm would not fully respond.

Jake shot again. It hit the ice in front of Drugov's head and shards of ice crystals sprayed his face. Another careless shot.

"You Bastard," Drugov yelled. He struggled to get up to one knee. He was forced to hold the gun with two hands and support both the weapon and his limp arm. He shot at Jake. It missed.

Jake needed to make the next shot count. He steadied the Berretta and calmed his breathing. Remember your training. One breath in and half of it out. Take careful aim. *"Sight alignment, trigger control."* The words of his coach echoed from the past.

He was sure he struck Drugov with the next shot but didn't know exactly where. Drugov reeled and fell to the ground, but just as quickly scrambled to his knee again. He supported his gun with both hands more carefully this time and took aim. Jake shot first.

Jake shot again and again. He struck Drugov several more times and kept firing until the Berretta was empty. Drugov lay motionless on the ice. Blood stained the ice around him.

Jake looked in the direction he had last seen Oksana and Felix run, but he could not see them. He ran back to Helo 15 and jumped into the pilot seat. He needed to get airborne fast and find Oksana and Felix before a crevasse found them. They could be running to their death.

He rushed the start checklist—NO, he *skipped* the start checklist: Fuel pump-ON. Hydraulics-ON. Push the starter button and hold it down.

The main rotor engaged at 10% RPM and began to turn slowly. He kept holding down the starter button, but it seemed like an eternity for the main rotor to work up to speed. Had he screwed up the start sequence? Finally, with the main rotor spinning freely at 40% RPM, he released the starter button and the calamitous noise and vibration of the rough start settled down. The engine RPM and rotation of the main rotor found its comfortable rhythm again. And though it felt like it had been an excruciatingly long time to get started, he was ready to fly in a minute.

Just after liftoff, Jake slowly rotated Helo 15 to his left to glimpse the carnage below. He could not see Drugov, and when he turned his head searching further, the blunt metal barrel of a gun was pressed hard against the back of Jake's neck.

"To my ship, you son of a bitch."

Where the hell did he come from?

Though Helo 15 was airborne quickly, Jake's abbreviated start sequence was enough of a delay and distraction to give Drugov time to recover and somehow crawl through the open cargo door of Helo 15 just as it lifted off.

Drugov squatted in a painful ball in the cargo bay behind Jake. He was forced to hold his gun in his left hand. He rested his limp right arm on the crate of meteorites. He was bleeding and losing strength.

"Fly to the ocean, you bastard." Drugov was breathing heavily. The gun wobbled in a precarious threat. Jake hoped Drugov wouldn't inadvertently fire a bullet into his brain. Drugov's right arm was clearly nonfunctional.

"Ocean... go to ice edge." Drugov let out a painful groan. His voice was broken. "Ship at ice edge... near Cape Royds."

Jake was silent. At their present location next to Scott's Hut, they were at sea level. Slowly they climbed above 1,000 feet in altitude. The ground was becoming hidden in the snow and ice. Both the barometric and radar altimeters in Helo 15 were in agreement—they both read 1,000 feet—and kept climbing. Soon they were lost in the milky haze of everything.

"Where are we?" Drugov was furious. "To my ship, you bastard."

They could not see the ground any longer.

Jake turned Helo 15's heading ever so gently to fly in a slightly different direction. Jake knew by heart where he wanted to fly. So gentle was the turn to their new heading, and slow the rate of their climb, that without a visual reference to the ground, the change was imperceptible to Drugov. The corrupt Russian Admiral was unaware that they were flying inland.

They passed 3,000 feet.

"Where is the ground? Get lower. Look for my ship."

They kept climbing.

"You're too high. Where is the ocean? Get down or I'll shoot you."

"Don't shoot or we'll both die."

Jake watched the barometric altimeter pass 6,000 feet.

Drugov was losing blood. "We should be there by now," he wailed.

The air was getting thinner as they passed 8,000 feet.

Drugov began to feel lightheaded. He knew he was losing too much blood and feared he might pass out if he didn't get back to his ship soon. "Hurry."

What the Russian Admiral didn't know was that they were now passing 10,000 feet.

The low air pressure differential in the Antarctic region also added another 2,000 feet to their pressure altitude. By 10,000 feet pressure altitude, humans become hypoxic. Not enough oxygen. Now they were feeling the effects of 12,000 feet pressure altitude.

It was hard to concentrate. Both Jake and Drugov suffered from the same hypoxia—oxygen starvation. They were well above the safe human threshold now. At this altitude, all but the fittest would start to pass out. Drugov's head became a dizzy mess. Jake's lungs were desperate for oxygen, and an acid pit grew in his stomach.

Jake began to question his judgment. The weather was terrible at this altitude. He could see nothing. He was putting all of his faith in what would otherwise be an insane choice.

Jake struggled to keep his head clear as he squinted to read the altimeter, 11,000 feet. It felt like 13,000 pressure altitude. *Not much further, where is it?* Soon, he knew, he would lose consciousness.

The aircraft also began to feel the effects of the thin air. Helo 15 strained to keep climbing. It was not designed to fly this high. *Come on, we're almost there.* A little more.

Jake was flying totally blind in a white Antarctic cloud. The barometric altimeter crept higher as Helo 15 struggled upward. It fought for every foot of altitude it gained. Jake compared both altimeters. Finally, at 11,200 feet on the barometric altimeter, unable to go any higher, the radar altimeter started to go down.

Soon he could see ice and rock again. "There," Jake said. "I see the ground." Looking through the foggy haze of his mind, Drugov gave a faint sigh of relief upon seeing the ground once more.

"There's the ground," Jake yelled at Drugov. "We're close now." Drugov's gun was too heavy in his left hand for him to hold it steady. His right arm worthlessly draped onto the crate of meteorites, his grip slipping.

The radar altimeter began to go down rapidly. But the barometric altimeter said they were still very high in altitude. The two altimeters seemed to be in disagreement.

Jake knew they weren't descending to the ground, but that the ground was rising up to meet them. His heading was good. His memory had served him well.

The odd scent of sulfur crept into the air. Drugov's mind was spinning. "What's that smell?" Confused, his head was empty of oxygen, but still full of hate.

Helo 15 could fly no higher. The air was too thin. *Come on, give me all you've got.*

Jake cranked the throttle as far as it would go. The engines screamed in obedience as they raced far past red line. They would not last much longer. The struggle for every foot in altitude, with every ounce of power, made Helo 15 heroic.

Only fifty feet now on the radar altimeter. Fifty feet above solid ground. The terrain was rising rapidly. Jake jumped when they almost hit a boulder just underneath Helo 15. *Come on, don't hit, a little more, we're almost there.*

The ground was very close now. Helo 15 was at the edge of Mount Erebus.

"We'll be there soon," Jake said. It was a small relief for Drugov. He was weak and felt gravely ill.

Suddenly, the radar altimeter needle jumped to 1,000 feet as they passed over the edge of Mount Erebus. They had crested the rim of the volcanic crater.

"Look there," Jake yelled. "Look out the door." Drugov leaned his head over the edge of the cargo bay. With the little strength he had remaining, he peered out the open cabin door. He didn't see his ship. He craned his neck further and loosened his tenuous grip on the crate of meteorites that he had been greedily holding with his weak right hand.

As aggressively as he could, Jake slammed Helo 15 over on its left side and then violently jerked it up and to the right. Jake watched Drugov tumble out the cabin door. He fell 1,000 feet into the mouth of the volcano. Jake looked down and followed Drugov's flailing body during its entire fall into the lava. A puff of smoke spit up when he hit.

EPILOGUE

A week passed before two LC-130 Hercules returned to Antarctica. A lot happened in that short time. The Commanding Officer of VXE-6 was replaced by the Executive Officer. And unlike the last ill-fated flight to McMurdo, there was no hurried rush to this mission. It was well planned. The weather had cleared, the aircrews were rested, and a second aircraft was added for safety.

The two Hercules flew south as a pair, one just ten minutes behind the other. Tim Rogers returned to McMurdo with another mountaineer to scout for hazards in the immediate area around the XD-03 crash site.

Cin, the two NCIS agents, and the disemboweled Russian corpse at Scott's Hut were to be flown off The Ice in one aircraft. The aircrew that had survived the whiteout landing, and Oksana, would fly back in the other.

Jake, Tim, and Felix had been sitting together quietly in Felix's office for a while when Jake finally spoke up. "You didn't expect to be back here so soon, did you, Tim?"

"I came back to say goodbye," Tim said.

"What?" Felix said. "You're not coming back next season?"

"I realize I can't be here forever and protect everyone all the time," he smiled. "Eight years in Antarctica is enough. It's time for me to move on."

"I thought you'd always be the Head Mountaineer," Jake said.

"Nope. I fly out tomorrow for the last time. I'll be escorting the bodies of Cynthia Brock and Special Agents Saunders and Morrow, and the Russian, at least what's left of him, back to America."

"Yeah..." Jake voiced sheepishly, somewhat dispassionately. "When I flew back to pick up Oksana and Felix, I knew we should have taken him back with us, but Oksana only wanted to bring Cin's body home to McMurdo. She said she owed Cin that much. She had sacrificed her life for Oksana."

"He was a bloody mess anyway," Felix said. "No way was I going to put him in the Helo with us."

"But by the time we returned to Scott's Hut with a snow track vehicle to retrieve his body, the Skuas had made a feast out of him," Jake said. "We found most of him. He fit in a couple of bags."

A soft knock came at the door. "Excuse me, gentlemen," Oksana walked into the room toward Felix's desk. "I've brought you something, Felix. It's another specimen for your collection."

Oksana needed less time than the week it took for the two Hercules to return to McMurdo to determine the true identity of her father's discovery. It was clear from the outset that the rocks were meteorites, and now she had confirmed they were from Mars, the most valuable meteorites ever found.

She knew all along. She believed because her father believed, and that faith proved to be more valuable to her than the meteorites themselves. The trust in her father not only led to the discovery, but it also freed her from her past. She would never have to worry about being hounded by Admiral Drugov. She would not have to run and hide in America. Rather, she was welcomed to the United States as a heroic scientist. She found much more in Antarctica than she ever expected. And the tough veneer she had maintained for so long, began to melt away.

Oksana approached Felix holding a fist-sized meteorite in her hand. "I wanted to leave you with one of my father's meteorites." She handed the black rock to Felix. "I selected this one especially for you. It's a particularly impressive example."

Felix stood up and graciously accepted her gift.

Respectfully, Jake and Tim also stood.

"Oksana Zverev is leaving us too," Felix announced to everyone. "She's been through a lot."

Oksana turned and faced Jake wanting to say something before leaving, but no words came. Jake was desperate to speak but stayed equally silent. What should he say? What could he say? He wanted her to stay, to be with her. He felt his heart pounding, but there were no words.

Oksana smiled warmly, turned, and was gone.

Felix broke the palpable silence. "We're giving her the opportunity to finish out the season in America. She will be allowed to bring the meteorites to NSF headquarters in Washington, DC and complete her work. A first."

"That's nice," Tim said. Jake stayed quiet.

Sharing her father's discovery with the world gave Oksana the privilege of naming the historic find. But true to the understated convention within the geological science community, the meteorites were simply recognized by a few letters and numbers. EAP, for East Antarctic Plateau, and numbered one through twenty-four. But Oksana added two more letters to her father's discovery—VZ—his initials. The first meteorite strewn field and their meteorites found in Antarctica would forevermore be known as EAPVZ1001-EAPVZ1024.

***

There's a place we go for peace. It's never very far. For some, it's a state of mind, no further than a thought—just close your eyes. For others, it may be a place—perhaps a quiet path through trees, or a walk to the top of a hill with a view. Sometimes it's right in front of you.

Today, for Jake, he found himself in a familiar place, back on Ob Hill next to the large wooden cross. He thought of what was, and what might have been, as he stood alone in the cold to watch the last two LC-130 Hercules depart Antarctica.

XD-06 took off first, followed exactly ten minutes later by XD-07. They climbed in effortless tandem into the sky.

The miracle of sunrise that happened every twenty-four hours around the rest of the world was still months away for McMurdo. But the closing kiss of twilight lingered to escort the last aircrews off The Ice safely. A prism of warm light arced high across the sky, weaving the final delicate red and orange wisps of the sun's afterglow into a subtle rose hue.

Jake stepped back from the wonderful light and touched the cross for what he imagined might be the last time for months to come during the long Antarctic night.

Jake turned to head back down the path toward McMurdo. He stopped and looked up. Cresting the hill was Oksana. She stopped and stood looking at him. Her heart beat surrender.

ACKNOWLEDGMENTS

Let me recognize some of the key people who encouraged me to write this novel. John Lipsett, my first reader, who read a very early rough draft and enthusiastically pushed me to continue. For months he bugged me to finish writing so he could find out what happened. Liz Craver, my sister, who read a final draft with a critical eye and offered excellent input. And thanks to all the other family and friends who supported my efforts and inspired me.

I'd like to give special thanks to "Rio" DeGennaro. We flew together often in Antarctica, he as the pilot, me as the navigator, for most of our three seasons on The Ice. He graciously read my final draft with a professional eye and offered important corrections and additions that needed to be included.

Finally, I want to thank all the squadron personnel I had the privilege of serving with in VXE-6, and the many members of the numerous other organizations affiliated with our tremendous Antarctic program: The National Science Foundation, The United States Antarctic Program, and Naval Support Force Antarctica. Your devotion and sacrifice in the name of science and peace will remain eternal.

Thank you all very much.

ABOUT THE AUTHOR

The setting for this story came about because of the dramatic change that occurred midway through my Navy career as a result of the end of the Cold War. My early Navy years had been dedicated to Anti-Submarine Warfare and the hunt for Soviet submarines. When the big change came, I transitioned to Antarctic Development Squadron Six, VXE-6, the squadron highlighted in this story.

As a squadron Department Head, and in my flying role as navigator, a position I enjoyed a lot, I knew how fortunate I was to be part of such an organization during this era of great change. I knew how fleeting these times would be. I felt privileged. I could touch, feel, and experience the changes as they were happening. Many of the old ways were going away. Many new things were introduced. I was one of the lucky few who had access to a desktop computer for my Operations Officer job when the world was starting to exchange emails. But I had no one to send an email to. My wife didn't have email back home. We wrote letters to each other—on paper. There wasn't anything that we would recognize today as the internet.

I still talked on High-Frequency radios from the aircraft. No satellite radios for us. Even if I had one, it wouldn't work—none of those types of satellites orbiting above the South Pole. They were all still parked over Russia. Cellular phones? Don't even think about it.

Navigation was still as much an art then as it was science. When the first military versions of GPS showed up at my navigation station in the aircraft, I remember thinking how it looked much like the cassette deck that I had once screwed under the dash of my girlfriend's (later wife) Volkswagen bug. "Try out this new gizmo," they said. "We want you to evaluate it and see if it works." That little box, hanging under my radios like an afterthought, didn't look MILSPEC to me, it looked like that old cheap VW cassette deck. I didn't trust it. Would you put your life on the line with something that looked like an old tape deck? It just seemed like a very accurate way to kill yourself.

I had often thought of writing about Antarctica ever since I was there so many years ago. I can't count the number of times I told my stories about The Ice, little vignettes I like to call them, to interested friends, family, or anyone who wanted to listen. And universally, everyone wanted to hear more about Antarctica. But too often, due to work, life, raising a family, whatever, I never got around to writing about my experiences on The Ice. Finally, I endeavored to collect all my vignettes and commit them to paper in a fashion that would essentially document my experiences. I think it's valuable.

So I started. But then I stopped. I realized I had waited too long. It had been so many years since my time on The Ice that the details were just too vague. I couldn't possibly remember all the dates, places, and names of so many disparate happenings. I couldn't accurately recall so many different experiences. It was heartbreaking.

Then I remembered a thought I had when I was in Antarctica that was very liberating. They always said we were operating at the bitter end of a very long food chain. Don't screw up. Don't get hurt. You could be dead before any help arrives. Minor incidents become major problems. And as often as I heard that ominous warning, I always said to myself, "Exactly, it would be a great place for a murder." Make it look like any other common accident that so often turned fatal. Why do I think this way sometimes? I don't know. I consider myself a fairly normal person most of the time. But sometimes I just let my imagination run.

So, if I had a story to tell, what about that murder idea? Let my vivid imagination run. Explore my memories from that grand experience to set the stage for a story. I hope my writing comes across with that same twinkle in my eye I get when I'm excitedly describing to someone how we would fly to the South Pole or land a plane on a glacier where no human had ever stepped before. I let all those vignettes be my inspiration. It really comes down to this: I need to tell you about my time in Antarctica, and I'm going to do it through a thriller novel.

AUTHOR BIO

Bill Craver was born in Manhattan, New York, grew up in Rochester, went to McQuaid Jesuit High School, and graduated from Syracuse University. He entered Aviation Officers Candidate School in Pensacola, Florida, was commissioned in the United States Navy, completed flight school, and earned his Wings of Gold. He retired from active duty in 1998 and created a successful financial services business which he has owned for the last 22 years.

Bill lives in Southern California with Antoinette, his wife of more than 38 years, and they have four beautiful children together.